FUMBLED ARRANGEMENT

S. JONES

Copyright@2024

S. Jones

All rights reserved.

No part of this publication may be reproduced, distributed, or transmitted in any form or by any means including but not limited to, the training, feeding, or creating any use of artificial intelligence, electronic, mechanical, photocopying, recording or otherwise without the prior written consent of the author.

This book is a work of fiction created without use of AI technology. Name, characters, places, and incidents are either products of authors imagination or are used fictitiously. Any resemblance to actual events or persons, living or dead, is coincidental and beyond the intent of the author or publisher.

Cover Design:

Sara Grin Sentz

Enchanting Romance Design

Editing:

Marla Selkow Esposito

Proofreading:

Virginia Tesi Carey

CHAPTER 1

NATALIE

"I NEED TO TELL YOU SOMETHING, BUT YOU HAVE TO promise you won't freak out."

I set my drink down and glanced at my friend Gina, who was eyeing me carefully. It was hard to hear over the loud music, so I leaned forward with a frown.

"I'll do my best, but I'm not making any promises." I rested my chin on my hand and moved my gaze over to Claudia. She was Gina's older sister by one year and they did everything together. Whatever Gina had to say, chances were about one hundred percent, Claudia was in agreement.

"Okay. That will have to do." She shifted in her seat and adjusted the white sash along her shoulder so the passing crowd could see the word "Bride" in big gold letters.

Claudia pushed a shot glass in front of me. "Do you want this before or after we tell you?"

"Whatever it is, just spit it out." I leaned my arms along the high-top table, wishing she would quit stalling.

Gina placed her hand over mine, trying to give me a

reassuring smile, but it wasn't working. "Hudson told me Levi is bringing Brittany as his plus one to my wedding."

My mouth opened and closed as I felt a burst of anger hit me at the sound of her name alone. Just when I thought things couldn't get any worse. Not only did I have to deal with seeing him, but I had to worry about seeing them together. I was still feeling bitter about him moving on with her so quickly after I left him.

We dated for four years. Marriage was in our future. We talked about it. We planned on it. I was faithful and studying my brains out in London while working on my master's degree. At the same time, he was playing hockey and hooking up with groupies.

What a stupid, naive girl I was.

It's only been a month, but then again, I shouldn't be surprised they were together. Brittany was the woman he knocked up right before I moved back to the States. Our relationship wasn't perfect by a long shot, but instead of calling it quits like I should have, I stuck it out and blamed our issues on dating long distance.

Gina grabbed the shot glass and placed it in my hands. I tossed the burning liquid down in one gulp, wishing I had the entire bottle in front of me.

"When were you going to tell me this?" I was surprised at how controlled my voice was.

Gina swallowed uncomfortably. She was stuck between a rock and a hard place, given that my ex, Levi, was best friends with her fiancé, Hudson. They played on the same NHL team together.

She swore up and down that she had no idea what was going on, and I believed her. We've been friends since our first year at Boston University. Things have been uncomfortable since my breakup, but I hoped this girls' weekend in Vegas would allow us to let go of the stress and relax a bit.

"I found out right before we left. I knew you were going to be upset about it. I wasn't going to say anything, but it's been eating away at me."

I sighed, swirling the ice around in my glass. I needed a refill. "So, he's bringing the woman he cheated on me with to our best friend's wedding? Am I understanding this correctly?"

She nodded her head. "I'm really sorry. Hudson and I got into a big fight about it. He said it's Hudson's plus one, and he is allowed to bring whoever he pleases."

I slumped back in my seat. I wanted to argue and complain about how wrong that was, but it wasn't my wedding. I had no right.

Claudia moved to my side and swung her arm along my shoulder. "He's not worth getting worked up over. You know what you should do? Bring a date of your own. That would be a sure way to piss him off."

"Where am I supposed to find this mystery man?"

She threw her arms out. "Hello, we are in Vegas, baby. Look around. There are plenty of men to choose from. Take your pick."

I glanced around the crowded club. She wasn't wrong. Most of the men were dressed in suits and designer clothes. While some were trying to start a fashion trend, others looked ridiculous.

Claudia tipped her chin to the guys in the VIP section in the back. "Holy hell, now there is a group of hot guys."

I knew exactly where she was going with this, so I took a sip of my drink, trying to hide behind my glass. Chances were, they were about to do something to embarrass me.

Gina stood on her tiptoes to see over the people in

front of us. "The ones in the corner?" She pointed, making it way too obvious.

"Jesus, will you two stop being so weird?" I sighed, rubbing my temples, when I noticed they were attracting unwanted attention to our table. It felt like everyone in the club was staring at me.

"How about that guy?" I followed Claudia's gaze and spotted him immediately. He was tall and dark and had a smile that could light up the entire club. He was with a group of well-dressed guys clustered in a booth, looking like they were enjoying their night. "You should go over there and introduce yourself."

"Absolutely not."

We were supposed to be celebrating and having fun. I had zero interest in meeting anyone tonight.

"Why not?" Gina nudged me with her elbow. "Life is too short. This is your chance to show yourself that you're better off without that jerk."

I turned toward her. "I just got out of a relationship. I'm not looking to get into another one."

The last thing on my mind was hooking up with a stranger. No matter how attractive the guy was. And let me be clear: the man she pointed out was way above average in the looks department.

"Just flirt with him and see how it goes." Claudia twisted in her seat to stare directly at their table. She would have been less discrete if she was peering through a pair of binoculars.

"With my luck lately, no thanks." I fidgeted with the hem of my dress, already over this scene. I meant what I said. I wasn't looking for anybody. I didn't need anybody. I wanted to wait for the right person, someone whose goals aligned with mine. Someone I could trust.

I made a promise to myself to start making better

decisions. When I decided to jump back into the dating pool again, it sure as hell wouldn't be with a random stranger I met at a Vegas nightclub.

"Maybe your luck is about to change. Besides, what's the worst that can happen?" Gina tipped her drink back with a grin. At the rate these drinks were going down, we would be paying dearly for this night tomorrow morning.

My eyes drifted over to the guy in a white button-down. He lounged comfortably with his arm resting along the back of the booth. His hair was slightly wavy on top but clipped short on the sides. He had this type of energy swirling around him that pulled people in. A blush hit my cheeks because the man was undoubtedly one of the hottest guys I'd ever seen. He also looked vaguely familiar.

"They look like football players," I whispered. "The Super Bowl was last weekend. What if he plays on Beau's team?"

That would make him off-limits in more ways than one. I started work for the Atlanta Arrows next week, so there would be no mixing business with pleasure. Not to mention, my ex was an athlete, and he ended up being the biggest jerk. I swore to myself that I was done with that type of man.

Claudia stepped closer, the corners of her lips tipping into a smirk. "If he's a player, we should have taken Uncle Beau up on his offer and gone to the game."

My uncle's team played in the championship game last weekend and he offered me tickets. Since my friends weren't interested in football and we had plans to celebrate in Vegas the following week, I declined his offer.

"If he is a player, that would make him a hard pass. The last thing I need is another guy who loves attention and doesn't know how to keep his dick in his pants."

"No, you need to find out," Gina said, still looking at

him. "Go flirt with him. You do remember how to flirt, right? Because if he's fair game, you should go for it."

I shook my head at the same time Claudia said, "She won't do it. She is too chickenshit."

"Don't try to peer pressure me." These two were relentless. Why couldn't we just laugh, drink, and have fun?

Claudia, who was always the more direct of the two, leaned in. "You need to get out of your head and have some fun. You could have your pick of any guy here in the club. If not him, we will find someone else."

"I don't need to find someone." I scrunched my nose up because they didn't seem to get it. "What I need is to get through Gina's wedding next month without getting arrested."

Gina sighed. "God, this is going to be so stressful. I don't know how I'm going to be able to enjoy myself with the three of you in the same room together."

I took offense because I didn't create this problem. Was I just supposed to pretend that none of this ever happened? If she was so concerned about drama on her wedding day, she could have put her foot down and told Levi that he couldn't bring Brittany.

"I'm not sure how I ended up as the bad guy here?" I took a hefty sip of my drink, reminding myself not to let my emotions get the better of me. I was trying. Really, I was, but failing miserably.

Gina's eyes widened. "Gosh, I didn't mean it like that. Of course, none of this is your fault."

Claudia chimed in. "No one is saying you are to blame for anything. We just don't put it past Levi to try to mess with your head."

"I'll manage," I said, trying to reassure them both. Somebody had to be the bigger person. It was one day. I could do it.

They looked like they didn't believe me. Did they think I was so fragile that I couldn't handle being in his mere presence without falling apart? Would it be hard? Absolutely. But after everything he put me through, I was focused on putting that part of my life in the rearview mirror. I would prefer he not bring the woman he cheated on me with to the wedding, but there wasn't anything I could do about that.

"What do I have to do to convince you both that I'm serious?"

Tonight was supposed to be about us having fun. I didn't want to make it all about Levi.

"I know it's going to be hard for you to see him." Gina leaned closer so I could hear over the loud music. "A little distraction will do you some good. Maybe finding someone will help take your mind off things."

"We're back to this again." I rolled my eyes. I had an underlying suspicion that she was more worried about my ability to handle my emotions and causing a scene on her wedding day than anything else.

"Yes," Claudia said, as a matter of fact. "It doesn't have to be the perfect guy. You don't have to leave with anybody or get married; just have some fun. Put yourself out there again and see what happens."

I eyed them skeptically. "You both will get off my back if I do?"

"Pinky promise." Gina held her finger out and wrapped it around mine.

I groaned when Claudia reached out and grabbed my other finger. "I swear you are both going through a midlife crisis."

"We're too young for that." Claudia shook her head and pointed at me. "Now, I dare you to find a random man and flirt with him."

"You dare me?" I chuckled at the idea. I should have been irritated, but this was turning comical.

"Yes, because we know you won't do it." Gina raised her eyebrow in challenge.

I appreciated what they were trying to do, but I wasn't sure I was ready to put myself out there again. I needed to put my life back together first.

"You guys are both nuts." I stood up and grabbed my clutch. "I'm going to grab another round. Try not to get any more crazy ideas in your head."

I weaved around the tables, stepped up to the bar, and slowly started pursuing my choices. I needed a strong drink—something to take the edge off. I caught the bartender's attention and waited until he finished serving another customer.

"What can I get for you?" he asked, wiping his hands on a towel slung over his shoulder.

"Vodka with a splash of cranberry juice, please." I slid my glass across the counter for a refill.

"Sure thing." He gave me a quick nod and turned to the shelves lined with liquor bottles.

As I watched him give me a generous pour, I felt the back of my neck tingle.

"You can put it on my tab," said the deep southern drawl behind me.

I turned slowly, and holy hell, my gaze settled on a pair of warm brown eyes and a face so gorgeous that it threw me off. I tried to say something, but I was too stunned to talk. Thank goodness I had already ordered a drink because my throat felt dry as a desert.

It was the hot guy in the white shirt.

CHAPTER 2
RHETT

The boys and I were chilling in the club's VIP section, which was set aside for our crew, while the DJ dropped beats good enough to keep the crowd hyped up. My gaze swept over all the scantily-clad dressed women milling around, hoping to get noticed. We were riding high after winning the biggest game of the year with top-shelf liquor and no shortage of professional cleat chasers to pick from. Life didn't get much better than this.

"Hey, big spender. How much did you win at the tables?" my teammate Mitch Morris asked before downing his shot. A replacement was placed in front of him before the empty glass hit the table.

"A few grand." I drained the rest of my glass and started tapping my feet to the beat of the music. I was getting antsy from sitting for so long.

"You are so damn lucky at cards," grumbled our quarterback, Brent Wilson. "Probably get lucky with other things tonight too."

"I've been stuck in the hotel for the past week, and now I'm itching to let loose," I said, stretching out to get comfy. No one understood the mental and physical strain we went through during the season. Leading up to the final game was no different. The players had to stay at a remote location, twenty-five miles away from all the women, booze, and general chaos. We weren't allowed anywhere near the Strip. The coaches didn't want us to have any temptations around us. We got to have dinner with our families earlier in the week, but then it was practice, press conferences, and team meetings until kickoff.

My eyes flickered over to a group of girls scoping us out. For the life of me, I couldn't figure out why I wasn't interested. It wasn't because I didn't want to have sex, because I loved sex. I was just tired of feeling so empty afterward. Lately, I'd been craving something better and more fulfilling.

"Hey." Elliott, one of our defensive linemen, slid into the overcrowded booth. His wrist was in a cast, so he shifted in his seat, trying to find a comfortable position to rest his arm. The guy took a beating during our last game and ended up with a plate and six screws in his wrist. "I'm going to head to the casino with the rest of the team. Are you guys coming or staying?"

JP Watson, our latest retiree, slid his eyes to mine. "I've already donated enough of my money tonight to the casino. I'm out."

"Are you nervous that cash will be tight now that you won't be collecting a paycheck?" I teased.

JP wasn't just a teammate. He was my best friend. His retirement kind of snuck up on me. I was having a hard time accepting that he was moving on.

"I'm off the market now. I can't be hitting the clubs and the casinos like you single guys with wallets filled with cash and condoms."

"Ahh, so you just want to get back home to Rylee then, huh?"

He waited until the cocktail waitress finished refilling our drinks. "Yup, and I'm man enough to admit that I'm in love and can't wait to make her my wife."

I groaned. "I swear, it's something in the water. I'm going to request that maintenance check the water pipes. First Mav, now you."

Mav was our mutual friend, who retired two years ago. JP was engaged to his sister, Rylee. While I was happy for my boys, I was sad things were changing.

As the conversation resumed, my phone buzzed in my pocket. I pulled it out and unlocked the screen. A tension headache started creeping in as my eyes scanned the message.

> **Claire**
> Congrats on the Super Bowl win. I looked for you after the game but couldn't find you. Let's celebrate when you get back into town.

Another text came through.

> **Mom**
> Claire has been trying to reach you. Please stop ignoring her. She is a nice girl. Just give her a chance.

JP looked over my shoulder as I was closing out the message. "Speaking of being tied down, is your mom still trying to wife you up?"

"Yep, if anything, she's been coming at me harder now that the season is done."

She liked to constantly remind me that at age thirty-one, I wasn't getting any younger. I've spent so many years trying to create my own identity and not live off my family name. I was panicking at the thought of what was waiting for me when this was all over.

Morris's hand rested on my shoulder. "At least it's not election season. You can enjoy your downtime and not have to worry about helping out with your dad's campaign."

He wasn't wrong.

Dad was a fifteen-term congressman, and my mom was a federal judge. My brother Ford, who was named after Gerald Ford, worked as a staff member. Then, there was my sister, Reagan, who was named after Ronald Reagan, and she was a DC lawyer turned lobbyist. See a theme there? If you were wondering how I ended up being named Rhett, let me tell you a little secret. Rhett was my middle name. My first name was Theodore, a name I would never use in this lifetime, and you could probably take a wild guess on which US president I was named after.

"True, but now I have to worry about my meddling mother trying to set me up with Clingy Claire."

From the time I entered the draft, I've tried to steer clear of my parents' political scene. It never felt right for me, so I carved out my own path, centered around football and just having a good time.

The only things they asked of me were to show up at political events when I could, to not do anything embarrassing, and to settle down when my football career ended. As luck would have it, my mom had the perfect woman in mind for me: Claire Settler. Her folks ran in the same social circles as mine and were big donors to my dad's reelection campaign each term.

JP's lips twisted. "Just block it out, man, like how we do

on the field. It's all outside noise. Focus on what makes you happy."

I rolled my shoulders back. "That's hard to do when all I hear is, 'Claire's a nice girl. She's perfect for you. You've got to stay on task and focus on your future.'"

JP leaned back and set his glass down. "Have you ever thought about finding a girl of your own? Maybe that would get her off your back."

Watching my buddy fall hard for the woman he'd been crushing on was a real treat. While I admired his commitment to her, I wasn't sure if that would ever be in the cards for me.

"Easier said than done, especially since I'm not looking to settle down," I grumbled and turned my attention away from the group.

I was scanning the crowd when my eyes snagged on a woman with long blond hair spilling down her back. Her red dress clung to her in all the right places and stopped right above her knees.

She was standing at the bar in a sea of beautiful women, but my gaze skimmed past every single one until it was completely glued on her. I brought my hand to my chest when I thought I felt a palpitation. Was that even possible? It had to be because I sure as hell felt it.

"Guys." I stood up and scooted out of the booth. "I'll be right back."

I watched in fascination as the knockout in the red dress leaned across the bar and ordered her drink. "Vodka with a splash of cranberry juice, please."

My mouth watered because I suddenly wanted to sink my fingers into those hips that God had blessed her with and run my mouth over every inch of her.

I pulled my card out and slid it across the bar. "You can put her drink on my tab."

Her body stilled, and when she turned, it felt like Cupid struck an arrow right through my heart. You could have knocked me over with a damn feather. I bit down on my fist because, hot damn, I was officially in love.

The most beautiful blue eyes I'd ever seen stared up at me.

"Thank you." She pushed a sigh past her lips like she wasn't sure what to do with herself. Christ, did I want to kiss this woman. "But you didn't need to do that."

"It was my pleasure." I pulled out one of the empty stools and gestured for her to slide in. "Why don't you have a seat, cutie."

She blinked, looking partially amused and partially annoyed. "Excuse me."

Flirting was something I was good at, so maybe she wasn't used to it.

"I saw you standing at the bar by yourself. You looked like you could use some company."

She tipped her head to the side. "Is that why you came over here? To be friendly?"

"Sure."

I came over for more than just a simple conversation, but I didn't think I should tell her that.

Her eyes narrowed. "Somehow, I find that hard to believe."

"How do you know that's not the truth?"

She held my stare. "Call it a hunch."

"Are your hunches always accurate?"

"Always." Her gaze dipped to my lips for a split second. She tried to hide it, but I still caught her looking.

Bingo.

I stood taller. "Does your boyfriend know you're here alone tonight?"

My pickup lines weren't the best. Sure, I got laid, but

that had more to do with my pretty boy face, and who I was rather than anything else. Women found me funny and charming, like a cute little golden retriever. I was fun to cuddle with, but rarely connected with someone beyond a surface level. For reasons I couldn't explain, I was eager to establish something deeper with the blonde beauty in front of me.

"If I had a boyfriend, I'm pretty sure he wouldn't appreciate you flirting with me right now."

"You got that right, sweetheart. If you were my girl, everybody in this room would know it." I grinned while admiring the little dimple on her left cheek.

"Charming." She gave her head a subtle shake and reached for the fresh drink that was just placed in front of us.

Jesus, this was fun. It's been too long since I flirted with a woman who wasn't a fan or someone my parents weren't trying to shove down my throat.

"Do you have a name, gorgeous?"

"Why don't you share yours with me first, then I'll tell you mine."

It took me a minute to realize she had no idea who I was. Granted, tight ends weren't the most recognized guys on the team, like quarterbacks and wide receivers, but after winning the biggest game of the year, our team was plastered everywhere leading up to the championship.

"Theo." I held my hand out and prayed to God that I wasn't coming on too strong.

I hadn't used my real name since kindergarten. Back then, kids were merciless, and having a name like mine made me an easy target. So, I ditched it and took on my middle name, "Rhett," which was way cooler. That's the name the world knew me by now.

She looked at my hand and paused for a moment before shaking it. "Natalie."

"Natalie. I like it. It suits you."

"I'm so glad you approve."

I touched my bearded jaw with my free hand, trying to think of all the ways I could convince the prettiest girl in the room to give me the time of day. I couldn't recall a single time in my life when I'd felt such a strong connection.

"Why don't you take a seat and have a drink with me?" I gestured to the stool I had pulled out for her. "We can get to know each other."

Did I sound pathetic? Probably, but this little encounter was the most excitement I had tonight.

"Is that what you want? To get to know me?"

Why did that feel like a trick question? Like I'm damned if I do and damned if I don't.

"Sure." I pulled on the collar of my dress shirt. It felt tight all of a sudden. "Unless you think I'm too boring to hang out with."

"And you would be okay if it ended with one drink?"

She was smart as a whip and calling me out on my bullshit. Why did that turn me on even more?

"Well, technically, I was planning on sweet-talking you into another one."

She patted my hand like a grandmother would a small child. "Thanks, lover boy, but I'm all set."

Huh! Maybe if she knew who I was, she would change her mind. Quitting wasn't in my blood, so throwing my name around might win me some brownie points.

"Do you watch sports?" I asked, pointing to one of the five TVs above the bar showing a Lakers game.

She blinked and narrowed her eyes. "Not really."

I raised an eyebrow, intrigued. "So, no favorite player, then?"

"Nope."

I sipped my drink, scanning the room for my friends, who seemed to have disappeared. "Why not?"

"The last guy I dated was an athlete, and it didn't end well. So, when it comes to my personal life, I steer clear of them."

My mouth opened and closed. This was downright painful. This was not a normal situation for me, and I never wanted to be someone else so badly in my life.

"What kind of men do you date?" Maybe I could consider retiring early and taking that desk job my dad had waiting for me.

"I don't." She was so matter-of-fact.

I whistled because, damn, did I have my work cut out for me.

"I must be down on my luck tonight."

"Maybe you can get lucky with one of those women over there." She gestured to the three girls who were eyeing our table earlier. There was no way I was screwing this up by looking over there.

"Nah, I'd rather take my chances and try to win you over instead."

She swirled the ice around in her glass and looked off to the side. "The redhead in the black dress keeps checking you out. I bet she wouldn't mind your company."

I should be pissed that she was trying to pass me off on someone else. Instead, the little show she was putting on went straight to my man parts.

"I don't see anyone but you, sweetheart."

She was on the verge of responding, when she suddenly looked over her shoulder and fixed me with a gaze full of urgency and silent pleading. "Will you do me a favor?"

Well, that was an interesting turn of events.

I cocked my head to the side, intrigued by this sudden request. "Depends on what it is?"

I was pretty sure I'd agree to anything at this point.

She looked me up and down. "I need you to let my friends think that we are going to hook up later."

I could feel the corner of my lips tug upward. "It would be my pleasure. When do I start?"

"Now." She curled herself into me. "Just play along."

"Any rules you want me to follow?" I asked, staring into her sapphire-blue eyes.

"Just make it believable and pretend you are really into me, and I'll do the same."

My grin widened. "I think I can manage that, although I should warn you. I plan on being pretty damn convincing."

There would be no pretending on my part.

My eyes followed hers as two girls strolled up to us. I had no idea who these ladies were or why she wanted me to lie, but this would be the easiest assignment I'd ever have to do.

"Am I allowed to kiss you?" I asked as the girls got closer. They looked like they could be sisters.

"Only if your life depends on it." She smiled through her teeth.

I guess she wasn't a fan of that idea.

I chuckled. "I'm not sure my pride will recover from this."

Her lips parted, but before she could say anything, the two girls were in front of us. They both looked genuinely surprised, and I couldn't help but feel a little smug.

"Natalie." The taller one's eyes moved back and forth

between us. "You've been gone a while, and we wanted to make sure you're okay."

They watched us with curiosity. I had to admit, I was just as intrigued as they were. My mind was going a thousand miles a minute, trying to figure out why she needed me to put on a show.

The two girls continued to stare with mild suspicion while Natalie shifted uncomfortably at my side. After a few more seconds of awkward silence, it became clear I would be the one to make the first move.

I placed one hand on the small of Natalie's back and held the other for them to shake. "Hello, ladies. I'm Theo. It's nice to meet you."

The shorter one's expression was more focused like she was dissecting every little detail. "I'm Gina, and this is my sister, Claudia."

I smiled at them both and took in Gina's sash. "Congratulations."

"Thank you." Her reply was short. If my instincts were right, she would be a tough one to win over.

"I hope you don't mind that I've stolen your girl away." I gave them a charming smile and dug my fingers into Natalie's back. Her sharp intake of breath told me she wasn't as unaffected as she was trying to come across. "We've been over here hitting it off, and I was hoping to get some more alone time with her."

"Really?" The older sister squinted her eyes at me. I waited and waited for the recognition to hit because what were the odds that none of these ladies had a clue who I was?

"Yeah, you don't mind, do you?" I asked, wrapping my hand around Natalie's waist. Out of the corner of my eye, I noticed a flush hit her cheeks.

"Natalie, what's going on?" the shorter one asked.

She smiled and brought her fingers up to my chest. The wisps of her hair tickled my chin. She was petite and barely reached my shoulders. "I'm just taking your advice."

"What advice is that?" I asked and gently placed a kiss on her temple. If she wanted me to play the part, I was going all in.

"They were encouraging me to put myself out there and find someone to talk to."

"Well, lucky me." I winked at her two friends.

Were they on my side or not? I couldn't tell.

"Okay," the bride-to-be said. "We are heading to the dance floor. Come find us when you're ready." She quickly finished her drink and left it on the bar.

"Make good choices, kids." The other sister winked over her shoulder and waved.

Natalie waited until they disappeared into the crowd before dropping her hands from my chest. "Thank you." She sighed with relief.

I casually draped my arm along the back of the stool. "It was no trouble at all, trust me."

She held my gaze as we silently asked what the hell to do now. I knew what I wanted to do. I wanted to buy her another drink, get to know her, take her back to my hotel, and fuck her until she forgot about all the reasons why she had sworn off men.

She wrung her hands in front of her. "Thanks again for going along with it. Maybe I'll see you around later."

My eyebrows shot up. "That's it?" I asked a little too quickly. "Why don't you let me buy you another drink?"

Yeah, my game was lame as fuck tonight, and it was doing weird things to my ego. I usually had skills, but this woman made me forget every single one of them.

She shook her head. "I'm the one who should be buying you a drink. I owe you."

"Well, if you want to repay me, I can think of a few…"

She swatted my shoulder. "Just when I thought you were being a gentleman."

"Relax, pretty thing. I was going to suggest a dance. I've been told I'm a good dancer and was hoping to impress you with my moves. Get your dirty mind out of the gutter."

She laughed. "You're trouble."

My eyes didn't leave hers. "And you're gorgeous."

She glanced away. "I should probably go find my friends."

Self-doubt started to creep inside my head. I felt like an inexperienced teenage boy trying to impress a girl rather than an all-star tight end who could have just about any other woman in the bar.

"What are you going to tell them? I thought you wanted them to think we were leaving together?"

I was grasping at straws and trying every game in the book to hold her attention and keep her talking.

"I'll tell them I turned you down."

My mouth dropped open. "Why am I the one getting dumped here? I feel like I deserve a better ending than that. I thought I did a good job of showing them how interested I was."

"Hmm." She tapped her lip like she was thinking it over. "Fair point. I'll tell them you got called away. Something came up with work. What do you do for a living?"

I hesitated for a moment. Did I tell her or give her another little white lie? Usually, I was an honest person, but things were going so well between us, so I opted for the latter.

"I run a not-for-profit."

That wasn't a total lie. I started it when I was first drafted into the league.

"Wow." Her eyes widened in surprise. "What kind of not-for-profit?"

"We help single mothers get back on their feet. Sometimes, we assist with getting them their GED or accepted into college."

I convinced myself that she would like me more if she thought I did something meaningful with my time as opposed to catching and running with a damn ball for a living.

"That's amazing." She nodded, clearly impressed.

I shoved my hands in my pockets, feeling unworthy of her praise. I also felt like a fraud because I wasn't as involved in the daily mission as much as she thought. The organization was very important to me, but I wasn't the white knight she assumed I was.

"How about a dance?" I stepped closer. "I've been known to tear up the dance floor a time or two."

She shook her head. "I don't think that's a good idea."

My heart sank. I couldn't believe she was shooting me down.

"Was it something I said?"

"Not at all. You really are a great guy. But I'm fresh out of a relationship and starting a new job next week. This is my last night out with my friends before we go our separate ways. If things were different, I would take you up on that drink, but we both know it wouldn't end there." She kissed my cheek. "It was nice meeting you, Theo."

My eyes never strayed from her retreating back as she made her way across the room. Away from me and back to her friends.

There was no way this attraction was one-sided. I

could feel it and sense it, and my instincts had never steered me wrong.

She was making me feel a certain way. I couldn't explain it, but I knew this wasn't the end. The night was still young; I had plenty of time to change her mind.

CHAPTER 3
NATALIE

Theo was in the middle of the dance floor, showing off his moves. The women were all formed in a circle, doing their best to flirt and smile. He was eating up the attention, drawing gazes from every direction. I knew the feeling; it felt like I was in a trance, making it hard to look away.

I was tempted to walk over and apologize, but he seemed preoccupied and not all that upset about me rejecting him.

I downed the rest of my drink and pushed my way through the throng of people where Gina and Claudia were taking up space on the far end of the dance floor. There were flashing lights everywhere, the music was loud, and the energy was unlike anything I'd ever experienced.

Claudia grabbed my arms and pulled me in. "Where is Mr. Hottie?"

"He had to take a business call, so I snuck away," I lied. "Now he's over there dancing with some friends. We agreed to meet up later if we're both still here."

"Are you sure you don't want to go over there?"

Claudia's hair swished from side to side as she looked for him on the dance floor.

"I don't want to seem too clingy, so maybe later. Right now, I just want to dance," I said, trying to carve out enough space to move without brushing up against someone else.

"Here, drink this. I'm already tipsy enough." Gina handed me her lemon drop martini. "Do you want to call it a night after this dance?" Her words were slurred. Clearly, the alcohol had done its job tonight.

My gaze drifted around the room. No matter how hard I tried, I couldn't stop thinking about him.

"It's your night. Your call," I said, giving my head a shake. I needed to get my shit together and focus on getting my life back on track. Not focus on a guy who could never be anything more than just a night of fun.

She held up a single finger. "One more."

The three of us threw our hands in the air and moved to the beat of the music. When the next song started playing, a warm palm landed on my waist, causing me to yelp in surprise. I knew exactly who it was by the shiver running down my spine. I turned, feeling my heart race at the grin playing at the corners of his mouth.

That grin probably had a lot of girls swiping right.

"Mind if I join you?" he asked, dipping his head and pressing his mouth against my ear. He was so close that my head began to swim at his intoxicating scent, which hit every one of my goddamn senses.

The smart thing to do would be to tell him no. Let him walk away and find someone else, but I couldn't find the words. There was something about that man I couldn't shake.

"Sure. I do owe you, after all." I forced a smile, trying to mask the fluttering of nerves in my stomach.

He pulled me against his chest. "You could sound slightly more interested."

"I wasn't sure if you would have any energy left. It looked like you were working up quite a sweat on the dance floor."

His finger brushed against my cheek, causing it to burn hot. "Just trying to get your attention."

A breathless laugh floated out of me. "You had my attention way before that."

His brown eyes were twinkling with a smile. "Are you flirting with me?"

I looked around to see if anyone was paying attention to us. "I don't know if I would go that far. I'm just being honest."

"Well, if we're being honest, I have a confession of my own."

"Let's hear it." My heart was skipping over its beats as I held his gaze.

He tucked a strand of hair behind my ear. "I haven't been able to take my eyes off you all night."

The man was too smooth for his own good, and something told me he knew it too. I needed to keep my guard up because he was making me feel weak in the knees and all kinds of stupid. I didn't usually fall for cheesy pickup lines, cute dimples, and nice abs. I'd been there, done that.

"I bet you say that to all the girls."

"If I have, I never truly meant it until tonight."

I pressed my hands against his white dress shirt, feeling those strong muscles ripple beneath my palms. "How often do you use that line?"

"First time."

I stared at him, blinking and trying to figure out why, in a club full of beautiful women, he would want to spend time with me when he could have had anyone he wanted.

"You expect me to believe that?"

"I sure hope you do because it's the God honest truth." He lifted my chin, and his eyes darted to my lips. "You are, hands down, the most beautiful woman in the room, and I want to kiss you so bad that I'm afraid if I don't, I'll never forgive myself."

"You don't waste any time, do you?" I tried to remain calm, but I was too distracted to think straight. Every touch, every stare, was making it hard to focus.

His hands roamed along my waist before spanning them along my lower back. "Not when there is something I want."

"You don't even know me," I said, not even realizing I was stepping into him. I looked up into his eyes, searching for a sign that he was being genuine and not just feeding me a line.

"You're right, but I want to get to know you." He brushed a piece of hair out of my eyes.

I wasn't sure what I was supposed to say to that. I was feeling out of sorts and acutely aware of how close we were. I wanted to kiss him as badly as he wanted to kiss me. But the idea of making the first move was terrifying.

As if sensing my hesitation, he moved closer and ran his thumb along my jaw. I tried to focus on the music and the swaying bodies around us instead of wondering what kissing him would feel like.

Before I could overthink more than I already had, I ran my hands along his shoulders, feeling a thrill of excitement when he pressed his lips to my mouth. I parted for him, feeling everything around us fade away. A simple touch shouldn't feel so good, but that was nothing compared to what his kiss felt like.

His hand went to the back of my neck, holding me in place and keeping me exactly where he wanted me. I hadn't felt this type of yearning in years. I convinced myself that I'd probably never feel it again. He was proving me wrong and making me forget all the reasons why I walked away from him in the first place.

The kiss only lasted for a minute, but when we stopped, I compared that kiss to every other one I'd had in my life.

This wasn't normal, and I was questioning my sanity. My lips tingled, and I had to remind myself to breathe.

He took a step back and rubbed a hand over his jaw. "I'm sorry, Natalie. That was really forward."

My heart was beating hard enough for him to feel it. "You don't need to apologize. I liked it."

He smiled back sheepishly. "Yeah?"

"Yeah, I wouldn't mind doing it again."

I wanted to hide my face in embarrassment. I couldn't believe I said that out loud. What the hell was wrong with me?

He stepped forward, looking like he had a few ideas on what he wanted to do next. I didn't trust myself or him, so I gently placed my hand on his chest, reminding us that we needed to slow down. "But you told me you were a good dancer, so I want to see more of those dance moves. I'm not sure I'm convinced yet."

Instead of looking disappointed, he gave me a lopsided grin. "I'm feeling pretty confident that I put whatever doubts you're having to rest."

"Oh, really?" I raised my eyebrows playfully. "I'll believe it when I see it."

He ran a shaky hand through his hair, and my eyes caught on an expensive-looking gold watch on his wrist. "Why does it feel like this is some kind of test?"

"I thought you were feeling pretty sure of yourself. Don't tell me you're having doubts now."

He gave me a boyish smile, one that was cute and innocent. "Challenge accepted. Prepare to be impressed."

I had a feeling his dancing skills weren't the only thing I would be impressed with.

I gave him a playful shove. "I hope you're as good as you say you are. I wouldn't want to be disappointed."

"Trust me," he assured me. "Just watch and learn, pretty thing."

As the music turned to something upbeat, Theo moved his body effortlessly. His confidence was infectious, and his gaze never wavered from mine. I was convinced the man could dance to cowbells and make it look sexy.

"See?" He pulled me into him when the song shifted to something slower. "Told you I was a natural."

I rolled my eyes. "Okay, fine. I admit, you're not half bad."

He pulled me closer. "Not half bad, huh? Just wait until you see what else I have up my sleeve."

His gaze was intense, and all I could focus on was him and how much I wanted to kiss him again. But how far was I willing to go?

In my head, I knew the right thing to do would be to go back to my hotel. But I didn't want to share a room with my two friends when I could spend more time with him.

This connection was unexpected. And while I might not have been a one-night stand kind of girl, I still wanted to have one with him. I might end up regretting this in the morning, but consequences be damned, I was going for it.

A night of fun couldn't hurt, right?

With a nervous smile and a fluttering heart, I leaned in

before I talked myself out of it. "Would you like to get out of here?"

His eyes widened momentarily, with a look of surprise flickering across his face. "Are you saying what I think you're saying?"

My cheeks grew warm; only I would screw this up. "Forget I asked."

He grabbed my elbow like he was afraid I would slip away. "I don't think so."

I didn't know what the hell I was doing, but for the first time in a long time, I was smiling. I was having fun, and it might have been just a small step, but I was grateful for it and tonight it was enough.

"This would be just for one night, right? Nothing else?"

"Are you okay with that, beautiful?"

I swallowed, feeling an overwhelming sense of certainty. "Yes. I just don't want you to get the wrong idea. I don't do this very often."

His teasing eyes were sparkling. "No one is judging you."

Nerves rattled through me. "Okay, your room or mine." I cringed. God, I was so bad at this. And what the hell was I thinking, offering up my room? I was sharing a suite with two queen beds and a pullout. Not the ideal setting, so where the hell were we supposed to have sex?

He rested his hands on my shoulders. "We're going to have to work on loosening you up a bit."

"Sorry," I said as he continued to smile down at me. "I was freaking out because I just realized if we go back to my hotel, we won't have any privacy."

He linked our hands together and watched me closely. "I have an entire king-sized bed all to myself and no roommate to worry about."

I slipped my hand into his. "Your room it is then."

He grabbed my chin. "Last chance to back out."

I shook my head, letting him know I was completely on board with this plan. "I just need to tell my friends I'm leaving with you."

He nodded and dropped his hand. "I get it. Go ahead."

I looked through the crowd but didn't see them, so I dug my phone out, pulled up our group chat and shot them a text.

The Gossip Girls
Me
Where are you?

Claudia
Bathroom.

Gina
I don't feel so great.

Me
Are you getting sick?

Gina was a lightweight. We would tease her in college because she would get drunk on one drink.

Gina

Not yet, but it might happen.

I slid my eyes closed. It would be shitty of me to leave my friend in that state.

Gina
Why? Where are you?

Me
Don't worry about it. I'll meet you by the bathrooms in five minutes.

Claudia
NATALIE EVANS!! DON'T YOU DARE? WE
SAW YOU DANCING WITH THAT MAN. I'VE
GOT THIS COVERED. SHE HASN'T
GOTTEN SICK YET. SHE JUST NEEDS HER
BED AND A BOTTLE OF WATER.

Gina
Can you please turn the caps off? It's
making my head hurt. Natalie, I agree with
my sister. Have fun. Just share your
location, please.

I looked up at Theo. He had his camera in front of his face, attempting to fix a few strands of hair that were out of place.

Me
I can't leave you when you're sick.

Claudia
Yes, you can.

Gina
I'll refuse your help if you come back here.

Me
You really want me to leave with him?

I rolled my lips together. My head was a mess of contradictions.

Claudia
We insist. She's feeling better already.

Me
I don't believe you.

> **Claudia**
> See for yourself.

The image came through. It was a selfie of the two of them leaning against the stall, smiling and giving me a thumbs-up.

I rolled my eyes.

> **Me**
> Fine, but please check in with me when you get back to the room.

Theo reached out and touched my elbow. "Everything okay?"

"Yeah." I shook my head and put my phone away. "Ready?"

Anticipation flooded through me as I took his hand and allowed him to lead me off the dance floor toward the exit.

CHAPTER 4

RHETT

She trailed behind me as we made our way out of the club, where a line of people were waiting to get in. As we stepped into the cool night air, all I could think about was the need to get this woman alone.

There were street performers and entertainers on every corner as we strolled down the Strip. A surge of anticipation buzzed inside me with each step closer we got to my hotel.

Natalie squeezed my hand, smiling the entire time, but I could sense something was off. We were two blocks away when her steps slowed, coming to a complete stop. "Theo, wait."

I stilled, and my gaze went to where she was trying to pull her hand away. "What's wrong?"

"I'm so sorry." She sounded visibly upset as she turned her head away from me. "I don't think I can do this."

I let go of her hand and searched her face for a clue on why she just did a one-eighty. "It's okay, but do you mind telling me why the change of heart? Be honest with me.

Did I do or say something that made you change your mind?"

Was I walking too fast? Trying too hard?

"No." She hesitated, looking torn on whether she should take my hand back or tell me to fuck off. "It's not you. It's me."

My chest deflated because that was the worst possible thing she could say. Well, not the worst, but you know what I mean. "Are you sure I wasn't forcing things along?"

She shook her head. "Trust me, you've done everything right. I'm just nervous. I'm fresh out of a long-term relationship, and this is so out of character for me. I'm sorry."

The woman was so damn adorable.

"We don't have to do anything," I assured her, not liking how she seemed flighty all of a sudden.

"Yeah, right."

I pinched my eyebrows together. "I'm serious."

What kind of guy did she take me for? I meant what I said. I would be perfectly comfortable just spending time with her. Disappointed? Sure, but I'd get over it. I could find a hookup anytime or place I wanted, but I didn't want that with anyone but her at the moment. If time was all we had, I'd take it.

"Come on, you expect me to believe that?"

"Of course I do." I flashed her a smile, trying to get her to relax. "Now, are you really going to let me walk back to my hotel by myself?"

"You'll be fine."

"I could get mugged or murdered."

She looked me up and down. "You look like you can take care of yourself."

"What if I trip and fall and crack my head open?"

That was stupid and lame, but my head was spinning

with alcohol. Not to mention, it dawned on me how our roles seemed to be reversed.

Normally, I was smooth with the ladies and had them eating out of my palm. With blondie, I felt like a lap dog begging for attention. This was so not cool.

"Let's go have a drink somewhere, please?" I dropped to my knees like a panhandler, begging for scraps. If there were paparazzi nearby with cameras, the guys would never let me live this down.

"What are you doing?" she whisper-shouted while frantically looking around.

"What does it look like? I'm pleading for a second more of your time."

She rolled her eyes. "You are being dramatic."

"I'm trying to be persuasive."

"Get up." She looked like she was one second away from wringing my neck. "People are starting to stare."

"Not until you agree to one drink with me."

"You are impossible." She gave me a swat on the shoulder. "Fine, now get up."

I took advantage of her outstretched hand and pulled myself off the ground. "See, was that so hard?" I asked, dusting my jeans off.

"Yes," she said, fighting a smile.

"Admit it. You find me charming." I bumped my shoulder into hers.

"Actually," she tilted her head to the side, "you seem a little high maintenance to me."

My mouth popped open at her playful jab. "Take that back." I poked her in the rib. "And for your information, I am low maintenance to the core, missy."

"Is that why I caught you fussing with your hair for ten minutes while looking at yourself in your phone camera when I was texting with my friends?"

I couldn't deny her observation, but in my defense, I was trying to look my best.

"You know, I barely know you, and you've insulted me more times tonight than in my short thirty-one years on this planet."

"Ew, you're thirty-one? That's old."

What. The. Fuck.

I stopped walking and shook my head when she broke out in a fit of giggles. "And just how old are you, young lady?"

"Old enough to know that you're trouble. Come on," she huffed. "I owe you a drink for helping me out earlier."

If she thought she was paying, she had another thing coming.

It was almost one in the morning, but the Strip was still full of life. I gently ushered her through the spinning doors of the first casino we happened upon.

I surveyed our options for themed bars and restaurants. There was a rowdy sports bar in the middle of the casino and a quiet lounge upstairs on the second level. There was no way in hell I was going to a sports bar.

"Are you okay with something a little more quiet and chill?" I asked over the whirl of slot machines in the background. It was hard to hear over the whooping and shouting. Some were celebrating wins, while others were moaning over their losses.

"Sure."

Thank God.

Natalie and I navigated through the sea of flashing lights and blackjack tables, trying not to inhale all the cigarette smoke. The lounge was packed, and almost every table was taken. We found a cozy booth off to the side, away from the chaos.

There was a live band playing jazz, which was not my favorite, but then again, I wasn't here for the music.

"How long are you and your girls in Vegas for?" I asked as the server set our drinks down.

She ran her finger over the rim of her glass. "This is our last night."

"Nice." I pushed a napkin her way so she could set it under her glass. "Have you guys been having fun lighting up the town?"

She swallowed. "It's been a blast. The three of us needed this time together."

"What's the deal with you and the two sisters anyway?"

She tilted her head to the side. "What do you mean?"

"Well, the whole reason why we're sitting here is because you had to put on a show for them?"

She winced. "Yeah, I recently went through a messy breakup, and they are afraid I won't be able to move on from it."

That's what I figured.

"What did he do?"

She glanced down at the floor, looking uncomfortable. "He got another girl pregnant while we were together."

"He's a fucking moron," I said, feeling pissed off on her behalf.

She dragged her gaze back up to mine. "That's too nice of a word for him."

"I hope you wrote him off for good." My jaw ticked. I didn't know the guy, but he sounded like a dumbass.

"As much as I can. Our best friends are getting married next month, so we have to put our differences aside and try to save face. It's going to be hard because he's bringing the pregnant girlfriend, which means I'll have to sit through the ceremony and the reception, watching the two of them, all the while enduring all the pity stares and whispered comments."

"That sounds horrible." I flagged the hostess over. "Bring us a bottle of tequila and a couple shot glasses, please."

Natalie raised her brows. "Are you ready to hold my hair back over the toilet bowl later when I'm puking my brains out?"

"Is that your subtle way of saying you plan on spending the night with me?"

Her laugh floated across the table. "I would need to get to know you better first."

"Go ahead and ask me anything," I told her while pouring the tequila into the two shot glasses.

"Why are you still single?"

I set the bottle down and tilted my head to the side. "That's your first question?"

She leaned forward, steepling her hands under her chin. "Yes, a guy who runs a shelter for single moms and helps women convince their friends that they're into each other. Theo, you're a great catch, but something seems off here."

"The work I do for the charity is nothing special," I told her, feeling slightly awkward and really fucking guilty.

I was starting to regret telling her that. And it felt weird hearing my real name come from her mouth.

"You're modest too and still haven't answered my question, so spill the beans."

"Maybe I'm just waiting for someone to keep up with me," I teased.

She raised an eyebrow. "I find that hard to believe."

I leaned against the booth so I could stretch my legs out. I loved that she wasn't trying to play games or use me for bragging rights. She had no idea who I was, and something told me she wouldn't care if she did.

"The truth is, my mother would be thrilled if I got married. In fact, she already has a willing prospect waiting for me when I decide to settle down."

She snatched her glass up and threw it back. "Sounds eighteenth century-ish."

I held her gaze. "My parents are very loving and supportive, but they are also old-fashioned. They expect certain things of me, and because of the pressure, I've rebelled a bit."

She sat up in her seat. "Finally, the conversation is getting interesting. Tell me more."

I chuckled. "My mom is afraid I'm going to die a lonely old man, and my dad is afraid that he failed me somehow as a parent. There were expectations of me growing up and a career path all laid out for me. Let's just say I was supposed to stay to the right, and I went as far left as I could possibly go."

She tilted her head to the side. "Are we talking politics now?"

I laughed while staring at my drink. "Honey, I was born into politics, and I've been running away from it my entire life."

"In that case, we can talk about something else."

I wasn't expecting this conversation to get so heavy. Maybe it was the alcohol that was making me so chatty.

"That's fine," I said, reaching for my shot glass. "I always said that the only way I would get married was if my life depended on it. The thought of commitment and settling down with one person scares me. My friends think I have Peter Pan Syndrome and am afraid of growing up."

She made a sour face. "Please don't tell me you still live with your parents."

"You got something against thirty-something-year-old guys who live in their mom's basement playing *Call of Duty*."

She tipped her glass at me. "Yes, because *Grand Theft Auto* is way cooler."

An impressed smile ghosted my lips. "For the record, I don't still live at home with my parents."

"Thank God for that." She breathed out a dramatic sigh. "Have you ever tried telling your mom that you're not interested?"

A light chuckle fell from my lips. "It's a bit more complicated than that."

"Isn't it always?"

We sat in silence for a minute, and I allowed my eyes to track over her face. She had the prettiest blue eyes, a cute little button nose, and lips so full and shiny with lip gloss that I was dying to kiss off of her.

"So, Natalie, what do you do for a living?" I asked, resting my hands along the back of the booth.

She pushed a strand of hair behind her ear. "I just finished grad school."

"Grad school?" I lifted a brow. I knew she looked a little on the younger side, but I didn't realize she was that young. "That makes you how old?"

"Twenty-six. I started a couple of years later."

"Why is that?" I sipped my Patron, feeling less like a dirty old man. Five years wasn't so bad.

She sighed. "Because I was stupid and in love and wanted to support my boyfriend."

"And he paid you back by cheating on you?"

"Yes, now do you see why my life is such a mess? Not to mention, I start my new job on Monday. This is supposed to be my fresh start, and instead of looking forward to it, I have to worry about sitting across from my ex and the woman he betrayed me with and pretend everything is totally fine."

"Sweetheart, if you think your life is messed up, try walking in my shoes. My mother probably already has my wedding venue picked out. She won't get off my damn back. She will find me a wife one way or another because, apparently, my parents don't think I can handle life on my own. The pressure they put on me stresses me out."

She clinked her glass with mine. "I say we get drunk and forget about all our problems."

I raised a brow. "Do you think getting drunk with me is smart?"

She leaned forward, and my gaze immediately dropped to her cleavage. I forced my eyes upward before I got myself in trouble. "Probably not, but what's the point of being in Vegas if you don't make at least one bad decision?"

Natalie and I spent the next few hours talking and laughing. As the night went on, every joke became funnier, and every story became more interesting. The drinks were flowing, and all the stress and tension I felt about the offseason melted away. An obvious connection was growing between us, and maybe it was the alcohol, but it felt like we were destined to meet.

There was a good chance I wasn't thinking straight, or maybe I was just overthinking, but I was picturing the two of us together. Her sitting by my side at family dinners and cheering me on at games. Spending time with her was fun, but what brought it home to me was how easily I opened up to her about personal things I didn't share with anyone.

I was being impulsive and ignoring the ringing bells in my head. Usually, I would take a step back and allow my brain to slow down, but it felt like the universe knew something I didn't.

CHAPTER 5
RHETT

Feeling the mattress shift, I cracked an eye open, trying to figure out where I was. It wasn't the first time I'd woken up in a strange city, trying to remember whose bed I was in.

There was a knot in my back, and my entire body felt sore. When I swallowed, not only did my throat feel dry, but it tasted like cow shit. What the hell was in that tequila last night? Getting blackout drunk seemed fun at the moment, but the pounding in my head made me regret every ounce of alcohol I put in my body.

I was getting too old for this. Not the mind-blowing sex but the drinking and partying. My body went through enough abuse during the season.

There was a rustling noise at the foot of the bed. I shifted my naked body under the sheets; my morning wood was rock-hard. Every muscle in my body ached, and my fuzzy head slowly started to clear.

A streak of blond hair and a naked silhouette that I memorized with my mouth and hands last night was now cursing and tripping over her own two feet.

I pushed up to a sitting position and rubbed my eyes. "Leaving so soon?"

She froze and glanced at me over her shoulder. "I planned on waking you up, but I wanted to get dressed first." She turned away and slipped her dress on. "What do you remember about last night?" she asked, walking over to pick up her shoes.

Her eagerness to run out of here wasn't good for my ego. Did I not perform well? No, that wasn't it. I remembered the sounds of her moans and how unbelievable she felt when I was inside her.

I shifted to the side and scratched my cheek. "I remember us having a little fun between the sheets."

"Fun between the sheets?" She stood taller like she wanted to smother me with a pillow.

"Yeah. Did you not have fun?"

My self-esteem would take a huge hit if she said no.

Her eyes turned hostile. "Do you have any idea what we did?"

Dragging both hands through my hair, I looked out the window, wondering what the hell she was so fired up about. It was way too early to deal with this little attitude. My fingers paused when I felt something foreign and heavy on my left finger.

Shooting up in the bed, I felt my sleepy eyes double in size at the gold band gleaming at me, and I had no recollection of how it got there. Awareness and panic hit me. Fucking hell. This had to be a nightmare. It couldn't be real.

"What the fuck is this?" I blinked, trying not to freak out, but the more I blinked, the harder my chest pounded. "We got married?"

"We sure did." She held out her hand to display her thin gold band.

My stomach roiled as pieces from last night started to click into place. Tequila, lots of tequila. Natalie not wanting to go to her friend's wedding alone. Me coming up with a brilliant idea on how to get my mom off my back. Natalie and I playing roulette with a big-ass side bet.

If it landed on black, we parted ways.

If it landed on red, we would get married.

Memories of us walking into a shady as fuck pawn shop. Paying off the Elvis impersonator to keep it a secret. All started to come into focus.

She sat down in the chair so she could slip her heels on.

Wait one hot minute.

"Where are you going?" I asked, feeling anxious and really fucking thirsty. I'd kill for a bottle of water and a few aspirin. My head was pounding, and the light coming through the window wasn't helping.

Her hands were shaking as she secured the strap along her ankle. "I have a plane to catch and still have to go back to my hotel and pack up the rest of my things."

Tilting my head, I squinted my eyes at her. "We have things we need to talk about."

Was she seriously going to bolt?

"Damn right, we do." She looked up at me with alarm in her eyes. "We shouldn't have gotten married."

A muscle in my jaw ticked. "A little too late for that, don't you think?"

She shot me a look that had my balls shriveling up. "You can't possibly be mad at me for saying that."

I should have been thrilled that she wasn't acting like a five-stage clinger. Usually, that would be exactly what I wanted, so why was I acting all bent out of shape?

"I'm not mad. I just need a minute to process this." This felt a lot like rejection, and I didn't like it. I shouldn't have felt this way. I should have agreed with her. But at the same time, I still wanted to get to know her.

Maybe I was still drunk.

She looked away, avoiding eye contact with me. "Last night was a mistake."

"Is marrying me the only thing you regret?"

I could accept her guilt over marrying someone she didn't know, but I'd never be able to get over it if she regretted being with me. Things might still be a little blurry, but from what I recall about the night we spent together, it felt real.

She blanched. "I don't regret spending the night with you, if that's what you're asking."

The pieces started coming together, each one becoming clearer. Some memories might still be fuzzy, but the spark I felt was as clear as day. There was a stirring of panic clawing inside me, but there was something else, too. Last night was one of the best nights of my life. I couldn't remember the last time a woman had gotten under my skin the way she did.

An idea started to take root in my head, and the longer I thought about it, the more it made sense. Normally, people regret waking up married. But instead of feeling like it was the biggest mistake of my life, it felt like it might be the best decision I ever made. This could be a win-win for both of us. It wasn't like this was forever. Once this was over, I could go back to doing whatever the hell I wanted. In the meantime, this little arrangement could work to my advantage.

"Good, because that's a start. I want to stay married. Just for a while," I stressed.

She blinked. "I'm sorry. What did you just say?"

"Just think about it, okay?"

"No."

I pinched the bridge of my nose. "Natalie, I don't want to have this marriage annulled right away, and your reaction is really starting to sting."

"Then take a deep breath or a pill to make yourself feel better. This is not normal. You can't be serious."

I closed my eyes, trying to put my thoughts and emotions into words.

"I've never been more serious in my life."

People always said I was a wildcard, but this was over the top, even for me. My friends were going to think I'd lost my damn mind. But it would be worth it if this got my mother off my back for a while.

She tilted her head, giving me a serious look. "Your jokes need some work because this isn't funny."

"Good, because I'm serious, so how about a favor for a favor? I need to get my mom off my back, and you need a date for a wedding."

"You must still be drunk if you think that this ridiculous marriage will solve all our problems."

On the contrary, this might be the only way to keep the peace with my family.

"You need a date, and I could use some help. Honestly, this scenario works best for both of us. Think about how pissed your ex would be. I would play the part of the devoted husband who couldn't keep his hand off you. It will drive him absolutely insane, trust me. And I bet I am a lot fuckin' hotter than Cheater Peter."

She blinked. "You really want to stay married?"

"Want and need are two different things. My team needs me next season. The fans are depending on me to deliver. I'm under a lot of pressure with the media. My family keeps riding my ass to quit and settle down."

"Your team? Media? What do you mean?" Her eyes

narrowed into slits. "You told me you ran a charity for single mothers."

I shoved a shaky hand through my hair. "Yeah, about that." I cleared my throat. "I have a confession to make. While I do run Born to Love, that's not my full-time job. It's a charity that I sponsor to help bring awareness to the cause. I'm actually a…"

She shook her head and slammed her eyes shut. "Don't say it. Please don't say it."

"I'm a tight end for the Atlanta Arrows."

Her eyes flew open, and holy hell, was she pissed. "You lied to me." She pointed her finger at me, and her voice might have gotten louder. "You told me you run a charity for single mothers; what the hell is wrong with you?"

I held my hand up. "It wasn't a complete lie. It is my charity. I'm sorry. I should have been upfront with you. But you didn't recognize me, and I ran with it."

I should have told her. I should have asked her more questions. There are lots of things we should have discussed, but instead of talking, we had sex. More than once, if my memory was accurate.

"Why didn't you tell me the truth?"

She wanted an explanation, and she deserved one. I didn't mean to deceive her, but it was easier to pretend to be just a regular guy.

I looked down at my ring and took a deep breath. "I got excited when I realized you had no idea who I was. By the way, my name really is Theo, but I go by my middle name, Rhett." She squinted her eyes at me, or maybe she glared. It was hard to tell. "Then you made it clear that you wanted nothing to do with athletes."

"Want to know why, other than my ex being a cheating asshole?" She inched closer and got on her tiptoes. "Because my uncle owns the team you play for!"

"What?" My eyebrows drew together as I allowed those words to sink in. This had to be some sick karma coming back to bite me in the ass for all the stupid shit I'd done over the years.

She smacked her lips together and shifted on her feet. "Beau Landers is my uncle."

Fuck! Of all the girls in Vegas. I had to get drunk and marry Beau Landers' niece. My stomach rolled with fear because there might not be a way out of this for me. Even if we did get the marriage annulled. No matter which way I looked at it, my career was in jeopardy. Something this big would be hard to hide. Maybe I could convince Big B to see my side of things. Prove that I could be responsible by owning up to what I did and hope he went easy on me. He was going to be pissed, but we had a decent relationship. He would get over it, right?

The tequila that was still flowing through me was telling me yes, while my brain was screaming: you're a fucking idiot, abort this plan right fucking now.

"Okay." I looked at her. "Let's come up with a plan. Is there anything else I should know?"

"I start work for the team on Monday in the public relations department."

I threw my head back and looked up at the ceiling. How was this my life? If this wasn't a crazy twist of fate, I didn't know what was. I drew in a deep breath, jumped from the bed, and threw on a pair of boxers.

I started pacing the room when a thought popped into my head. I spun around to face her. "You really had no idea who I was?"

She shook her head without even hesitating. "I swear to you, I had no idea."

I blinked. "How is that possible? Your uncle owns one of the best teams in the league."

"I've been living in London for two years, and before that, I was in Boston. Any time I saw Uncle Beau was during the offseason."

I had so many damn questions, but I didn't get a chance to ask any because Natalie's phone dinged.

"That's my Uber. I can't believe I have to leave like this." Her eyes frantically started moving across the room. "I have to go back to my hotel and pack. I can't miss my flight." Her eyes grew wide, and a look of pure horror filled her expression. "How the hell am I going to explain this to Beau? He's going to kill me." Her trembling hands went to her stomach. For a brief second, I was sure she was going to puke. "Oh my God, what have we done?"

Natalie was one step away from having a breakdown, and when tears started falling from those pretty blue eyes, I felt helpless.

"Breathe." I took her shaking hands in mine.

"Do you think anyone saw us leave together?"

I sure as fuck hoped not.

"We will figure all this out. Just give me your number, and I will call you tonight. Okay?" She shook her head, but she still looked pretty spooked. I walked over to the nightstand to grab my phone. "Put your number in while I get you a tissue."

Natalie started typing in her information but jumped when her phone started ringing. I grabbed a tissue from the bathroom while she talked to her driver.

She shoved her phone in her purse. "We can get this annulled, right?"

I grabbed my phone from her hand. "I'll call my attorney, and we will get things sorted out when we get back to Atlanta," I told her, briefly placing my hand on her lower back. When I opened the door, we both looked at each other.

Should we kiss? Hug? Shake hands?

The woman looked scared to death, so my instincts told me to be gentle. I opted for a kiss on the cheek. "Everything will be fine. We'll talk later." I guided her forward, trying to keep my boxer-clad body hidden from view. "Have a safe flight."

She looked back at me as she punched the elevator button. I waited until the doors closed behind her before ducking back into my suite. I slammed my eyes shut and dragged both hands through my hair.

I needed to call my agent and my lawyer. They were going to lecture the fuck out of me. This was something a rookie would do. The NFL warned you about stuff like this. My parents were going to disown me if they ever found out the truth. My coach was going to kill me, and my teammates were going to hold this over my head until the day they die. Now that I was sober and thinking more clearly, I knew in my heart that if Beau found out that I got drunk and married his niece in Vegas, then my life was over. Done. Finished. My reputation would never come back from this.

Fuck!

I walked into the bathroom and threw some cold water on my face. Seeing the ring on my finger did a funny thing in my chest. This was absolutely insane. This type of thing only happened in the movies, not in real life. I couldn't even look at my own damn reflection in the mirror.

I tapped on my agent's name and hit the call button.

"Rhett," Tony greeted, "how's Vegas? Did you win or lose?"

He had no idea.

I shifted uncomfortably. "Are you sitting down?"

"Of course, I'm sitting down; it's my day off. Is there a

reason why you're interrupting my Sunday breakfast?" he asked in between bites of his food.

"I got myself in a jam and I need your help." I moved my neck back and forth, trying to relieve some of the tension.

"Please tell me you didn't get arrested." I pictured him running his hands through his heavily gelled hair.

"I didn't get arrested." I chewed nervously on my bottom lip.

"Okay, then, whatever it is, we will deal with it."

I clenched my eyes shut, hoping and praying to God that was true. "I got married last night."

The line went silent for about five seconds, and then I heard the sounds of him shuffling through the restaurant and bells jingling through a door.

"Tell me you're fucking joking."

"I'm dead serious."

"Jesus, Christ, kid. You don't pay me enough for this shit."

My gaze narrowed. "You earn plenty."

The guy wasn't going to go easy on me, but it wasn't his job to hold my hand. I paid him to clean up my messes. And this was the deepest pile of shit I'd ever found myself in.

"I'm raising my hourly rate." I could hear him huffing and puffing through the line. Most likely lighting up a cigarette. He claimed to only smoke when he got stressed.

"Can you stop busting my ass and do what I pay you to do?" I muttered and ran a hand over the top of my head.

"Hold on. I'm going to check the news." He switched me to speaker phone and started tapping away against his screen. "I haven't seen anything online. How the fuck did you manage to slip into a Vegas wedding chapel, get married, and avoid the press from finding out?"

The man was on the Internet twenty-four seven. He hasn't missed a headline since Google was invented. It was a small miracle that the media hadn't gotten wind of this yet.

More pieces of last night started to come into focus. My shoulders tensed as each memory pushed its way through my mind.

"I paid to use a private entrance and offered up a Super Bowl suite to the next game."

"What the fuck! Do you know how much those suites cost? Two point five million dollars. That's fucking bananas."

"It is, but I was a little under the influence last night, so money was no object."

I cringed because holy shit! I clearly remembered offering that to my new friend Elvis and telling him, "We're *going to the Super Bowl next year. Even if I don't play, we're going to watch it together. You, me, and all our friends.*"

"Who is the mystery woman? I'm going to need her info."

A muscle in my jaw ticked, and I started pacing the room. "About that," I blew out a long breath, "her name is Natalie. I don't know her last name, but she's Beau Landers' niece."

"I'm sorry, can you repeat that please? We must have a bad connection. I thought I heard you say she was Beau Landers' niece."

"You heard me right."

"Listen, kid. I've been around a long time. I've heard some crazy shit over the years, but this is bonkers. I don't even know where to start with this dumpster fire."

"Well, I hope you figure it out soon because we will both be out of a job if you don't. "

He let out a frustrated sigh. "Do you know that your

contract is up after the next season? You need to stop behaving like a hillbilly fucking machine. Do you have any idea what the media will do with this news if it gets leaked? You'll be fucking toast, my friend, and you don't have enough bread and butter in your pantry to save yourself."

I was starting to regret telling him, but what other choice did I have?

"Look, I know you're pissed, but you can please just focus here for a second. I need you to get this annulled quickly and quietly."

He laughed. "You really think you can keep this quiet? Are you nuts? You were in Vegas celebrating winning the big game, got drunk, and married the niece of the owner of the team you play for. You're not exactly a nobody, Rhett. Your dad is in politics, and your mug is everywhere. What in the ever-loving hell were you thinking? Do you have any idea how much a story like that will go for? This will be blasted everywhere."

I dragged a hand over my face. "You better fucking hope not."

"Not to mention, I'm still cleaning up your mess from last week. The strip clubs, your drunken behavior at the after-party, the photos of you falling into the fountain at the Bellagio."

"Okay." I rubbed my temples. "I get it."

This past week was all about letting loose and enjoying a bit of freedom. I worked my ass off all year long. I didn't do anything illegal. I didn't get arrested. I was simply having fun.

"I will pay you extra to fix this."

"How fucking generous of you."

I hung up the phone and looked at the gold band on my left hand. It looks like a championship ring isn't the only ring I won in Vegas.

CHAPTER 6

NATALIE

I stared at the outside of the Atlanta Arrows corporate office, feeling my nervous fingers twitch against my coffee cup. It's been twenty-four hours since I found out I was a married woman and ran from that Vegas hotel room like it was on fire. I should be focusing on my job, not worrying about my uncle finding out that I got hitched to one of his players.

My legs felt wobbly as I trudged through the parking lot. Heels were not my friend, but it was my first day, and I wanted to make a good impression. The second I passed through security, scanned my key card and stepped inside the main lobby. I was shocked at how much had changed.

Uncle Beau had an intern meet me and walk me through department after department. The first floor contained the locker rooms and training facilities. There was also a huge hydrotherapy pool, rows of massage tables, a state-of-the-art kitchen, and a dining hall.

My intern, Patrick, introduced me to a few staff members as we passed by the white cubicles on the second level. Judging by the tall ceilings and wide hallways, you could tell these buildings were designed to accommodate football players. Everything was oversized and quiet due to this being the offseason. When I passed by a team photo on the wall, it took everything in me not to stop and stare at my husband in his team uniform.

Rhett's dark brown hair was floppy and hanging along his forehead. His smile was big, and his eyes were sparkling. Just looking at him gave me butterflies. Jesus. I needed to get a grip.

Patrick led me to one of the meeting rooms, where I sat at the end of the large, glass, sleek table. I took a deep breath and pulled my iPad out of my bag. I tossed my phone on the desk, feeling my stomach twist in knots while I waited for a team member to drop off a list of training materials to review.

Knock. Knock.

A short, younger woman with long red hair popped her head into the room.

"Hi, Natalie. I'm Penny, one of the head marking directors."

She breezed into the room, and I stood to greet her. "Hi, it's nice to meet you."

We had spoken several times on the phone, but this was our first time meeting in person.

"Beau is finishing up with a meeting. He'll be in shortly," she said, holding out a small white box with a bakery logo on the top. "Are you ready for your first day?"

"I am," I said, accepting the pastry box from her. "Is this for me?"

She nodded and smiled. "Beau said you liked blueberry muffins, and these are the best. I hope you like them."

"They are my favorite, thank you." I set the box down. "Please help yourself." I flipped the lid open so she could take one.

She shook her head. "Nope, those are all yours."

"That was very thoughtful."

"It's just a small welcome gift." She smiled as she lowered herself into the empty chair across from mine. "Do you have any questions for me?"

"Yes, and I apologize if you're not the right person to answer this, but my offer letter indicated that I would be mostly working with the shareholders and investors on managing our national and media coverage. The revised paperwork sent to my email stated that my role would be more community relations targeted. "

"Good eye. You're just as smart as Beau said you were. The V.P. you were originally reporting to, took a different position, so the marketing department had to shift things around a bit."

"So, my role will be focused more on local programs as opposed to national targeting?"

"From my understanding, yes." She tilted her head to the side. "Is that going to be a problem for you?"

That was a good question because it meant I would be more involved with the players' charities and their volunteer work. I wasn't planning on working so closely with the team, well, one team member in particular.

I shifted in my chair and gave her a tight smile. "I'll just have to verify a few things with HR. I'm sure it will be fine," I lied and berated myself for my lack of judgment in Vegas.

"Okay, great." She stood up and straightened her shirt. "I gotta run. Here is your schedule for today. You have my number if you need anything. Beau will be in shortly."

"Thank you."

"Also, here is an employee benefits booklet and a few government forms you need to fill out so you can get paid. You don't need to complete those right now, but if you can get them finished by the end of the day, that would be great."

I placed them in the folder and started writing everything down. I was fortunate that Beau gave me this opportunity, so I didn't want to screw this up. I was worried that people would assume I only got this job because I was related to the owner.

If I hadn't made such a stupid decision over the weekend, I would have held my hands up in celebration.

I thumbed through the training materials and was about to complete the last task on the checklist when Uncle Beau came strolling in. He was dressed in a blue suit with an orange tie.

His face was buried in his phone when he looked up. "Hey, sweetie."

I dropped my pen and walked around the desk. "I'm sorry I didn't get a chance to see you when my plane landed yesterday."

He set his phone inside his pocket. "No worries. Did you get settled in okay?"

"Yes, but you went overboard on the snacks." I laughed as he pulled me into his chest for a hug.

He chuckled and squeezed me tight. "I remember how much you love your chips and Twizzlers."

I patted his shoulder. "And don't forget the blueberry muffins."

"I'm just trying to help ensure you have everything you need."

"The room is more than enough. Thank you."

My suite in Uncle Beau's mansion was almost the size of a small house. I had my own living room, bathroom, and balcony. As nice as it was, I yearned for something more intimate: my own space, something I could call my own.

"Good. In a couple weeks, you'll have the whole place to yourself, so feel free to invite a few friends over."

"I'll keep that in mind, and I really appreciate you letting me stay with you while I look for something more permanent."

I originally planned on crashing at a hotel until I could find a place of my own, but he insisted I take one of the guest wings. It was only temporary, but the house still felt big and lonely, especially with him and Aunt Suzie not being there very often.

"You can stay as long as you need. I'm just so happy to have you here." He smiled and tapped my nose. "I'm sorry I won't be around much."

"No need to apologize. I know you do a lot of traveling during the offseason and split your time between here and LA."

Uncle Beau also ran an investment business that was headquartered in California. Despite the geographical distance, he was able to balance both responsibilities.

"Yeah." He rubbed his chin. "I need to wrap up a few things before I leave for South Africa. Which reminds me, I'm hosting a dinner tomorrow night for the team after the parade. It's nothing fancy, but I'm hoping you will be able to join us."

"Oh, that's right. You have your victory parade downtown."

He tilted his head. "Yes. The weather is supposed to be beautiful, so we are expecting a huge crowd. You are more than welcome to come as my guest."

"I would love to, but I need to stay behind and get caught up to speed. I know nothing about football, so I feel like I have a lot to learn."

He leaned forward. "I'm going to give you a piece of advice. Your job isn't to learn plays and keep track of stats." He swept a hand, gesturing to the window that overlooked the city of Atlanta. "Your job is to nurture relationships and make sure the guys are having a positive impact on the community. If anyone can keep them in line and make them roll up their sleeves and do some good work instead of just writing a check, it's you."

"About that." I swallowed nervously. "I was hoping you could provide some clarification of the revised email that I received this morning. The job description is slightly different from what I was originally hired for."

"Sorry about the short notice, but we are doing some restructuring. The position I originally assigned you was not very stable. That department is going through too many changes, and due to the rise of social media, I thought it would be best to have someone younger start to foster our commitments in the community. I figured you would be much better served working with the athletes and individual charities, as opposed to sitting behind a desk, drafting up media posts. I know your skill set. I know your personality, and I think you would be the perfect person to help promote the team's brand in the community."

"But what about the public relations position?"

I wasn't trying to come across as ungrateful, but I was hired to do a specific job, one that I'd prepared for.

"That wasn't a permanent position, and there was no guarantee we would be able to keep you on after the first year. This is a similar role, with more flexibility and stability."

"Got it. I was concerned when I saw the email, but I feel better now," I said, tacking on a smile at the end.

"I know I'm throwing you a curve ball here, but this will benefit you in the long run. You're not just my niece, you're also my employee, and I need to do what's best for my business. Tracy, the woman you will be reporting to, has the experience to teach you all you need to know. There is no doubt in my mind that you will thrive under her guidance."

If Beau had that much confidence in her and felt this strongly about it, then I had no doubt that this was the right move for me. I was just starting out without a nickel to my name. Most people would kill for this opportunity, and I might have already had a foot in the door, thanks to who Beau was to me, but I still wanted to make him proud.

"I understand. I know you have to get going. Is there anything else I should be made aware of?"

He held up his hand. "One more thing. While I'm excited to have you join the organization, I want to make something very clear. Under no circumstances are you allowed to have any type of romantic relationship with anyone in this building. I know these guys, and I know how tempting they can be. They're not all bad, but you just got out of a relationship, and I'll be damned if I allow any of those young punks to take advantage of you, and trust me, they will try. If they do and I find out, they will be gone quicker than cupcakes at a kid's birthday party." My face went white, but somehow, I managed to simply smile and blink as he continued. "We had a scandal a few years ago that involved a big player and our physical therapist. The guys know I mean business, so when the season starts, I will be sure to remind them that you are off-limits."

I never truly understood how much I would regret my actions until this moment. Beau has been one of my biggest supporters in everything I've done. The thought of disappointing him filled me with dread.

"Now that we got that talk out of the way, do you have any last-minute questions for me?"

"I can't think of anything at the moment."

He nodded and rose from his chair. "Don't hesitate to

reach out with any questions." I stood to meet him halfway, feeling unsteady on my feet. "I think you're going to be very happy here." He smiled and gave me one last hug before walking out of the room.

I gripped the edge of my desk before pulling the gold band out of my purse and staring at it. The events over the last weekend came rolling through my mind. My heart raced with anxiety about how he would react if he ever found out. He would see this as a betrayal, and Rhett could lose his spot on the team.

I couldn't let that happen.

Now, I had to find a way to divorce my husband before Beau found out the truth.

CHAPTER 7

RHETT

"Hey, are you going to be okay, man?" JP clapped me on the back hard enough to almost make me spill my beer.

I adjusted my collar for what felt like the hundredth time. "I hope so."

"You look tense, so you might want to loosen up a bit."

I glanced around. Beau's mansion was filled with the sound of my teammates chatting and laughing. Everyone was stoked for a break and looking forward to leaving the pressure behind for a few months. I, however, was too nervous to enjoy myself.

"What the hell am I supposed to say to her when I see her?" I whispered, hoping no one was in earshot.

After I talked to my agent, I called JP to get his advice. He was the only friend I trusted to keep his mouth shut.

"Probably should have thought about that before you married her."

My eyes widened when Morris started heading our way. "Can you keep it down a bit?" I asked, feeling really on edge. I had no clue how I was going to keep up the act and engage in conversation when I was this distracted.

"Why does this feel like a total sausage fest?" Morris asked, with a broad grin on his face. He took a gulp of his beer, looking relaxed as always.

"Because all the guys left their wives and girlfriends at home," I answered, taking a gulp of my own, hoping it would calm my nerves.

"Which is why I'm headed out soon. I have an early morning meeting with my financial advisor. You know, to talk about what I'm going to do with all my millions now that I'm retired." JP glanced at me with a smirk.

He was so full of shit.

I pointed my beer at him and called him out. "Stop acting like you're not itching to get out of here so you can go home to Rylee."

He smiled, not even denying it. "What can I say? When things are good, they're good."

Morris clapped me on the shoulder. "Are you going out later, Rhett? Or did you do enough damage last week?"

He was referring to my shenanigans at the team's after-party the night of the Super Bowl. I suffered a bit of backlash after images of my drunken behavior surfaced online. I could only imagine the heat I would get if the media found out about my impromptu nuptials.

"I think I'm going to stay in tonight," I said, scanning the room for a particular blonde.

Morris nudged JP playfully. "Do you think the party boy is slowing down?"

They were just teasing me in good fun, but I was too wound up tonight to participate. I rolled my eyes and found my mind drifting away from my friends.

I looked toward the front of the room and spotted her as she descended the staircase. My eyes tracked her every movement. I licked my lips and swallowed hard, hoping I wasn't being too obvious.

Man, I thought I remembered how gorgeous she was. After looking at her now, I couldn't seem to pull my eyes away from her. A warm feeling spread across my chest, but I quickly shoved it away. I shouldn't be thinking those thoughts while standing two feet away from her uncle. Not unless I planned on digging a grave for myself in his backyard.

"Boys." Big B stepped in front of us. I wasn't sure how I was supposed to handle this, so I stuffed my hands in my pockets without saying a word. Staying quiet was the only way to ensure that I didn't do or say something stupid.

"Have you guys met my niece, Natalie? She's going to be working in the PR department, so you better treat her well, but not too well." He pointed his finger at us in warning, or maybe it was just me.

"Hello, Rhett. It's good to see you again." She held her hand out for me to shake like we were casual acquaintances instead of two people who spent the night together and woke up married.

A handshake? Really? I wanted to laugh, but nothing about this was funny.

"Uh, yeah, you too." I sounded like a damn idiot and was making things ten times more awkward. "How is your first week of work going?" I stepped back and tried to put some distance between us. I didn't have the first clue about what I was doing, but knowing my track record, I would probably fuck it all up somehow.

"It's just orientation and getting caught up to speed, but so far, it's been great."

Beau kept his attention on me, and I swear to God, I felt a bead of sweat start to form on my upper lip. "So, have you two met? I hope Rhett was a perfect gentleman."

Kill me now. If he knew half of the things I did to his niece when we were in the hotel room, he'd probably pluck my eyeballs out with a pair of tweezers. The same ones he kept in the top drawer of his desk. The pair he used to pull out his nose hair when he thought people weren't looking.

"Of course." She kept her face completely composed. I, on the other hand, felt like I was shitting bricks.

I thought I could handle seeing her. Living in the same city seemed like fun. Yet, here I was, stumbling over words and trying not to stare at her chest. I could barely breathe around the woman.

Beau threw an arm around her shoulder. "Rhett had a little too much fun at the after-parties last week. He's a wild one, but I'm sure you can come up with a few creative ideas on how to keep him on his best behavior."

This was bad. So damn bad. I could feel my heart beating like a set of bongos at a Bob Marley concert. Unfortunately, when I got nervous, I had a bad habit of rambling like an idiot.

"Don't worry, Big B. It was just a little celebration fun. I was just practicing my touchdown dance when I fell into the fountain. Gotta keep those skills sharp, right?"

I could feel the glares from my teammates drilling holes in the side of my head. I was just trying to make light of the situation, not sound like a moron.

Thankfully, Beau laughed, although he was probably tempted to call the team doctor and have me tested for a concussion. "That's a good one. You guys keep me young. If you will excuse me, I need to do some socializing." He patted Natalie's arms and gave us a nod before making his way across the room.

Natalie finally looked up at me. "Can I talk to you for a second, please? Outside."

My buddies gave each other a quick look, but luckily, nobody spoke.

Natalie didn't wait for my response. Without looking

back, she strutted toward the terrace, the click-clack of her strappy heels resonating through the air with each step. I trailed behind her, admiring her long silver dress. It hugged her curves in all the right places. Curves I had my hands on last weekend, and skin I'd love to touch again. When I noticed her right shoulder and arm were bare, I wanted to slip my coat over her entire body and cover it up to avoid letting my teammates get a look at her.

When she whipped around to face me, it was clear she didn't bring me here for a quick romp on Beau's patio.

"Have you talked to your attorney yet?"

I raked a hand through my hair. "Yes. He's working on it."

She looked over her shoulder and then back to me, like she was terrified that someone might overhear us. "Have you told anyone that we…"

I shoved my hands in my pocket instead of reaching out and pulling her into me like I wanted to. "The only people who know are my agent, attorney, and my friend, JP."

She didn't look happy with that last one.

"Can you trust him?"

I nodded my head in reassurance, noticing she looked like a bundle of nerves ready to pop at any second. "With my life, and the only reason why he knows is because I was freaking out and needed to talk to someone. I called him after you left."

"No one else." She pointed at me in warning. "Especially after my conversation with Beau. He made it perfectly clear that he doesn't want me involved with anyone on the team."

I could see the fear in her eyes, so I stepped forward when her lip started trembling. "Natalie, don't panic."

She crossed her arms over her chest and let out a shaky

exhale. "He said there was a situation a few years back involving a physical therapist and one of the players."

I threw my head back and looked up at the night sky. Fucking Della.

"Yeah, she caused a giant shitshow, and things were ugly for a while. It dominated the tabloids for weeks. She was sleeping with a couple of guys on the team."

Her face pinched tight. "He obviously doesn't want history to repeat itself."

"Listen." I scrubbed a hand across my face. "Nowhere in my contract does it dictate who I can or cannot date."

"He'll trade you."

I blinked, feeling sick to my stomach. "He said that?"

"He implied it."

What a complete clusterfuck.

She looked over her shoulder and tried to keep her voice down. "We are both going to be in deep shit if he finds out about this. But your shit will be deeper than mine. You could lose your spot on the team. We can't let him find out. We really need to handle this as soon as possible. We can't afford any delays."

This sucked balls. I finally found a girl I liked and had to give her up. I would fight for her if I thought she wanted it. But she was right. I miscalculated and messed up big time. Now, I had to make sure I fixed it.

I said my goodbyes and waited until I got inside my car to call my lawyer.

"Vince Bradly speaking."

I shook my head because the guy had caller ID and knew it was me.

"Vince, it's Rhett. I need an update. Did you start the paperwork for the divorce or the annulment or whatever the hell it's called?"

There was a long stretch of silence before he finally spoke. "I just spoke with Tony and was about to call you."

My eyebrows crinkled. "This doesn't sound good."

He coughed into the phone. "There is a bit of a holdup."

"What's the issue?"

"The judge overseeing the annulment is a guy I went to law school with, and he's not my biggest fan. He is using your case as leverage to fuck with me."

My hands tightened around the phone. "Vince, I swear to God. My career is on the line. You need to clean this shit up and get it sorted."

I was mentally kicking myself for being so reckless. I was going to pay the price for this in more ways than one.

He sighed. "I'm doing what I can, but maybe you can use this to your advantage."

"I'm not following," I said, staring through the windshield of my truck, wondering what the fuck he was getting at.

"You really like this girl. Maybe use the time to get to know her. See if there's something there."

I scratched my head. There was no denying that I wanted to take my time and see if this connection turned into something. But that wasn't an option, right? I couldn't force her to stay married to me, but I could take advantage of this little delay.

Maybe use the time to get to know her. See if there's something there.

Perhaps Vince was onto something.

CHAPTER 8

RHETT

I was driving myself crazy, so I drove around for an hour, trying to clear my head, before I found myself sitting in JP's driveway. I put my car in park, hoping he would know what to do.

I picked up the pizza box and the twelve-pack from my passenger seat and trudged up the driveway; balancing the food and drinks in one hand, I twisted the knob with the other, only to find that it was locked. The lights were on inside, so I knew he was home.

I rang the bell and waved into the Ring camera in case he was looking.

A few seconds later, the front door swung open. "Rhett, what are you doing here? I thought you were still at Beau's?"

"Wow," I said, breezing past my buddy. "Some greeting."

He closed the door while I kicked my shoes off. "We've talked about this," he said gently like he was afraid he would hurt my feelings. "Rylee and I are engaged, and this

70

is her house now too. You can't just show up unannounced whenever you want."

My eyes rounded. "Are you saying I'm unwelcome?"

He scrubbed a hand over his beard. "You are always welcome, but Rylee and I are living together, and you know, we could be doing things."

I raised an eyebrow at him, noticing his rumpled shirt and messed up hair. "What kind of things would you be doing? Because judging by your appearance, I can take a wild guess."

He gave me a murderous glare, and I laughed. It wasn't his job to entertain me, and it wasn't like I couldn't keep myself busy. I liked being around the guy but with him settled down, we didn't see each other all that often anymore.

"Where is that lovely fiancée of yours?" I called out and set the pizza and beer on the table.

He looked up at the top of the stairs. "None of your damn business."

I fought back a laugh and flipped open the pizza box. "Easy there, big guy."

"So, how did things go with Natalie?"

"Not great," I said, patting their golden retriever, Oakley, as he came up to rest his blocky head on my lap.

"What happened?" He walked back into the kitchen to grab a bottle opener.

"She doesn't want to drag this out. She wants a divorce." I sighed and popped my beer open.

He pushed a coaster my way. It was another new house rule since Rylee moved in. "That's good. You can't hide this forever, and with her being Beau's niece, that makes things really complicated for you."

I rested my head against the back of the couch. "Dude,

you don't know the half of it. Big B told her that he would get rid of anyone who tried to make a move on her."

"Damn. That's rough, and Big B isn't known for his sarcasm either. So, what's your plan now?" he asked, taking a seat next to me.

"I was hoping you would give me one."

Sleeping with the owner's niece was crossing a line. Secretly marrying her was career suicide. But even knowing who she was, I still didn't regret it.

He shook his head. "Not going to happen, buddy. Time to start acting like a grown-up and take some responsibility for your actions."

"She's really eager to put this behind her and move on," I told him, staring straight ahead.

"That's good, right?"

I shrugged. "I'm not so sure."

He moved a scented candle out of the way so he could set his beer down. "Rhett, what's going on? You can't possibly want this. I know you want your mom off your back, but there has to be another way. You barely know each other."

I played with the label on my bottle. "Maybe I want to get to know her."

His eyes grew big. "Then date her first. Ease your way into this. Find out if you have anything in common and go from there."

"She won't date me."

"Try being her friend, then."

I mulled over his words. "I don't want to be her friend. This is going to sound crazy, but there is something about her. I've never felt this way before."

His head tilted to the side, and he looked at me like he couldn't believe we were having this conversation. "That's a pretty big statement coming from you."

I looked up at the ceiling, pondering how to explain this in a way he would understand. "I feel a connection to her that doesn't feel forced. I've never been in love before, but if it were to happen with anyone, I think it could be with her."

"Rhett, come on." He laughed. "You are not being rational right now. You barely know the woman."

I rolled my lips together and felt myself getting defensive. "Just because I don't know all the personal details doesn't mean I can't learn them over time. But she doesn't want that with me and it bums me out, man, and I know it shouldn't, but it does. I should be focused on my career and not landing myself in hot water with the owner of the team."

He pushed his beer aside and leaned forward. "I am having a hard time wrapping my head around this. You have spent your entire life avoiding relationships because you didn't want anything serious. This is so out of character for you."

"Maybe, for the first time in my life, I'm being honest with myself about what I want. My gut instinct is telling me she's the one, and I've spent too many years relying on that to stop now."

JP grabbed his phone and started texting someone.

"What are you doing?"

He lifted his phone. "This is too much for me to handle on my own. Mav is on his way."

I rolled my eyes. "Now you're being dramatic, and I promised Natalie I wouldn't tell anyone else."

"Too late." He looked at his screen. "He'll be here in thirty."

As the ex-team captain, Maverick Cross was like our team Dad, which could be really irritating at times. He was one of the last people I would want to talk to about this.

Over the years, even after his retirement, we maintained a solid friendship. I still looked up to him to this day, but the thing with Mav, he was serious as fuck and called a spade a spade. I wasn't sure I wanted to hear the truth.

"I'm not waiting for him to eat," I said, grabbing a slice of pepperoni and taking a huge bite.

JP was in the middle of lecturing me about the toll this would take on my career and how it would affect the team when the doorbell rang. I couldn't believe I honestly came here to loosen up. Instead, I was feeling more irritated than when I first got here.

Mav walked through the door holding what looked like to be a pie. "What's going on? What's the emergency?"

"There is no emergency," I said, standing up to greet him.

"That's not what JP said." He lifted a brow and handed me a glass pan covered in foil.

"You brought dessert?" I lifted the lid to peek inside. "How domesticated of you."

"Shut up." He laughed. "Kinley was up all night baking. Mila has been stuffy and coughing. Between the two kids, Kinley and I haven't gotten much sleep. Kinley finds baking therapeutic."

"At least she doesn't find painting relaxing like Rylee. I'd rather suffer through eating a few pies as opposed to sanding down walls and spending hours looking at swatches of gray paint that all look the same."

"Dude." Maverick exhaled, looking exhausted. "At least you get to sleep at night."

I smacked Mav on the back. "Enough of this pie and painting shit. When did we become a bunch of boring old men?"

"When we grew up and settled down." JP smirked over the rim of his beer. "Buckle up, buttercup."

Maverick laughed and squeezed my shoulder. "Enjoy the single life, my friend."

I could feel JP's stare on the side of my head, so I avoided eye contact. Mav was smart as a whip, so I knew it wouldn't be long before he started putting the puzzle pieces together. Now was as good a time as any to spill the truth. He wasn't known to have a big mouth, so I wasn't too worried about anything getting leaked.

What's one more person, right?

"Yeah, about that," I said, looking at Mav. "I'm not exactly single at the moment."

His eyes widened, looking caught off guard. "You're dating someone?"

"I got married in Vegas."

Mav's eyebrows shot up in surprise. "You did what?"

JP jerked his chin toward the backyard. "Let's take this Dr. Phil session out back and finish whatever pizza is left in the box."

Mav shook his head. "I can't believe you got married."

"It gets worse," JP said, and I glared.

We walked through the house and grabbed a few more beers to take outside.

"So, who is the mystery girl?" Mav asked, helping himself to a slice of pizza.

"Beau's niece," I said, cutting straight to the chase.

Mav dropped his plate on the table and turned to me. "I don't even remember him having a niece, and when the hell did you two start dating?"

I knew before I even explained this that he would give me an unwanted lecture about breaking the rules and crossing lines.

My jaw worked back and forth as I geared up for the pending lecture. "We haven't actually dated. I met Natalie at one of the clubs in Vegas. We had a little too much to drink and ended up getting married at one of those little wedding chapels off the Strip. I didn't know who she was until the next morning," I said, giving him the short version.

He shook his head like he was disappointed in me. "Rhett, what the hell were you thinking? There is a difference between getting drunk and being reckless. You aren't some rookie who doesn't know how to exercise self-control. You've been in the league long enough to know better." His reaction was exactly what I expected. He was always the serious one of the group, which made him a damn good team captain back when he played. "It's ten ways of fucked up. You crossed a line that you can't uncross."

I sighed, running a hand through my hair, struggling to find the right words. "I would think you'd be a little more understanding about my situation, seeing you slept with your sister's best friend and didn't even know who she was."

"Whoop, there it is." JP clapped and raised his hands in the air. I reached over for a high five. Mr. Serious narrowed his eyes at us. He hated every time someone threw that in his face. In his defense, he did marry her, but it sure was fun yanking his chain.

Mav shook his head. "Now that you got yourself in this mess, what are you going to do about it?"

I reached for my Blue Moon. "That's a good question."

Mav shook his head. "I can't imagine Beau being very happy about this."

"He doesn't know."

He pinned me with a serious gaze. "You are planning on telling him, right?"

I scratched the side of my head. "Not exactly. We are

in the process of getting the marriage annulled, and I don't know all the details, but there is a delay with the paperwork."

"Rhett." Concern was heavy in Mav's gaze. "This is going to blow up in your face. The longer this goes on, the more you have to lose. Beau Landers is not the type of guy you fuck with. I don't know how close they are, but I can't imagine he would take being lied to lightly. You need to find a way out of this dumpster fire before you lose everything."

I leaned forward, resting my hands on my knees. "Maybe I don't want a way out. Maybe this is a sign that we should at least try to work through this mess."

Mav raised an eyebrow, and it was hard to miss the solemn expression on his face. "I'm not sure what signs you are looking at, buddy, but all I see are 'Job Wanted' and 'Apartment for Rent' signs in your future."

JP cleared his throat. "You seem pretty into her. Just be smart about this. This is your career. Beau is the owner, he could cut you from the team if he doesn't like the color of your hair if he wanted."

"Do you really think he would trade me?"

He implied to Natalie that he would, but would he actually do it? Everything has been happening so fast that I haven't had time for the gravity of the situation to sink in. I was at the top of my game, but I had to look at the bigger picture. The potential impact on the team made my stomach feel unsettled.

"Anything is possible." JP dropped the pie down in front of me and took a seat. "So, if you and Natalie find yourselves on the same page and decide to do this thing for real, you better hope to hell that Beau will jump on board. Chances are he won't, so proceed with caution."

I stared into my beer, feeling my throat grow tight. I couldn't even allow myself to think of the worst-case scenario, but I needed to take this seriously.

Mav was right, as usual. There was a good chance this could blow up in my face.

CHAPTER 9

NATALIE

"Thank you." I smiled at the doorman and breezed through the double doors to Rhett's high-rise. He had a key card dropped off with a code that would give me access to the elevators. I didn't know why I was so nervous; we were only going to talk.

The second I stepped inside the elevator, I re-read our text exchange from earlier.

Rhett
Have dinner with me tonight.

Me
No. I asked for a divorce, not dinner.

Rhett
I have an update from my lawyer.

Me
Why haven't you called me?

Rhett
I want to talk in person.

Me
Is there a problem?

Rhett
I'll fill you in when you get here. I'll text you my address. What time are you off from work?

Me
Six. I'll be there to talk, but I won't eat.

Rhett
I ordered Italian.

Me
I'm coming to talk about the divorce, not load up on carbs.

Rhett
Do you really want to talk on an empty stomach?

Me
I'll make sure to eat a big lunch.

Rhett
I'll save you a plate.

Me
I AM NOT EATING!

Rhett
I'll take my chances. See you at six.

I shook my head at his silly nonsense and walked down the hall, almost bumping into a guy who was yelling at someone on his phone. When I reached the door, my palms were sweating, and my heart was racing.

I knocked and glanced down at my black flats. They

were a welcome relief from wearing heels all day. Now that I was here, I was second-guessing wearing just a simple sweater and a pair of black leggings.

When the door swung open, my breath caught in my lungs.

"You're early." My shirtless husband smirked like he could read my mind. The man was barefoot in dark jeans and nothing else. His hair was damp from the shower, and he smelled amazing.

I thought I was prepared to face him, but oh, how wrong I was. My gaze lingered and wandered, feeling thrown off. It took every ounce of strength I had to drag my eyes upward.

Everywhere, from head to toe, was cut and carved. How did I miss all this last weekend in Vegas? What the hell kind of exercises did the coaches make these guys do in the weight room?

Rhett lifted an eyebrow, prompting me to string some words together. "Can I come in?"

He opened the door slightly, but I still had to twist my body to the side because he wasn't moving an inch. I could feel the warmth of his chest as I squeezed past him, and the asshole looked amused too.

"You could have given me more room."

"And miss the feel of your breast against my chest, no thanks," he teased. The man enjoyed toying with me, and I loved putting him through the paces. We were quite the match.

"You are impossible," I said on a shaky inhale. "And for the love of God, please put a shirt on."

"It's nothing you haven't seen before." He closed the door and laughed.

Yes, but my brain was soaked with so much tequila that I felt like I missed it. I should have touched and memorized him more; maybe then I wouldn't be so enticed to keep staring.

He shoved his hands in the front pockets of his jeans. He was so close; all I could think about was how I wanted him closer.

"I had dinner delivered."

"I told you no to dinner," I said, walking further into the room.

Rhett's apartment was modern and weirdly decorated. The living room had a brown sectional with two recliners. Along one wall sat a huge TV screen above the fireplace and video game consoles. The other end had built-in cabinets that were empty—not a picture, a trophy, or even a book on a shelf. It was small and modern and nothing like him at all.

"Sorry, I was hungry." He rubbed his flat stomach, bypassing a formal-looking dining room without a single chair. "If you want, you can sit and watch me eat," he said, sliding onto one of the barstools at the kitchen island.

My eyes narrowed. "Don't you think that's a little rude?"

"No more than refusing to have dinner with your husband."

Heat crept up into my face. "Stop calling yourself that."

He cocked his head to the side. "Why? It's the truth, isn't it?" he challenged.

He was correct, but that would be changing soon.

"Rhett." I rubbed a hand over my forehead. "We need to establish some boundaries to prevent things from getting too complicated."

A smile split his cheek. God, why did he have to be so cute? "Are we setting these boundaries to keep you from falling in love with me?"

I shifted on my feet, not acknowledging that, yes, I was indeed worried about that. If I wanted to get out of this in one piece, I needed to draw a line in the sand and make sure neither of us crossed it.

"This marriage will end. There will be no touching, and no kissing, no more sex. Now, what is the update?"

"Sounds like a regular marriage to me." He shrugged.

I pressed my thumbs to my temples. "Can you please be serious for a second."

"You want to know what I think?"

"Probably not."

"Your rules suck."

"Well, too bad. They are in place for a reason. Now, tell me what your lawyer said."

He walked over to the recliner and slipped on a thick, oversized hoodie in vibrant colors that looked softer than my bedsheets. "We have a problem."

"What kind of problem?"

A growing sense of unease churned in my gut. I did a little research online today. Getting married in Vegas under the influence was textbook grounds for annulment. This was supposed to be easy, so I wasn't expecting any problems.

He ran a hand through his hair. "The judge who is overseeing the case has beef with my attorney."

I tilted my head to the side, feeling confused. "How does a judge in Nevada know your attorney?"

He ran the pad of his thumb along his bottom lip. "I don't know the specifics, only that they went to law school together, and he's holding things up and playing hardball. The judge knows the circumstances and the people involved. He's trying to show my attorney who holds all the power in this case. I guess shit like this happens all the time."

"You have money and influence. Don't you have people that can help you?"

None of this made sense to me. How was I supposed to stay married to a man I barely knew? I looked down to the floor, feeling panic bubble up inside me. What an unexpected turn my life had taken. Never again was I drinking tequila.

"I'd rather let my lawyers do the job that I pay them a fortune to do."

While I understood where he was coming from, I wasn't thrilled with that plan.

"How long will this go on for?"

He shrugged and walked into the kitchen. "I'm not sure. I was told, maybe a few weeks, possibly months, but that's the worst-case scenario."

I slumped onto one of the stools at the counter. This was bad. Really bad. Rhett reached for a bottle of wine and poured the cabernet into a glass. He slid it my way and picked up a half-finished beer bottle.

"Thank you." I lifted my wineglass. "Now what?"

He started moving around the kitchen and plated the pasta he had ordered. "I was going to ask you the same thing."

"We need to come up with a plan until we can find a way out of this." I sighed, staring at my phone, trying to think of someone I could call to help me. I just wanted to bury my head in a pillow and cry.

He placed a plate full of food before me and pulled on the back of his neck. "I'm assuming you still want to keep this under wraps."

"Why? Do you have a better idea?" My head was scrambling, trying to figure out a way around this. Lying wasn't something I was comfortable with. There had to be another angle we could consider.

"I do, but you're probably not going to like it." He swirled the angel hair around his fork. How could he be so casual about this? Why was he not freaking out like me?

"If you are going to suggest that we tell Beau the truth, I'm not sure if I'm ready for that. I mean, I know it's the right thing to do, but I'm scared. He will never forgive me, and I'm afraid of what he will do to you."

He held his hand up. "Relax. I'm not going to let you take the fall for this. Before we go any further, who knows about this?"

"Not a soul."

He raised a brow. "Not even the two sisters?"

"All they know is that we spent the night together. I haven't talked to them since we left Vegas."

He popped a meatball in his mouth. "I thought you guys were close?"

My face grew tight. "We are."

And yet, I haven't said a word to them about this. We used to talk almost every day; however, since I broke up with Levi, we haven't remained as close as we used to be. I assumed it was mostly because I moved to Atlanta, and Gina and Claudia were busy planning the wedding. Maybe it was more than that. Perhaps it was just my imagination. I wasn't sure of anything at the moment.

"Here's what we're going to do." He set his fork down. "We take this day by day and keep this under wraps."

The knot in my chest eased slightly, making breathing a little easier. "Okay, and Beau will be out of the country for the next three weeks, at least. That should make it easier."

"That's right. He's going on his annual hunting and fishing expedition in South Africa."

"Yes, so that should buy us some time."

"You're still planning on bringing me as your plus one to the wedding?"

"Do you think that's smart?" I asked, leveling my gaze on his. "Wouldn't people find out about us? Wouldn't that defeat the whole purpose of us trying to keep this a secret?"

"I mean, yeah, Beau is our only concern. The fewer people that know, the better, but as long as you and I don't post anything on social media, we are good."

He was making it sound so simple, but I wasn't convinced it would be a good idea.

"But what if people recognize you and take pictures?"

"You're only bringing me as your plus one. No one needs to know anything more than that. You just need to flaunt me in front of your ex. He doesn't need to know who I am to you."

I bit my bottom lip. "You make it sound manageable, but It's probably not the smartest move. Not to mention, it could potentially lead to more problems."

"I disagree. How awesome would it be if you took me with you? It would be a good way to say fuck you to whatever his name is."

"Levi."

"His name is Levi?" he asked, sitting back and giving me his undivided attention.

I nodded, feeling nerves prickle my skin. Maybe if he knew who Levi was, he would change his mind. "Levi James."

He pushed his sleeves up his forearms. "Why does that name sound familiar?"

"He plays in the NHL."

He tilted his head. "Jammer James is your ex, huh? I don't know him personally, but he doesn't have the best reputation. He holds the league's record for most slashing and penalties. I never would have pictured you with someone like him."

I sighed and leaned back. "He's changed over the years."

At the start of his career, Levi was driven and focused, but as time went on, he got caught up in the fame and struggled under pressure. He had been slipping away from me long before we ended. I thought moving in with him and finally being able to live in the same city would restore some balance in his life. But I realized quickly that the man I fell in love with was replaced by someone I barely recognized.

"I bet he has changed." He shook his head and grinned. "Think of it like this. What better way to show him up than bringing an NFL all-star tight end who just won the Super Bowl as your date."

"And yet, you're so famous that I didn't even recognize you." I tried to keep a straight face, but my smile slipped out.

He laughed, not even taking offense to that. "Well, I do wear my helmet a lot, so that's probably why." He winked. "I'm not trying to brag, but my name is a lot more well-known. He will be jealous as fuck. I guarantee you, it will eat away at him."

My eyes went to the ceiling. "You're proposing all this just to get your mother off your back? Can't you just find someone to date?"

"I don't want to date."

I grumbled under my breath and prayed for patience. "Then pay someone."

He scoffed. "Please."

"Fine," I huffed. "But are you sure you still want to go with me?" I asked, giving him one last chance to back out. He was being so nice and accommodating, and I was worried that this would blow up in our faces.

"I told you I would."

"You don't have to," I said, letting him know that he didn't have to stick with the original plan.

"It's part of my husband duties."

I rolled my eyes. "I have a feeling you're going to play that card as often as you can."

He leaned forward and squeezed my knee. "We probably shouldn't tell my parents about this, especially if we are going to get divorced so quickly."

"But that was the whole point of this."

He shook his head with a sigh. "Trust me, I know, and I'm not even mad about it. We can't help the situation. It is what it is. We'll just have to make the best of what we have."

I looked at my lap. This had disaster written all over it. I wanted to scream at the universe, but this was one of those situations where I wasn't in control. The last thing I wanted to do was complicate his life more than it already was. He was going way too easy on me when he didn't have to. I couldn't even live up to my end of the bargain, and he was okay with that?

There was so much I still didn't know about him, but from what little I did know, I liked a lot. More than I should. No doubt, I could do a hell of a lot worse.

As if he could read my mind, he reached for my hand. "I don't know how to handle this either. I'm still trying to figure this all out myself. So, I'm going to be candid with you for a second. I like you, Natalie. You make me feel things that I'm not used to feeling. I know you're looking for a way out, but in the meantime, maybe we could take advantage of the time we have. Let's get to know each other and make the best of it."

"What are you saying?"

I came here thinking we would be talking about signing divorce papers, not trying to see if there was something worth holding on to. If he was implying what I think he was, I wasn't sure what I was supposed to say. There were so many ways this could go wrong. But as I looked at him and saw how excited he was about the possibility, I started wondering if maybe we should give it a try.

He squeezed my hand. "I'm saying I want to take advantage of the opportunity we've been given and explore whatever this is. When the time is up, if you still want to end it, we can at least say we tried."

My brows pulled together. "Are you saying you like me and want to have a real relationship?"

Why did that thought make me smile? Why was he making it so hard to walk away? None of this made sense, and I couldn't figure him out.

"This is a mess, so I'm not going to sugarcoat it." He studied my face, searching for a reaction. "But yes, to both. Do you think you could at least give it some thought before shutting me down?"

"I don't know what to say." I was so confused, but something about the way he watched me had me holding my breath, making it hard to tell him no.

A slow smile passed over his face, and I really liked being the recipient of it. It was playful and warm and had me imagining things and wondering if we could really do this.

"Say yes to getting to know me. Let me take you on a few dates."

We were already on slippery ground, so entertaining this idea would be pushing it. I knew in my head that this would only make things ten times harder, so why couldn't I say no?

"I'll give it some thought." He caressed my thumb. Just a simple touch had me melting into a puddle. I wasn't a big believer in fate, but I didn't have any other explanation for how I was feeling. All I knew was that I wanted to learn more about him before I considered his offer. "Is that okay?"

He licked his lips deliberately as if he knew he had the upper hand and had won this round. I didn't even need to say the words. The truth was written all over my face.

How was I supposed to keep my hands off my husband when he was making it clear he wanted to do the exact opposite?

CHAPTER 10
NATALIE

"I'm sorry I'm late," I said to my boss, feeling all eyes on me as I rushed through the coffee shop. A sweat broke out at the nape of my neck from running across the parking lot in heels. If it was this warm at the end of February, I could only imagine how hot Atlanta would be in the summer.

"No worries." Tracy waved me off as I settled into the booth. "You mentioned something about your Uber driver being pulled over?"

I mustered up a smile and draped my purse strap along the back of the chair. "Yeah, I had scheduled a ride, but he called and said he got pulled over for speeding. It took me a few minutes to schedule a new one."

She didn't seem annoyed or on the verge of firing me, which helped me relax. "I didn't realize you didn't have a car," she said.

"That's next on my list. I'm actually going to look for something later today with a friend."

"Any idea what you will get?" she asked, taking a sip of her iced coffee.

This was only our second meeting, and I liked Tracy. She was the type of boss that you could go to for anything. I could see us becoming friends, but I reminded myself to be careful about how much I shared with her this early in our relationship. In this case, less was more.

"Probably an SUV, like a Jeep Cherokee or a Nissan Rogue," I said, allowing my gaze to slide over the menu. "I'm short and like sitting up higher so I can see better in traffic."

The waitress came over, and I ordered a regular coffee and a bagel with cream cheese. After living abroad for two years, I learned to appreciate the simplicity of ordering a plain cup of black coffee.

"I love my Audi," she said, picking up a knife to butter her toast.

"My dream car. I drove a Nissan in college, and I loved it. I need to do some more research."

I had to be smart about money. My Uncle Beau wanted to buy me a car, but I said no. I told him I was good with my job. I also knew I had to find my own place to live, because crashing at my uncle's couldn't last forever.

"Speaking of research. How much do you know about football?"

I rubbed my hands along my knees. "I'm learning more every day."

"Trust me, the rules are always changing, so it's hard to keep up sometimes, especially with those guys. They are a fun group to work with, but they all have different passions. I emailed you a spreadsheet with a list of players and their individual charities. It will give you a better idea of their interests for when you assign them to events."

I wiped my mouth with my napkin. "I'm really excited about this opportunity."

"Speaking of which." She reached over and grabbed a

folder from her bag. "I have your first assignment. One of our players has an annual event coming up. It's a shelter for single mothers called Born to Love. Your job will be to handle the PR campaign and manage the social media presence."

I blinked, wishing I had a minute to process this. As I read through the details, I forced myself to keep a neutral expression.

"Sounds easy enough." I smiled and sipped my water, hoping I didn't look as guilty as I felt.

Her eyes sparkled with excitement. "I figured I would start you off on a simpler project and let you get your feet wet. The player you will be working with is Rhett Daniels. He's a great guy, and the fans love him."

"I can't wait." I swallowed hard, trying not to lose my shit, as she handed me the folder.

She laughed. "I can tell you're nervous. You'll have plenty of time to review the materials and prepare."

I nodded and clutched the folder in a tight grip. I was forcing myself to stay calm. I couldn't afford to have a panic attack.

She handed me another folder. "Unlike some of these guys, Rhett loves attention and knows how to handle the press, but you will learn quickly that some of these boys would rather sell a kidney than commit to an interview. The reality is, we need the positive coverage to help fill the stadium and sell our merchandise, so you must really stay on top of them at all times."

"I understand," I assured her and took the plate from the busy waitress as she was about to set it down.

Tracy took a bite of her eggs and leaned back in her chair. "Another important point to keep in mind is there will be controversies, and when situations happen, you won't be alone. We have crisis teams, lawyers, and consulting firms to help find solutions." As if she could read the fear on my face, she took her glasses off and gave me a reassuring smile. "I know this sounds daunting, but we have teams ready to spring into action whenever we need. Remember, your role is to ensure a healthy public image. It's always best to get ahead of the curve regarding scandals."

I smiled, trying to hide the fact that instead of preventing a scandal, I might end up being the cause of one of the biggest PR nightmares this team has ever experienced.

Tracy left for another appointment. As I was writing a recap of my notes, a text popped up.

Rhett
Is your meeting over?

Me
Yes, do you know anything about me being assigned to the Born to Love benefit?

Rhett
Wow! What a coincidence.

His response came too quickly.

Me
You knew, didn't you?

Rhett
I requested you.

I shook my head and groaned.

Me
I'm going to kill you.

> **Rhett**
> Relax, you've got this.

> **Me**
> No, I don't. I wasn't prepared for this.

> **Rhett**
> You'll be great. We'll talk about it later. I'm
> five minutes away.

> **Me**
> I'm still mad at you, but I appreciate you
> taking me today.

When I mentioned that I was going to look for a car, he insisted on going with me.

> **Rhett**
> I was planning on telling you.

> **Me**
> No more surprises.

I closed out the chat, paid my bill, and walked outside to meet him.

———

"I can't believe you orchestrated this," I grumbled while sliding into the passenger seat of Rhett's truck. He was wearing a pair of jeans and another bright-colored hoodie. He looked hot, and when he flipped his baseball hat backward, I would have thrown myself at him if I wasn't so pissed.

"Natalie, we can't avoid each other completely. That will be way too obvious."

"I know." I sighed. "But you don't think requesting me is going to raise any red flags?"

"I wouldn't put you in that position."

I took a deep breath, trying to calm down. "Why didn't you tell me before my meeting today?"

He shifted in his seat and started tapping his fingers on the steering wheel. "I talked to Tracy last night. I told her I would need someone for PR and social media. She asked if I wanted anyone specific. I requested the 'new girl.' I thought it would be a good way for you to get some experience."

He looked sincere, so I decided to go easy on him. "I appreciate that, but we must be careful from now on, okay?"

"I promise." His gaze slid down my legs with a frown. "Is that how you always dress for work?"

I glanced at my outfit. "Do you have something against skirts and heels?"

"Yeah, they are going to get me arrested."

I rolled my eyes and buckled my seat belt. "You are being dramatic."

His hand tightened around the steering wheel. "My teammates are a bunch of horny men filled with so much testosterone, they could bottle it up and put Viagra out of business if they wanted to."

"I can't help it if they stare. You'll just have to learn to check your temper at the door."

The veins in his neck bulged. "I'm not trying to sound like a controlling asshole, but some of these guys won't give a shit if you're Beau's niece or not. If they think you're available, they will do more than stare."

He glanced at my bare ring finger, and his jaw worked back and forth. Shivers raced down my spine in a way they shouldn't have. He wasn't wearing his ring either, so he had no reason to be mad at me.

"Will you knock it off and give me a little credit," I said, sagging into my seat. "I know how to dress, and I know how to handle myself. I promise, the only horny asshole who will ever know what's under my skirt is you."

He cracked a smile. "Is that an invitation for another peek?"

I turned in my seat and crossed my legs. "No."

"You realize I might never get married again, right? You are denying me a once-in-a-lifetime experience of unlimited marital sex."

I tilted my head to the side. "Didn't you just imply the other day that most married couples don't have sex very often?"

His grin turned into a full-blown smile. "That would not be the case for us. I'm a big guy with a big appetite, and I'm not just talking about food, sweetheart."

Okay, then. I picked up my water bottle and tried to hide my blush.

The ride to the car dealership took about half an hour. Rhett spent the entire time asking me questions that made me want to pull my hair out.

What cylinder do you prefer? Four or six?
All-wheel or four-wheel drive?
Electric, hybrid, or gas?
A car! I screeched.

I just wanted four wheels to get me from point A to point B. I didn't need anything fancy or top-of-the-line. I didn't need a champagne chiller in my back seat or biometric secure stowage. What the hell was that, anyway?

When we finally pulled up to the front of the building,

I sighed with relief. Rhett jumped out of the truck and came around to help me down. I laughed at the scowl on his face when the breeze lifted my skirt up. He was kind of cute when he was all grumpy.

I looped my arm through his. "If it will make you feel better, I'll hold on to you extra tight to keep all the predators away."

He stopped and tilted my chin up to meet his eyes. "You should be more worried about me than them."

"You don't scare me, big guy." I patted him on the cheek, hoping to get him to lighten up a bit. He'd been Mr. Serious since he picked me up, and I was starting to miss his usual juvenile nonsense.

We walked side by side, moving from row to row, looking at the price stickers on all the windows.

"I can't believe you talked me out of the Audi. It even had pink interior lights. How cute was that?"

I showed him a picture of an ad I found online, and he immediately shot it down.

Rhett shook his head. "They are too expensive to fix."

"And what exactly was wrong with the Volvo?"

"Too unreliable."

"And the Ford?"

"I only like the trucks. I don't trust their SUVs."

That's how we ended up at the Toyota dealership. Rhett drove a Camry when he was a teenager and loved it. He said I should stick with a Nissan or Toyota if I were looking for something practical and reliable.

We stopped at an SUV that was bigger than I'd ever need. "You expect me to drive this thing?" I looked inside the window. It had beige leather interior, and the dashboard was filled with fancy tech gadgets.

"Have you ever driven one before?" he asked, opening the door and peeking inside.

"Why would I need something this big when it's only me?"

"Because they are safer than a car?"

"Says, who?"

"Says, me."

A short, stocky salesman came across the parking lot, looking slightly out of breath by the time he reached us. I snuck a peek at the sticker price and cringed when I realized it was out of my price range. It wouldn't be long until I was collecting a steady paycheck. Until then, I'd have to be careful with my cash.

"Hello, folks, my name is Don. Can I help you guys with anything?" He stopped and sputtered when he noticed who was at my side. "No fucking way! You're Rhett Daniels."

Rhett flipped his hat around, pulling the brim down above his eyes. "Nice to meet you."

"Congratulations on the win, man."

"Thanks. I appreciate it." He gave him a nod and looked at me. "This is Natalie. She's looking for a car today."

"I can help you find whatever you need," he replied happily. When he stepped forward, I had to itch my nose and turn my head. Somebody needed to tell the poor guy that he didn't need to use an entire bottle of cologne.

"I think she likes this one right here." Rhett pointed to the white Toyota Highlander.

"Great choice. It's all wheel drive, heated seats, a nice touch screen to connect your phone to, and enough horsepower to pull a boat or small camper."

I laughed. "That's good to know if I ever decide to buy a boat or a camper."

"And because I'm a huge Atlanta Arrows fan, I can cut

you a great deal." He smiled up at Rhett. "I'll even give you an extended warranty for half the regular price."

Rhett cleared his throat. "That's great, but she's the one buying a car, not me. Maybe you should try sucking up to her."

"Of course." He laughed nervously at being called out. "You want to take this for a test drive, sweetie pie?"

Sweetie pie?

"Sure."

Rhett winked and held the door open for me. "Get in and see if you like it."

"I'll go grab the keys." Don started walking away, but Rhett put his hand out.

"I'm just going to put this out there, and I'm not trying to be a dick, so I hope you understand. I'm here helping a friend. I don't want any attention. If you want an autograph or a picture, I'll give you one when we are done. If you post anything online, then the deal is off."

Don gulped loudly. "I got it." He gave him a shaky thumbs-up. "You can count on me."

He hurried away, and I studied my new husband. This was a version of him I'd never seen before, and I was surprised at how much I liked it.

Our salesman came back less than a minute later and handed me the key fob. "Just give me a minute to screw on the license plate."

I hopped into the Highlander and ran my hand along the leather, thoroughly looking over the rest of the interior. "I wish this was black instead of beige."

Rhett buckled his seat belt and stretched his long legs out in front of him. "Black gets too hot during the summer."

"I didn't know you were such a car expert." I side-eyed him with a smirk while adjusting the mirrors and seat.

"I know enough." He winked and reached into the glove box to pull out the instruction manual.

Don tapped on the window and motioned for me to roll it down. He then spent the next few minutes reviewing all the safety features and showing me how to operate everything.

"You kids take your time. I'll be waiting for you inside."

Rhett tapped my leg and motioned for me to start moving. "You lived in London for too long. I want to make sure you remember which side of the road you're supposed to drive on."

I pushed the start button and listened for the engine to fire up. I shifted into reverse and backed out of the parking spot. "Would you look at that?" I smiled as I inched slowly out onto the road. "I remembered how to drive."

"You know you can go over ten miles an hour, right?"

I held the steering wheel with a death grip. "I'm nervous. What if I get into an accident?"

His hand came out and squeezed my knee. "You won't crash the car. They have insurance, and even if they didn't, I would pay for it."

It took me a couple of minutes to get used to it. The vehicle still felt big, so I was surprised at how smoothly it rolled down the boulevard. I started to relax and ran a hand over the steering wheel.

Rhett stared out the window. "You're doing good."

I rolled my eyes. "I've had my license since I was sixteen. You act like I've never driven a car before."

"Then why are you so nervous?"

I squirmed in my seat. "Because I feel like you're judging and critiquing my driving skills."

He busted out laughing. "I'm not a driving instructor. I just want you to find something you'll feel comfortable with."

I eased my foot on the brake when we approached the stoplight. "I think I'm going to buy it," I told him. I had enough in my savings for a decent deposit, so the monthly payments should be doable. "Now I just need to find a place to live. I can't stay with Beau forever, and I already feel like I'm mooching off of him."

He looked at me out of the corner of his eyes. "You know, you could always stay with your husband."

"I don't know about that." I turned to him, wishing I didn't like that idea so much. "We are going to be getting a divorce soon. You don't want me cramping your style when you start bringing random women home again."

The thought itself sent a sharp pain through my heart. I didn't want to think about Rhett with other women. It was nice being the center of his attention, but it wouldn't last. That's why I needed to keep my walls up before he got any closer.

When I glanced at him, I noticed his jaw was clenched. "Like you said, it wouldn't be forever, right."

This conversation distracted me, so I focused on the road when the light turned green. "I appreciate the offer, but I can't do that."

"Why not? I have the room, and you need a place to stay. Beau is going to be out of the country for the next month. You said yourself you don't feel right staying there."

"I don't know if I feel right staying with you, either."

The reasons for that were completely different than staying with my uncle. We were already putting ourselves in situations that weren't good for us. I wasn't sure I'd be able to survive being around him day in and day out without wanting more.

"Why not? We're friends after all."

I glanced at him quickly, trying my hardest not to smile. "Is that what we are?"

He knew the effect he had on me. Just like I knew, these feelings would be my downfall.

"I'd like to add the benefits part to our arrangement, but you're against that idea, so I guess we are just friends who are planning a divorce."

I laughed. "Why can't we be like normal people? Why did we have to get married before we got to know each other?"

"I think it adds a bit more mystery and intrigue to the whole situation."

"I think it makes us sound even more crazy." I shook my head and swerved around a tire in the middle of the road.

Rhett's hand flew to the dashboard. "Jesus! You don't need to jerk the wheel so hard."

"Would you rather have me hit the tire instead?"

"Just be a little gentler next time." He eased back in his seat. "Now, back to your living arrangements," he said, studying the road in front of us like he was afraid and wanted to prepare himself. "Do you really want to stay in that big, cold, lonely old mansion by yourself?"

"Not really," I said, easing up to the stop sign.

He rested his elbow against the window. "If it makes you feel any better, the mattress in the guest bedroom is really comfortable."

"Really?" My cheeks split into a smile.

"Yep. It's a top-of-the-line memory foam."

"What else does the apartment come with?"

"It comes with a chef, a housekeeper, and a great fucking view."

Was I seriously warming up to the idea? Living with Rhett was probably reckless. But it would be nice to have company around so I didn't feel so alone. After all, it would only be temporary. I wouldn't have to rush into a new lease. I could take my time until I found the right area. If Beau asked, I could tell him I was staying with a friend. He was barely around anyway. He basically lived in California during the offseason.

All those reasons sounded great in my head, but if I were being honest with myself, that type of arrangement would only complicate an already messy situation.

"Moving in together would only make things worse." I admitted something we both already knew.

"I disagree. Also, my birthday is coming up, so instead of getting me a present, you can agree to be my roommate. It would make my entire year if you did."

My gaze slid to his. "You are so full of shit. Your birthday was last November."

His lips quirked up on the one side, causing his dimples to poke out. "Ah, you googled me, huh?"

"Obviously. I had to make sure I didn't marry a crazy person."

He laughed while glancing in the side mirror as I changed lanes. "I'm not full of shit. My birthday is coming up." He paused and leaned forward. "At the end of the year. So, what else did you find?"

"That you're annoying."

God, why did he have to be so playful when I was trying to remind him of all the reasons why this wouldn't work?

When we pulled into the front of the dealership, I couldn't wait to get out of this car.

I killed the engine, grabbed my purse, and reached for the handle. Rhett climbed out of his seat and jogged to my side.

"Thank you." I smiled as he helped me out.

"Thanks for saying yes." He smiled and shut the door.

"I didn't say yes," I yelled out as he started walking away.

"You will." He winked over his shoulder.

"What makes you so sure?" I asked, finally catching up to him.

He ran his hand across his stubbled jaw. "I guess I'm feeling pretty confident that if I could convince you to marry me, then I should have no trouble convincing you to move in with me."

I groaned because I was pretty sure he could convince me to buy a beach house in Arizona without even trying.

I was in big trouble.

CHAPTER 11

RHETT

I checked the time on my phone and cursed under my breath. Navigating the streets of Buckhead could sometimes be as challenging as downtown Atlanta. I was twenty minutes late by the time I reached the Capital Grille. My mom wasn't going to be happy, but there wasn't much I could do about the traffic.

When I walked into the dark restaurant, I spotted my mom sitting near the window, and she wasn't alone. Claire Settler smiled at me from her seat at the table. I let out a long groan as I entered the dining room. If there was the slightest chance I could sneak away and avoid this little setup, I would. But there she was, waving her arm, motioning for me to join them.

Fuck my life.

"Hey, Mom, sorry I'm late," I offered her a sheepish apology as I leaned in to kiss her cheek.

"No worries, darling. Claire and I were just catching up. I forgot to mention that I invited her to join us."

I should have known that it was a setup.

"Claire." I waved. "It's good to see you."

"Hi, Rhett. I hope you don't mind that I'm crashing your lunch," she said over the rim of her wineglass. "I thought it would be fun to surprise you."

I hated surprises. "Of course."

I went to take the seat next to my mother, but she quickly placed her purse and sweater on the seat, leaving the one next to Claire open. Claire scooted her chair closer to mine as soon as I sat down.

"So, I have some news," my mother began. "I'm organizing a charity event for our veterans. Our local VA hospital is seeking funding to upgrade its mental health clinic. Claire has been appointed chair of the fundraising committee, and I offered your help."

"I would be more than happy to make a few calls," I replied, looking down at my watch. I was already counting the minutes until I could peel out of there. "I can send you an email once I receive the confirmation of who is donating what."

She waved her hand. "That would be great, but seeing that this is the offseason, I was hoping you would be more directly involved."

Claire rested her hand on my leg. "And I will be there every step of the way for whatever you need." Her hand slid lower, but I shot my arm downward and seized her wrist before she made it any further. The thing with Claire was that you needed to be direct, or she would get the wrong idea. I learned that lesson the hard way.

I made the mistake of hooking up with her a few years back. I thought it would be harmless fun until she got the wrong idea and convinced my parents we were together when I made it crystal fucking clear we weren't. She went crying to my mom over a broken heart, and it didn't matter what I said. Claire had the perfect pedigree and connections. She came from a respected family, and my parents thought she would be the ideal person to settle down with once I was done playing the field.

Well, they would be waiting forever.

"Mom. I'll have to look at my calendar and get back to you. You can count on me to make some calls, but I can't commit to anything today until I talk to my assistant."

"Rhett, I worry about you. You never take a break."

My parents never understood that my commitment to football lasted well beyond the six months we played. We had sponsorship obligations, fundraising dinners, and celebrity tournaments, and I had my own charity to run.

"You know I hate sitting around doing nothing. I need to keep busy." I pushed my silverware to the side. "If anyone should understand that it's you."

Both of my parents were workaholics. So, it was ironic that she was preaching to me about working too much when she rarely took a break herself.

She leveled her gaze on mine. "Even I take vacations from time to time. You need to find balance in your life. Please promise to take better care of yourself."

"I promise, Mom, you have nothing to worry about." I winked, hoping to put her mind at ease a bit.

The waitress came over and took our order. Claire slung her arm along the back of my chair and ordered another chardonnay. "Did I tell you that I am going to be on the June cover of *Southern Bells*?"

I took a sip of my water. "You mentioned it."

She's told me no less than fifty times. She seemed to be under the impression that I gave a shit. I couldn't care less.

"Oh, yes. I'm sure I have. I'm just so excited. There is going to be a launch party, and I was hoping you could go with me."

She was getting more forward with her advances. I've been doing my best to drop subtle hints and ignore all her calls and texts, but the woman was like a bulldozer who didn't know when to stop digging. "Unfortunately, my schedule is booked solid. Sorry."

My mom folded her hands on the table. "Rhett, surely you can find time in your busy schedule."

If I was interested in her, I probably could. But I wasn't.

"I don't want to add anything more to my plate," I said, picking up my menu and studying it. Then, I remembered I had already ordered, so I set it back down. "If something changes, I'll let you know."

Claire smiled, and I immediately regretted it because I didn't want to give her any false hope. As the conversation progressed, Claire went on about a fashion show she was invited to next month in Milan. She gushed about the lavish resort she and her friends were jet-setting off to this summer. She lost me somewhere between chartered yachts and VIP access to nightclubs.

"Oh, no. I just got a message. I'm sorry." My mom stood with a speed that was impressive for her age. "But I have to go. Rhett, would you mind bringing Claire home? She drove with me."

My mom needed a hobby because this was getting ridiculous. I knew she meant well—she always did—but she needed to understand that the idea of me settling down with Claire was never going to happen.

"I'm sorry, but I have a meeting across town. She should have no trouble finding an Uber." I stood and pulled her chair out.

"You will do no such thing," she openly scolded me. "Be the gentleman that I raised you to be, and make sure she gets home safely."

I sighed, resigning myself to driving Claire home and mentally preparing for an awkward car ride.

I sat back down and gave Claire a strained smile. "I hope you don't mind, but we're going to have to leave as soon as you're finished eating. I'm short on time today."

She tilted her head to the side. I was expecting her to look disappointed, but instead, she seemed unfazed. "Okay, but I'm free later if you want some company."

Been there, done that. No thanks.

I leaned back, and my eyes wandered through the restaurant, looking for an escape route. Everything slowed to a stop when I spotted honey-blond hair, pretty blue eyes, and perfect pink lips.

I blinked, making sure my eyes weren't playing a trick on me. My wife had just walked in. This had to be a joke, right? What were the chances? As if she could feel the weight of my stare, she turned, and her mouth fell open.

Her eyes bounced back and forth between my lunch companion and me. Her lip curled into a frown. I didn't need to guess what was happening in her head. I could feel her jealousy across the room.

She'd been avoiding me since I asked her to move in. During that time, I'd been going back and forth on reaching out or allowing the silence to continue.

I wasn't the type of guy who sat by the phone, waiting for it to ring or got this worked up over a woman. Yet here I was, holding my breath, waiting for her to acknowledge me.

Her hands tightened around her purse strap, and I almost smiled but thought better of it. Instead, I sipped my drink, wondering how this would play out. Would she come over and say hello or ignore me and pretend I didn't exist?

When she slid her small frame into the booth, effectively giving me her back, I knew I had my answer.

I slipped my phone out and shot her a text.

> **Me**
> Meet me by the bathrooms.

I watched and waited for her to read the message on her phone. Claire was prattling on about what I couldn't tell you. I nodded and looked up every few seconds, pretending to be listening.

Natalie picked up her phone, glanced at it quickly, and flipped it face down on the table. I gave her a minute to respond, but after two passed, it became clear she was ignoring me, so I sent another one.

> **Me**
> Now, or I will walk up to your table and cause a scene.

I was full of shit, and she most likely knew that, but chances were, she wouldn't risk it.

When Natalie got up to go to the bathroom, she had to walk right by my table. I hastily excused myself, barely acknowledging Claire's confused stare. My heart raced as I rounded the corner and made my way toward the hallway where the restrooms were located.

My foot rested against the wall as I waited impatiently for her to finish up. I pulled my phone out, trying to distract myself, when the door finally swung open.

Instead of her usual skirt or dress, she was wearing black leather pants with a matching blazer. I cracked a smile when, in reality, I wanted to rip the leather material from her body and show her what she'd been missing out on.

"Hey." I moved away from the wall. "Fancy meeting you here, huh?"

She stepped toward me, keeping those baby-blue eyes locked on mine. "I'm surprised you even noticed me."

I raised my eyebrow, playing it cool. "Of course, I noticed you."

"Funny, it didn't look like it to me," she replied, crossing her arms defensively across her stomach.

I hesitated, unsure how to ease the tension between us. "Did I do something wrong?" I glanced over my shoulder to make sure we were alone. "You seem upset with me?"

She scoffed. "I'm not upset with you. Now, if you'll excuse me." She tried to sidestep me, but I gripped her by the elbow.

"I don't think so, sweetheart."

"What do you want?"

Her! I wanted her and to stop playing these damn games.

I arched my neck and stared up at the ceiling. "I wanted to talk to you."

Her attention flickered toward the dining room. "Is your date not able to carry on a conversation?"

"She's not my date," I explained. "I came here to meet my mother and realized it was a setup."

She tilted her head to the side. "That's the woman your mom has picked out for you?"

I nodded. "That's the one."

"She's really pretty. You could do a lot worse."

"Looks can be deceiving," I said, keeping my eyes steady on hers.

"You're really not interested in her?"

"I wouldn't be here with you right now if I were."

My gaze dropped to her mouth, and it took every bit of strength I had not to close the distance between us.

I wanted to taste those lips more than I wanted my next breath.

"Why are you looking at me like that?" she asked, even though she already knew the answer.

It was probably foolish and reckless, but I closed the gap, towering over her. I dragged my nose to the side of her neck and brought my mouth to the shell of her ear. "I'm tempted to kiss the jealousy right out of you and put whatever doubts you have about me to rest."

"I'm not jealous." She said on a shaky breath that wasn't very convincing.

"Then prove it." I leaned in closer. "Kiss me, right here and right now."

She frowned. "How does that prove I'm not jealous?"

I kept my tone light but my eyes serious. "If it doesn't bother you then you'll walk away without thinking twice."

Her brows bent together. "That's ridiculous. Your logic makes no sense."

"Maybe not." I smiled at her stubbornness. "So prove me wrong. Because if you're not jealous than you won't care if I take Claire home with me and fuck her, right?"

She hesitated for a second. Her eyes flashed with a mixture of anger and hurt, but she quickly composed herself. I thought maybe I had pushed her too far. So, I sighed, taking a step back, ready to apologize.

"Fine." She yanked on my hand and led me out the back door. She looked to the left and to the right like there was a wrong way and she wanted to make sure she was headed in the right direction. She finally turned to the left, away from the pedestrians and parked cars, and continued down the pavement, never once stopping or telling me where we were going. If I had to guess, wherever it was, she didn't want to be around people. We navigated our way through the parking lot and cut through a path where the only things surrounding us were trees and bushes.

She stopped abruptly when we were out of view, and just as I was about to ask what she had in store for me, she reached up on her tiptoes and shoved me against the tree trunk.

"Just so we are clear," she brought her lips to my ear. "I'm not jealous. I'm just here to prove a point."

I chuckled and wrapped an arm around her waist. "Yeah, right. You're not jealous at all." I pulled her closer. "Your words may say one thing, but your eyes tell a different story."

There was a flicker of vulnerability in her expression. She cared more than she let on.

"You're technically my husband, so your mother needs to stop trying to set you up with other women."

"Are you ready to claim me as yours?" I asked, daring her to admit to something we both wanted. "So my mom and the entire world will know that I'm taken?"

"I'm just setting some boundaries and making sure when you walk back through that door that you won't forget who I am to you."

"What exactly are you to me?" I asked, resting my forehead against hers.

"I'm your wife, and as long as we are married, there will be no one else for either of us."

She reached up and dipped her face forward, and in the next second, her lips were on mine, taking me by surprise. My palms cupped her cheeks as her tongue urgently sought access to my mouth. There was no hesitation on my end.

Her body moved closer, like she couldn't help herself, so I allowed her to take the lead. There wasn't a sliver of space between us. It felt like we were the only two people who existed, lost in a world of our own making.

She was on her tiptoes, so I angled my head to deepen the kiss. Her hands fisted in my hair. The grip she had on me was so tight I could barely breathe. She could have asked me for anything, and I would find a way to make it happen. I would give her anything she wanted.

I poured every ounce of emotion into the kiss. It was so consuming that I felt my entire world tilt on its axis. Her arm tightened around me, making it impossible to think straight. If I didn't unleash some of this pent-up frustration soon, I was going to lose my mind.

Someone could walk by and hear us, but I didn't care as long she kept doing what she was doing.

Her hand palmed my erection, and the rubber band holding me together snapped. Her lips moved down my neck, and she sucked hard, taunting and teasing me when I was already craving her next touch. She was pushing me to my limit when her hand moved down to my belt. Overwhelming desire was all I could feel.

I clenched my teeth together when she slid my zipper down and pulled my dick out. "Natalie," I gritted out when she started stroking me. There wasn't time to think or look to see if anyone was within hearing distance. All I could think about was how good it felt to have her hand wrapped around me. I swelled and thickened in her hand as she continued to stroke harder, like this was a game of foreplay that she was intent on winning.

There wasn't much restraint left in me when she slid her finger over my balls. How could I be this turned on by just watching her try to get me off?

"To be clear, this isn't what I had in mind when I pulled you out here," she said, squeezing my arousal so tight that it sent chills shooting up my spine. If she was trying to inflict pain on me, I'd let her try all night long.

"You won't hear any complaints from me."

A moan flew from my mouth when she started pumping with a possessiveness that added to the already overwhelming sensations. She stretched and pulled, and it was the best type of torture I'd ever felt in my life.

My cock jerked in her hand. "I'm going to come if you keep that up."

"You better be quiet then because I'm not stopping," she said without an ounce of shame.

Her fingers were wound so tight as she pulled and squeezed my pulsing cock. My hips flexed forward. I could barely contain myself. It was growing thick and heavy, so I clenched my hand around her hair to keep myself upright. With each tug, I had to suck in a breath. With each squeeze, I hissed through gritted teeth.

My fingers dug into her scalp as she picked up the pace. Our eyes met and held. My breathing was erratic as a bead of pre-cum glistened at the tip.

It had never been like this with anyone before, and I didn't think it ever would be.

Her movements became harder and faster, and I was done. The sensation was too much. Her touch was too intense. "You asked for it." I shot my hips forward with her name on my tongue. I was lost. I had no sense of my surroundings. The woman was consuming me in the best possible way. My legs shook, my eyes closed, and I finally let go.

I should have been embarrassed at how quickly I came. She made me feel things, things I couldn't explain. Something stirred inside me, and I tried to figure out what it meant.

When I finally opened my heavy lids, my gaze landed on her hand, which was coated with my arousal. I wasn't sure where the insatiable need came from, but my dick felt like it was coming back to life.

She shook her head and looked away as if she were ashamed of herself. "I can't believe I got carried away like that. This isn't me. Why do you make me crazy like this?"

My breath stopped, and I stared into her blue eyes, which were swimming with emotion. She liked me, maybe more than liked me. If she didn't care, it wouldn't have bothered her to see me with someone else.

"Probably the same reason why you make me feel so damn weak?" I was panting hard and feeling off-balance. "What if I told you that I have real feelings for you? That I haven't been able to think about anyone else since Vegas? That you are all I want."

"But there is still so much that we don't know about each other."

"Then let's take advantage of the time we have and learn. Move in with me. Get to know me. The real me. Give me one month."

"One month?" Her resolve was weakening, as if she was finally opening herself up to the idea.

"That's all I need." My eyes held her captive. If this was my one chance, I wasn't going to waste it.

She looked down at the ground and back to me. "What if this doesn't work out?"

"Then at least we tried." I replied. "We can't live our life in fear of what might go wrong. We need to take chances on things that could go right."

She bit her lip. I could see the internal battle she was fighting. "Fine. I'll stay with you, but I'm still going to look for my own place."

I pulled in a quick breath. "You can take all the time you need."

She arched an eyebrow. "No promises and no expectations."

I grinned. "Whatever you say, boss."

She took a step back. "I'm sorry if I've been sending

you mixed signals. I'm just trying to keep a level head about this. I feel something for you too, that's what makes this so scary."

I reached out, lifting her chin and forcing her to look at me. "I'm scared too, but I'm more scared of missing out on something amazing because I was too afraid to try."

"One step at a time, right?"

I smiled. "Right."

Her expression softened. "Thanks for being so understanding."

"I'll never push you beyond anything you're not comfortable with."

She looked down at her hands. "I need to get cleaned up and get back to my table. I'm meeting with one of the interns."

I looked down at my dick. I had a mess on my hands. "I gotta do the same, but you go back in before me." I reached out and pulled her in for one last kiss. "And for the record, you can claim me whenever you want. I'm all yours."

Her mouth opened like she wanted say something, but instead, she turned and headed back to the restaurant. I watched through the bushes as the door closed behind her and sank against the tree. I glanced up at the sky with a grin.

Maybe jealousy wasn't such a bad thing after all.

CHAPTER 12
NATALIE

"Here, let me help you." Rhett grabbed my bag off my shoulder and rolled my suitcase inside the condo.

"I still can't believe I let you talk me into this."

"I mean, it makes sense if you think about it. I live in a secure building, and I have plenty of room." He shrugged as if it was no big deal. "Like I told you, I'm not around that much, but at least you won't be totally alone."

I wish I could say that was what sold me, but I would be lying. There wasn't a doubt in my mind that living together would further complicate things, but I liked the idea of having him just a few feet away more than I should have.

We walked down the hallway, and I followed him into my bedroom. I expected it to look sparse like the rest of his apartment. Instead of bare walls and minimal furniture, I blinked, momentarily stunned.

"This is really nice." I spun around, noticing the walls were a warm gray, almost with a faint blue tint. The king-sized bed had a white comforter with light lavender accent pillows. I set the cardboard box down next to a writing desk and a big, oversized white chair in the corner. Sheer long curtains hung in the window, and a vase of fresh flowers was on each end table.

"Did you do all this for me?" I asked, feeling a flutter of excitement in my chest.

He shoved his hands in the front pockets of his jeans. "I know it's not as fancy as Beau's mansion, but I wanted you to feel comfortable here."

Everything inside me went soft. "That was very thoughtful. I love it. Thank you."

He tilted his head and smiled. "I'm glad you like it, but wanna know what the best part is?"

"What's that?"

"I'm just a knock-knock away on the other side of that wall if you need anything."

I bit down on my lip to keep myself from smiling. "I'll keep that in mind."

After a few more trips from the parking garage, we finally had all my stuff in the room, ready to be put away.

Rhett reached into one of my smaller bags, pulled out a perfume bottle, sniffed it, and closed his eyes. "I can't tell you how many times I've dreamed of this scent since Vegas."

He looked perfectly at ease while sniffing my perfume and reminding me of our night together. Something tightened in my stomach, and I had no damn clue how I was going to survive this little arrangement.

He put a lot of effort into making me feel at home. I knew he wanted more, but I had to make sure we wanted the same things before I gave in to him. I needed to be strong and smart and not lose touch with reality.

He set the bottle of perfume down and spun around. "I have a Zoom call with one of my sponsors. It shouldn't take long. Do you want to order in for dinner?"

I played with the hem of my sweatshirt, wishing I had a clue as to why I was so nervous around him. "I would like to cook if that's okay."

He rubbed his stomach. "A home-cooked meal sounds pretty damned good."

"I'll order what I need online," I said, picking up my phone and opening the app.

Rhett reached into his back pocket and pulled out his wallet. "I'll give you my credit card."

I held my hand out. "Nope. You are not going to win this one."

His eyes narrowed. "Wanna bet?"

"Rhett." I exhaled. "You are refusing to charge me rent. This is my contribution. Please, let me do this, or I will move back in with Beau."

He pursed his lips and moved his eyes across the room. "Fine."

My eyebrows drew together. That was way too easy. "You're up to something."

He shrugged. "I guess you'll have to wait and see." He smirked and left the room before I could say anything else.

My eyes rolled up to the ceiling. I wondered if it was too late to change my mind. This could potentially end up being one huge mistake. I'd been harboring feelings for him since Vegas, and now that we would be sharing a space together, I had no idea how I was going to keep my emotions in check.

I wandered over to the bed and unpacked my bigger suitcase first. What if living together only made these feelings stronger? How was I going to hide the way my heart raced whenever he was near? There was no way he didn't pick up on it. Probably got off on it. Speaking of getting off, I still can't believe I pulled him into the bushes and gave him a hand job, all because I was jealous.

I still didn't know why seeing them together bothered me so much. I knew he wasn't interested in her. Maybe I just needed the reassurance.

I closed my eyes; what I needed was a therapist. The man was driving me insane.

After hanging up all my clothes and putting everything away in the dresser, I grabbed the three pillows I always slept with and started slipping on the pillowcases. I could feel Rhett hovering in the doorway.

"Are you here to supervise, or are you planning on helping me?" I teased.

He rolled his eyes. "I don't want to mess up your organizational system."

I threw a pillow at him. "Stop making excuses."

"Is there something wrong with the pillows that I had on the bed?"

I hesitated. "Do you promise to not make fun of me?"

A grin was already starting to spread across his face. "I'll do my best."

"I'm a pillow snob."

"A what?" He laughed.

"I'm picky," I admitted while clutching my favorite one. "I only like foam pillows."

I moved around the room and pretended to fold a T-shirt I had already folded.

He plopped on the bed and picked up one of the pillows. "Why three?"

"Because they all have a purpose," I said, still unable to meet his gaze.

He raised an eyebrow. "Other than building a pillow fort, why would you need three?"

"One is for my head. One is for snuggling, and one is for in-between my legs."

His eyes sparkled. "Babe, if you need something firm

between your legs, I have something that will make you feel a hell of a lot better than a foam pillow."

I ducked my head, feeling my cheeks heat. If they got any hotter, they would melt right off. "I walked right into that one."

"You sure did," he said, still laughing.

"Don't you have something to do? Like, watch SportsCenter or something?"

He folded his arms along the back of his neck. "Nah, I'll just lay here and rest my head, or maybe I'll put one of these pillows between my legs and see what's so special about it."

"Don't you dare." I snatched the pillow away and finished getting my room organized.

Thankfully, Rhett got bored and went off to do God knows what.

A couple of hours later, I was in the kitchen when I heard footsteps coming down the hall. "Something smells amazing." Rhett leaned forward to peek at what was on the stove.

"I was trying to surprise you. It's almost finished if you want to pour yourself a drink."

"I didn't know you could cook," he said, fumbling through the cabinets, grabbing plates and glasses for dinner.

"There are a lot of things you don't know about me." I winked and turned off the stove.

"Oh, yeah, do you bake too?"

I scrunched my nose up. "I can bake a cake if it comes in a box or packaged cookie dough that just needs to be pressed on a baking sheet and thrown in the oven. Even then, there is no guarantee that the cake won't stick to the pan or the cookies won't come out hard as rocks."

"So, no dessert with dinner, then. Got it," he said,

placing two glasses under the faucet. It didn't go unnoticed how he intentionally brushed his arm against mine.

"So, where did you learn to cook? Your mom?"

His question hit me like a punch in the gut. My smile faltered, and I took a deep breath, trying to steady myself.

"I did. She was a great cook."

"Was?"

I set the plate down and picked up my wine. I was hoping to avoid talking about this. It's not that I couldn't. I just didn't like to. Rhett has never lost anyone like I have; at least, I didn't think he had.

"My parents died in a car accident when I was a teenager."

Rhett's eyes widened, and his face softened in concern. "I'm sorry, Natalie. I had no idea."

"It's okay," I said through a shaky voice. "It happened a long time ago, but sometimes it feels like yesterday."

He reached across the table, taking my hand in his. "Can you talk about it, or is it too much?"

I sighed and pushed my hair back with my free hand. "I was at a friend's house, and they were on the way to pick me up. I waited for hours, and they never showed. It wasn't until Uncle Beau came and picked me up the next morning that I found out they both had died."

I carried the weight around for so long, even though I wasn't the one behind the wheel. I knew they would still be here today if they didn't have to pick me up that night. It was hard not to blame myself. But I always wondered how different things would have been if I just stayed home.

"Big B is a good man. I'm sure he didn't hesitate to step in and help," he said, his eyes softening with empathy.

I nodded. "He really is, especially since he and my mom were estranged."

"That sucks that they never had a chance to make peace." He grabbed the back of my hand and kissed it.

I swallowed. "They were never going to make peace as long as she was with my dad. He was a very sick man, and it was hard for Uncle Beau to watch him struggle with his alcohol addiction."

"So, your mom stuck by him?"

I nodded. "She was a woman of strong faith and refused to leave him. That decision ended up costing her her life."

I watched as his expression switched from concern to understanding. "He was driving that night?"

The words wouldn't come out. All I could do was nod.

Rhett leaned back in his seat, unsure how to respond. "Natalie, that's terrible. I'm so sorry."

"Not too many people know. Beau has gone to great lengths to protect me."

"So, Beau has been a solid figure in your life ever since?"

I looked down, thankful that I wasn't being pitied. "We've always been close. He's not just my uncle, he's also my godfather."

He rolled his eyes. "Great. He is going to fucking kill me."

I laughed, feeling a bit lighter. "You should probably prepare. Maybe consider leaving the country."

"Glad to see you're so worried about me," he said, scooping a helping of the sausage cream pasta and shoving it in his mouth.

Rhett had a rare gift for bringing lightness into the heaviest moments, and I'd never been more grateful for it.

We laughed and talked throughout the rest of our meal. As the evening wore on, I realized that I was developing real feelings for him, and I could tell he felt the same.

There was something more going on between us than just two people trying to figure things out. I could see myself falling for him. Maybe I was already starting.

———

I was in a blissful sleep when I felt a nudge on my shoulder. "Time to wake up, sleepyhead. You've got places to go and people to meet."

"Go away." I groaned and tried to burrow farther into the covers. Rhett wasn't kidding. This mattress felt like heaven.

"Do you have any idea what time it is?" His cheerful voice was way too loud.

I cracked an eye open and glared at him. "Yes, it's way too early."

He grinned and plopped down next to me on the bed. "Natalie, you have to wake up."

"Come back in an hour." I tried to pull the comforter over me, but in one swift motion, he yanked it off.

"You're meeting my friends today, remember?"

Oh, right. The anxiety I felt over meeting them for the first time came rushing back. These weren't just his closest friends. They also knew my uncle. Rhett has assured me countless times that I had nothing to worry about, but the fear of our secret getting out filled my body with panic.

He must have seen the concern on my face. "Don't worry. You're going to love them. I promise."

I sighed and leaned against the pillow, wishing I could stay in bed all day. "You make everything sound so simple."

He kissed my temple. "Because it is. Now get up and get dressed. We have a big day ahead."

Begrudgingly, I swung my legs out from the bed and stood up. "Fine." I stretched my arms up over my head. Rhett swallowed when my camisole rose over my stomach. "Any idea on what I should wear?"

"Wear something that makes you feel good."

"So, should I wear my 'will trade for coffee' shirt with an arrow pointing to you, then?"

"I didn't realize you could be such a smartass. I don't think you'll have anything to worry about. You're going to fit right in."

I smiled, feeling a bit more at ease.

After a quick shower and feeling somewhat more human, I got dressed and went to join Rhett in the living room. Only he wasn't there. I walked toward his bedroom, ready to give him a hard time about not being ready yet, but he was nowhere to be found.

Huh?

Instead of going back to the living room and waiting for him, I decided to peek inside his bedroom. The man was such a mystery to me, and I was feeling a little nosy.

I pushed the door fully open, and the first thing I noticed was an orange and yellow beta fish swimming in a small aquarium. I had so many damn questions, but I didn't have much time and didn't want to explain myself if I got caught, so I wandered over to a shelf above his dresser with a collection of pictures. There were photos of friends and teammates; one was a snapshot of him with two little girls.

"Those are my nieces."

"Jesus." I dropped the picture and immediately placed it back in its place. "You scared the crap out of me."

I spun around to see Rhett leaning against the

doorjamb, his bare feet crossed at his ankles as he casually sipped from a water bottle. Did I also mention his chest was bare, too? And don't get me started on those gray sweatpants hanging low on his hips.

I had no idea how I was going to survive this, but it would be a good test of my restraint.

"If you wanted a tour of my bedroom, all you had to do was ask," he said, forcing my gaze from his broad chest to his face.

"I wasn't snooping," I blurted out, sounding guilty as hell.

He raised a brow that said *you are so full of shit.*

"Okay." I raised my hand. "Guilty."

He strolled into the room. "Find anything interesting?"

Yeah, your body. One I wouldn't mind getting acquainted with again.

I cleared my throat and pointed to the small aquarium, needing to focus on something other than how badly I wanted to run my fingers through the soft dusting of hair on his chest. "I didn't realize you had a fish."

"That's Tito."

"You named your fish after a bottle of vodka?"

He laughed. "It's a long story that involves a drunken night with friends and a bet."

I fiddled with my hands. "Why are you not dressed?"

He rubbed at the scruff peppering his jaw. "I wanted to get a quick workout in and didn't expect you to get ready so fast." He moved over to the closet and swung the double doors open. "Do you want to pick out an outfit for me while I take a quick shower?"

I peeked my head inside, and my eyes doubled in size. This wasn't a closet, but a mini room filled with rows of designer shirts neatly hung on hangers. I ran my fingers over the soft cashmere sweaters and silky button-downs. As

I moved further into the closet, I was met with a rack of expensive-looking suits filling the space.

I spun around and stared at the man who was such a mystery to me. "I married a fashionista."

He shrugged. "What can I say? I like to look sharp."

My forehead wrinkled. "I can understand the clothes, but this?" I pointed to the wall dedicated just to shoes. There were shelves of sneakers from floor to ceiling—every color, shape, and style ever invented.

He picked up a pair of turquoise and black high-top sneakers. "Some are custom designed, some are from working with a specific company, and a few are from designers who gifted me a pair to promote their brand."

"This is a lot." I spun around in a circle.

"I have to make a lot of public appearances, so I try to make sure I'm not photographed wearing the same outfit twice."

"What?" I glanced at the closet and back to him. "You're serious?"

He shrugged. "You just saw my entire closet."

I parked my hands on my hips. "And you gave me shit about my pillows."

He turned toward the bathroom. "Seeing that you're so fascinated with my wardrobe, why don't you pick out something I'll look good in."

"You trust me alone in here?" I raised an eyebrow, smirking.

He chuckled. "Yes. Just don't make me look like a clown."

I waved him off. "I can't make any promises."

When I heard the shower start, I started flipping through his shirts. I picked up a crisp white button-down and a pair of jeans. He would probably think it was boring, but it reminded me of the night we met.

I laid the clothes on the bed and chuckled when I heard him humming some off-key pop song.

Instead of leaving the room like I should have, my eyes zeroed in on his nightstand. A quick peek wouldn't hurt, right?

A pang of guilt hit me for invading his privacy, but I couldn't resist learning every little detail about the man I would be living with for the next month. He was one big puzzle waiting to be pieced together.

I pulled open the drawer and shifted through a tangled-up phone charger, a flashlight, earbuds, and a half-eaten pack of Skittles. I was expecting to find a bottle of lube and a box of condoms. The man continued to surprise me at every turn.

I didn't hear the footsteps approaching until it was almost too late. I quickly shut the drawer and jumped on the mattress before being caught red-handed.

Rhett emerged from the bathroom, a towel wrapped around his waist and water droplets still clinging to his chest. Lord, help me. His steps faltered when he saw me on his bed. He stood there staring at me while running his hands through his damp hair.

"What are you doing?"

"Oh, just looking for a pair of socks," I said, playing dumb.

He crossed his arms across his chest. "Sure you were."

"I was." I gave him my most innocent smile and let my gaze travel down his towel-clad body. "But then I got distracted."

He stood there, watching me. I had no idea what he was thinking, because his expression was unreadable. The air between us rippled with tension. His eyes searched mine as if asking for permission. For what? I didn't know.

What I did know was there was no way I wouldn't let

him touch me right now if he wanted to. I lifted my chin, daring him to either walk away or come closer.

I gulped when he walked to the bed and dipped his knee into the mattress. I grabbed a pillow and clutched it in a death grip, not feeling as bold as I did a few seconds ago. My stomach wobbled when he leaned forward and threw it aside. He lowered his face and ran the tip of his nose along mine. "Don't you even feel a little guilty?"

Oh, shit. He was really doing this.

"Why would I need to feel guilty?"

His hot breath dusted against my lips. "For being a little snoop. That's twice I caught you today."

"I told you, I was looking for socks."

He raised a brow. "In my nightstand?"

"You never know where you're going to find one."

He narrowed his eyes at me. "Is that how you're going to play this?"

"You think I'm playing with you?" I sucked in a breath when his fingers slowly brushed against my cheek. Bolts of heat shot through me. He had me exactly where he wanted me, and he knew it too.

He shifted his weight and inched closer. "Yep. So, why don't you do the right thing and admit what you were really doing."

"I'm sorry." I sighed as he ran his free hand down my rib cage. "I was curious and got carried away."

"Hmm…" He brushed his lips to the shell of my ear. "I married a little sneak. What should I do with you?"

"I can think of a few things," I said, feeling my heart race. He was turning the tables on me, and I couldn't even be mad about it.

His hand reached out and pushed the hair back from my face. "I have a few ideas of my own."

He slid the strap of my dress to the side so he could

sweep his tongue across my shoulder. Every cell in my body was on high alert. I sucked in a breath while his mouth kissed its way along my bare skin.

There were a million reasons why this was a bad idea, but I couldn't remember a single one.

"Rhett." I moaned, feeling a bolt of pleasure as his hand dipped beneath the fabric of my dress.

"So beautiful," he said as the pad of his thumb skimmed up my bare leg. "You're the kind of beautiful that makes a man go crazy."

"Oh, God." I squeezed my eyes shut and rolled my hips into him when he started stroking his fingers along my entrance.

"If I want to go down on you right now, will you let me?" he asked, pressing his finger against my clit.

There was no way in hell I would stop him.

"Why don't you take my underwear off and find out for yourself," I murmured while he continued to tease me with his fingers. I lifted my hips, begging him for more. He had me teetering on the edge, and he'd barely touched me.

He laughed and pulled away. When I glanced up, a look of satisfaction filled his face.

"What are you doing?"

I was so freaking confused. I was panting, and it was still unclear as to why he was leaning back on his knees instead of between my legs where I wanted him.

"Getting you back for that stunt you pulled at the restaurant. You had me by the balls, literally. Just wanted you to know what it felt like to be at someone's mercy."

"Are you serious right now?" I leaned my head back and groaned. "You got off, asshole. You're really going to leave me hanging?"

He looked down at his erection that was poking out underneath the towel. "I told you that I play to win. I'm not going to fuck you again until I know for sure that you're ready."

"What makes you think I don't want this? I'm basically giving you my consent."

He regarded me cautiously as he headed toward the door. "I don't want just your body, and the sooner you figure that out, the sooner we can stop playing these games. Now, if you'll excuse me, I need to go to the bathroom and take care of this." He winked and strolled out of the room.

What the hell just happened?

CHAPTER 13
RHETT

THE GRAVEL CRUNCHED BENEATH OUR FEET AS NATALIE AND I walked up the path to Mav's enormous McMansion. The ride was silent, and every time I glanced over, hoping to catch her eyes, she would just stare straight ahead.

I hoped we would talk about what happened earlier, but every time I tried to bring it up, the words wouldn't come. I knew she was feeling the same awkwardness as I was because she was going out of her way to avoid me.

There was so much uncertainty about our future, and I wanted to assure her that everything would be okay, but how could I when I wasn't sure myself?

When Mav's front door came into view, I said the hell with it. "Natalie, about earlier."

She turned to look at me; her eyes were wide. "I know we need to talk, but not now, okay? I'm nervous as it is about meeting your friend's."

"Fine. I just wanted you to know that I've been thinking about it a lot. We can't keep avoiding these conversations. We need to figure some things out."

She gripped my hand and squeezed it tightly. "We will. I promise."

"Fair enough." My eyes connected with hers. "And I told you, you have nothing to worry about.

My friends already knew the real story. I had already answered the girls' questions, and they couldn't wait to meet Natalie. Kinley and Rylee thought I was crazy. I couldn't help but think they understood my feelings in a way that no one else did. They reminded me to protect my heart and keep a level head about this. They didn't pity me, judge me, or bust my chops like their men did.

"Tell me again who everyone is."

"Mav used to be our starting quarterback before he retired. He's the mother hen of the group. Kinley is his wife and the only person on the planet who can put him in his place. JP used to be our top wide receiver and the one everyone goes to for advice. He's engaged to Mav's sister, Rylee."

She tilted her head to look at me. "And they all know the truth?"

I reached out to take her hand and entwined our fingers. "Yes, and they are dying to meet you."

"I hope they're not disappointed."

I cupped her cheek. "They won't be, and even if they are, I don't care."

This connection was undeniable, and I was ready to embrace it with everything I had. I wanted her to see this side of me, the one that allowed me to be myself without any expectations. I wanted her to fit in with my friends, but I never considered what would happen if she didn't.

But after looking into her eyes and seeing how nervous she was, I realized I didn't care about anyone else's opinion.

"Well, let's hope I make a good impression and pass their test." She squeezed my hand before letting go.

I guided her through the foyer and toward the kitchen.

"Hi." Rylee smiled, walking right up to us. "You must be Natalie. I'm JP's fiancée, Rylee."

"It's nice to meet you." Natalie held her hand out with a bright smile, but Rylee surprised us when she pulled Natalie into a hug.

"Sorry, I am a hugger." Rylee winked at me over Natalie's shoulder and pulled away.

"Don't I get a hug?" I held my arms out and lifted my brow.

"Of course you do, especially since you brought something other than just a twelve-pack of beer this time." She grinned.

I loved the woman to death, but she loved to bust my balls and to keep myself out of hot water with her brother and fiancé, I let her.

Given that Rylee was Mav's sister, I've known her for years, but we grew close when she started dating my buddy JP.

"Something smells good," I said, feeling my stomach growl at the smell of warm cinnamon and apples. My eyes moved around the kitchen and landed on the pie resting on the stove.

"Don't even think about touching that pie," Kinley warned as she came into the kitchen, balancing baby Mila in her arms. "It's scorching hot, and you'll burn yourself."

"I wouldn't dream of it. I swear," I teased, flashing her a grin before quickly glancing back at the stove.

Mav stepped into the kitchen, holding a trash bag. He set the bag down and extended his hand to Natalie. "I'm Mav, it's nice to finally meet you."

"You too. Thanks for inviting me." She pushed her hair behind her ear and blushed.

If she hadn't been so nervous, I would have teased her about being so dazzled by his pretty boy face. She had mentioned in the car that she'd seen photos of Maverick at the office and thought he was cute. At least she wasn't fumbling over words and making a fool of herself like most women did when they met him for the first time.

I pulled Natalie to my side and handed Mav the bottle of wine we brought.

He took it and whistled. "Wine and a wife. Who are you, and what have you done to my friend?"

Kinley turned to Natalie. Her tone was filled with genuine warmth. "We've been looking forward to meeting you since we found out that Rhett was bringing you."

Mav leaned against the counter. "She's not wrong. It's not every day that we get to meet the woman who has the patience to put up with this big fella." He winked at me.

"Glad to see you're not making a big deal about this," I joked.

After being single all my life, I never understood the appeal of being in a committed relationship. It never made sense to me how my buddies would get so stupid over their woman and bend over backward to ensure their happiness. Slowly, I was starting to get it and the more time I spent with Natalie, the more I wanted what they had.

"Where's JP?" I asked and leaned in to kiss Mila on her tiny head.

"He's out back with Zander." Kinley smiled as she passed the baby to Mav so she could grab the pitcher of iced tea from the fridge.

There were bowls of chips and appetizer trays waiting to be carried outside. I immediately picked up a couple and carefully balanced them in my hands.

"Can I help you with anything?" Natalie asked as Rylee grabbed the mason jars filled with silverware off the counter.

"Just come on out and have a drink with us." Rylee smiled as she headed toward the sliding glass door. "I hope you're hungry because we have plenty of food."

Maverick opened the door, and Natalie grabbed one of the trays from my hand as we made our way outside. The smell of the meat cooking on the grill made my stomach growl.

We set everything down and I turned just in time to catch a football coming my way. Out of instinct, I jumped up to catch it.

"You playing quarterback now?" I yelled out to JP and made my way across the yard with Natalie.

Mav's boy, Zander ran in circles while JP pretended to run from him.

"It's good to see you again, Natalie." He held his hand out as Zander wrapped himself around his tree trunk of a leg. The kid was shy around ladies, probably because he was used to women fawning all over his father, thanks to quarterbacks getting all the love. We all had our fair share of fan girls, but Mav's was on a whole other level.

"You too." She waved to Zander, who was peeking at her from behind JP. His brown eyes shined with interest once he got a good look at the woman at my side. She was in a cute little sundress that she picked out just for today. She had been nervous and mentioned that it felt more like a date, and she wasn't sure how she was supposed to act around my friends. Adding kids to the mix scared her because she never knew what to say or how to talk to them. Judging by the adorable smile Zander was shooting her way, it was safe to say she was doing just fine.

"What's up, little man?" I held my fist out for a bump.

He giggled when I pulled my hand away, pretending that he hit me hard enough to hurt. "You're strong, just like your daddy, huh?" I ruffled his hair as he ran off to play with JP and Rylee's golden retriever, Oakley.

"Something smells good," Natalie said as Rylee handed her a frozen margarita.

"I just pulled some brisket off the smoker." JP threw an arm around Rylee's shoulder as she put her drink up to his lips so he could take a sip.

I glanced at the table that was loaded up with more food than we could ever eat. JP went all out with brisket, burgers, grilled chicken, macaroni salad, coleslaw, and fruit. The guy loved to cook, so everyone let him, because we all knew everything he prepared would be amazing.

After grabbing our drinks, we all settled in at the table and started making small talk.

"So, Natalie, will we be seeing you at the Born to Love benefit next week?" Rylee eyed her over the rim of her glass.

"I'll actually be there taking pictures for the team's social media department."

Natalie shifted in her seat, so I rested my hand on her thigh to get her to relax. Her nerves were stamped all over her face.

Rylee's eyes bounced between us. "You'll be working it like me, then?"

I smiled, keeping my voice casual, even though the disappointment gnawed at me. "I can't exactly bring her as my date, but I still want her there. And I might have convinced Tracy that I needed someone to take pictures for my social media."

Although this was way below Natalie's job description, she still needed to start somewhere.

"So, basically, poor Natalie has to follow your butt

around and snap pictures all night?" Kinley asked, setting her glass down.

Natalie laughed. "I'll mostly just be assisting with whatever Rhett needs me to do."

I threw an arm around the back of her chair. "I can think of a few things that might require your *assistance*."

"I don't think that's what Tracy meant." She rolled her eyes and nudged me in the ribs.

"Don't worry, Natalie. I'm the event coordinator, which makes me the boss." Rylee smirked at me from across the table. "So I'll make sure you don't get stuck by his side all night."

"That will probably be for the best," Mav said, taking a sip of his beer. "Considering you guys need to keep a low profile."

"Really, Mav?" I frowned. This was already a delicate topic, so I didn't want Natalie to feel uncomfortable.

He set his napkin down. "I'm not trying to be a dick. I'm just looking out for you."

JP sliced into his brisket. "We just want you to be careful, Rhett."

"I'm not going to do anything stupid," I reassured them. "Have a little faith in me."

Natalie sat up and straightened her shoulders. "Rhett and I plan on keeping this a secret for the time being. I will be there strictly in a business capacity."

It sucked that we would both be there together, but I couldn't bring her as my date. I wanted her by my side, but as Mav bluntly pointed out, we had to keep things professional. There would be cameras everywhere and various people from the Arrows organization. The last thing I wanted to do was piss Beau Landers off.

Although, I'd be lying if I said I wasn't jealous that

Mav and JP could both bring their women, that they didn't have to lie and sneak around. But I couldn't let any of that stop me. I had one month to convince her to give me a real shot. If, by some miracle, she decided to give this thing a go, then there would be no more reasons to hide and pretend.

I rested my hand on her leg and squeezed. She peered up at me, and I was expecting her to push my hand off her thigh. Instead, she smiled and rested one of hers over mine. What did that mean? Was she just being nice, or did it mean something else?

We started talking about the upcoming season, but I was only half listening; I was too focused on how easily Natalie was bonding with my friends and how hard it would be if she chose to walk away. My skin got damp just thinking about it. I tried to play it cool as the conversation around me continued, but I kept envisioning Natalie and me together. Having backyard dinners like this with our friends, quiet nights at home watching movies, and her running onto the field after every game to congratulate me. I had to close my eyes because that wasn't our reality, but damn, I wanted it to be.

We got to our feet and started clearing off the table. The girls pulled Natalie into the kitchen for another margarita while the guys hung back with Zander and Mila.

"I wasn't expecting you to look so happy," Mav said before snapping a picture of Zander trying to spike a football.

My eyes went to the house. Through the big kitchen window, I could see Natalie's blond hair. She threw her head back and laughed, and their giggles could be heard all the way out here. I was hit with a deep sense of contentment.

JP followed my gaze. "You deserve this, Rhett. I know you guys are still testing the waters, but I've been watching her tonight, and she looks at you the same way you look at her."

I reached over to grab a cookie off the table. "How do I look at her?"

JP flipped his baseball cap around his head. "I don't know what's going on with you two, but there is genuine affection there. I was expecting physical chemistry, but from what I can tell, it's more than that."

Mav scooped baby Mila out of her bouncer seat when she started to fuss. "What's the status with you guys?" he asked as she laid her tiny head against his chest. "Because from the looks of it, you have feelings for her. And not just any feelings, but strong ones."

"I asked her to give me a month," I explained and took a bite of my chocolate chip cookie.

"You're really not worried about Beau finding out that she's staying with you?" JP leveled his gaze on me.

"He's in South Africa and then going to California," I stated as if that would be enough to settle their doubts.

Mav sipped his beer. "Still seems risky."

"We all know how much I love to walk on the wild side," I teased, trying to turn this heavy conversation around. I was already confused, and quite frankly, I was sick of having to explain myself. They didn't get it, and I didn't care if they ever did. This was between Natalie and me.

JP kicked his feet up on the free chair. "We're not trying to bust your ass. We just want you to be happy."

Mav set his beer down so he could adjust Mila in his arms. "Yeah. And if she makes you happy, then we are all for it, but you can't expect us to not be concerned about you."

I turned to my friend. "I appreciate the concern, but I'm a big boy, Mav."

"You obviously care about her," he said, gentling his tone. "You've never had a serious relationship before. While we are happy that you are finally ready for that, what are you going to do when it all blows up in your face?"

I could always count on Mav to not mince words. I couldn't be mad at him because he was only looking out for me.

"Why are you so sure that's going to happen?" I asked, sitting straight up in my seat.

He gave me a serious look—the same one he used on game day when he served the team a piece of humble pie with a side of stone-cold truth. "Let's be real for a second and allow me to play devil's advocate. What do you think is the worst thing that can happen?"

"I get traded."

He raised an eyebrow. "You think so?"

Jesus. No wonder guys twice his size were intimidated by him. The dude had a serious rod stuck up his ass sometimes.

"What are you getting at?" I asked, feeling annoyed with this line of questioning.

"Unless something has changed, you guys are still planning on getting divorced."

He was getting under my skin, so I pulled on the sleeves of my shirt a little aggressively. "We're trying to work things out."

At least, that's what I thought we were doing. After what happened at the restaurant and with the way she responded to me this morning, I was feeling pretty damn confident that we were making progress and headed in the right direction.

JP leaned forward to cut in. "What if things don't go the way you want them to go? Are you going to be okay with that?"

I sighed. "I don't know what to tell you guys other than Natalie is special."

"You're proving our point," JP said, resting his hands on his knees. "There is a good chance you could end up with a broken heart and playing for a new team. Is she worth it?"

"Yes," I snapped. The thought of losing everything put a knot in my stomach. Getting traded wasn't something I wanted, but if I got to keep Natalie, I think I could handle it.

"Then we will be here for you. Whatever you need."

As the night wore on, the kids grew tired, so Mav and Kinley put them to bed while Natalie and Rylee bonded over a few more margaritas. With each drink, their laughs got louder, and after each joke, their smiles got bigger. I would have been content to sit back and watch the two of them all night.

I was elated that Natalie hit it off so well with Kinley and Rylee. I could tell she was desperate for some female companionship. Moving to a new city and starting fresh could be challenging enough. And while I'd like to think I was great company, it wasn't the same as having a girlfriend to do girly shit with.

We played a quick game of flag football, guys versus girls, and let the girls win. According to the guys, it was the only way they would be getting laid tonight.

The rest of the time was spent sitting around the fire shooting the shit, and every now and then, the guys would tell Natalie a story to get a rise out of me.

When we said our goodbyes, the three girls made plans

to go to the salon before the Born to Love benefit next week.

Tonight was nothing like I expected it to be, and everything I didn't know I needed. The more time I spent with my temporary wife, the more I wanted it to be permanent.

CHAPTER 14
NATALIE

My stomach buzzed with a mixture of excitement and nerves as Rhett and I pulled up to the venue of tonight's charity event. The valet opened my door, and I stepped out, smoothing a hand down my pink dress. It was short with a graceful fit that still looked classy. Best of all, it was comfortable.

Rhett rounded the truck in a dark suit that looked custom-tailored to fit him perfectly. His dark brown hair was styled, taming whatever little wave he had. He looked every bit of the NFL playboy that the media made him out to be.

"How come your parents won't be here tonight?" I asked as we made our way up the grand steps of the hotel.

I assumed his entire family would want to support him, but I overheard him talking to his sister on the phone when he picked me up from the spa earlier.

"My folks are in Washington for a White House event. My brother had a prior engagement, and my sister has the flu. This is the first year where my family has had to miss it."

He didn't seem all that upset, but this was a big deal to him, and I would think they would want to be there.

"It doesn't bother you?"

"Nah, everyone has their own lives. This event is about raising money for the mission. They sent their donations in, and tonight is about focusing on the people that are here rather than the people who aren't."

This was the sixth year in a row that the tickets have been sold out. According to Rylee, the event continued to get bigger and bigger. He was downplaying the impact he made. The money coming in tonight wouldn't be possible if it weren't for him.

"Well, judging by how many tickets were sold, I think tonight is going to be a huge success. That should make you feel good."

He gave me a modest shrug. "I haven't really done anything. Rylee has done most of the planning. All I'm doing is bringing my pretty boy face and charming the guests."

I raised an eyebrow, giving him a playful nudge. "You don't give yourself enough credit. You're the reason all these people are here tonight."

He chuckled. "You make me sound like I'm some kind of superhero."

"I bet to some people you are."

He shook his head. "Maybe I'll add that into my speech tonight."

"You better."

He looked at me, his eyes softening. "I'm glad you're here."

"So am I." I squeezed his hand briefly before he opened the door for me.

When we stepped inside, the ballroom was alive with chatter and laughter. As we made our way through the crowd, people approached Rhett from all angles. I was so busy watching him charm his way through conversations that I almost forgot to snap a few photos. He chatted easily with each guest who approached him, and I couldn't help but feel a surge of pride in my chest.

There were only a handful of people I recognized, so I excused myself and made my way to the other ballroom, where we were holding the auction later in the night.

Instead of having items on the table for people to bid on, I convinced Rhett to have a live auction. I thought it would be more fun and engaging, and Rylee agreed.

Speak of the devil. When I rounded the corner, Rylee and JP were walking toward me.

I set my champagne down and slipped my phone out to get a few close-up shots.

"You look stunning," I said, admiring the emerald-green dress that clung to her in all the right places. A few men had turned their heads and were having a hard time looking away.

JP snaked an arm around her waist and glared at the group in tuxedos who were caught staring.

"Like you're one to talk." She smiled so I could snap a couple more pictures. "Where is the man of the hour?"

"He's mingling." I clicked on the screen and tucked my phone back in my clutch.

"Good to see you, Natalie." JP's eyes darted around, seeming impressed. "It looks like you guys are going to be bringing in the big bucks tonight."

"I hope so." I picked up my glass of champagne. "Your fiancée did all the work. She deserves all the credit."

He looked down at her with affection. "Rylee is the best, but I think you're being modest. I heard you were able to get one of the hottest chefs in Atlanta to donate his services."

"It was nothing." I smiled at how easy and friendly he was. "I just threw my uncle's name around and did a little sweet talking."

"How much sweet talking?" Rhett stepped up to my side and raised an eyebrow.

"Enough for him to say yes." I gave him a coy smile and blinked up at him. It was hard not to admire every six-foot two inches of him and the way his suit hugged his broad shoulders.

"Maybe you should save some of that sweet talking for me." He pinched my side playfully.

Rylee glanced around while sipping her wine. "This place is gorgeous. It might just make me change my mind about an outdoor wedding."

"Have you guys set a date yet?" I asked them as she played with the engagement ring on her finger. They have been going back and forth because Rylee wanted a fall wedding, and JP wanted it to happen before the season started so all his friends could be there.

"We're getting closer." She rested her head against JP's shoulder.

A pang of jealousy hit my chest just from watching them. I shouldn't feel it. I shouldn't be thinking about how there were times when I wished my marriage was real or that Rhett would look at me the same way JP looked at Rylee.

My phone dinged with a notification, so I dug it out of my clutch and glanced at the screen. "I'm sorry. Will you guys excuse me for a minute? I need to grab the auction paddles for later."

"Need any help?" Rylee asked, stepping forward.

"Nope." I squeezed her arm. "You have already done enough, so try to enjoy yourself. I'll see you in a bit."

I turned and started walking toward the service

elevators, smiling and greeting guests as they passed by. I didn't want to be running back and forth all night, so I reviewed my checklist to ensure I didn't forget anything.

I grabbed the paddles off the shelf and went down the long corridor. Just as I was rounding a corner, I bumped into someone.

"Shit," I said, watching the paddles land all over the floor. "I'm so sorry." I looked up at the woman scowling at me.

She placed her hands on her hips. "Watch where you're going."

I squinted my eyes, trying to pinpoint where I knew her from, but she stormed away before I could get a word in. I was impressed that she could even move that fast, seeing how tight her dress was. Normally, I would lecture her on treating people with kindness, but I didn't have time to deal with petty people today.

I leaned down, started shoving all the paddles back in the bin, and hurried toward the ballroom. Once everything was organized, I turned and collided with a muscular chest.

"Jesus," I cursed. Rhett instinctively wrapped his arms around me and held me in place.

"What are you doing?" I stepped back once I gained my footing.

"I just wanted a minute alone with you," he whispered.

I tilted my head to the side, noticing he seemed a little off. "Is everything okay?"

"Yeah." He ran a hand through his hair. "I just needed a break. Everyone wants to talk to me, and when they're not, they're staring."

I laughed. "I thought you enjoyed the spotlight?"

He looked off to the side, never settling on one spot for too long. His tension was obvious. "I'm not sure how to answer that. This charity means everything to me. It's the securing sponsors and rubbing elbows part that stresses me out. It reminds me of being forced to attend fundraisers for my dad. I hated every second of that part of my life. But I know all this is necessary to ensure the charity's success."

I grabbed his hand in mine as chatter and laughter could be heard outside the double doors. "I understand this might not be your favorite part, but you are making an incredible impact, and these people just want to support you."

He nodded. "Speaking of support, I appreciate all the extra work you put in. You've gone above and beyond."

"You don't need to thank me. I am happy to help you in whatever way I can. I'm proud of you."

His eyes shined with warmth. "You have no idea how badly I want to kiss you right now."

"I would like that too, but I think people would get the wrong idea about us." I glanced around to make sure no one could see us.

He slipped a hand around the back of my neck. "You should be more afraid of people getting the *right* idea about us." He leaned in close and angled his mouth right at my lips. "Now, open that mouth for me, wife."

My breath hitched as his knuckles slowly drifted across my cheek. My brain was acutely aware of how dangerous this was. Anyone could walk in, but my body said the hell with it.

I gripped his suit jacket, not giving a damn that we were pressing our luck and could get caught at any moment.

My lips parted open, and a soft moan came out. His mouth moved slowly against mine, in a rhythm that overwhelmed my senses. The gentle pressure and the slight teasing of his tongue made me acutely aware of every little detail. The warmth of his breath, the smell of his cologne and the way his palm burned through my skin. Kissing him felt like the most natural thing in the world.

Little by little, he's been stealing pieces of my heart, making it impossible to even think about leaving him when our month was up. It was crazy how much I wanted to abandon my responsibilities and give this thing with him a real shot.

Rhett walked me backward until I was against a wall. He shoved his legs in between my thighs. "Why does kissing you always feel so good?" His voice came out in pants as he rained kisses across my face. "Why does touching you drive me crazy?"

I didn't know, but if he kept talking like that, we would end up doing a lot more than kissing.

One of the doors started to push open. Rhett turned around, and I brought my trembling hand to my mouth. He glanced back at me over his shoulder and watched me adjust my dress and attempt to fix my hair. I didn't need a mirror to know that I looked like a hot mess.

A woman in a tight, black, sequined dress strode our way. I recognized her immediately. It was the lady with the snotty attitude from earlier, the one who bumped into me and left me to pick up the auction paddles after scolding me about not paying attention to my surroundings.

She clutched her wineglass and gave me a once-over. The diamonds along her wrist glistened under the chandelier. She was dripping in money, and I didn't like to judge, but she looked like a stuck-up snob who was fed with a silver spoon her entire life.

"Rhett." She slid up next to him with an exaggerated sway to her hips. "I've been looking for you."

"Claire, I had no idea you would be here tonight." He shifted uncomfortably, trying to keep her at arm's length.

Ah, this was the woman from the restaurant—the one his mom was trying to set him up with. Everything was starting to make sense.

"Of course, I would be here, silly. I love supporting your little cause." She lingered against his arm, eyeing me curiously. "I was actually coming to find you to see if you wanted to dance."

His eyes flickered to mine briefly, and he offered her a polite smile. "I appreciate the support tonight, but as far as the dance, I'm a little busy at the moment."

Her smile never faltered. "You need to find time for fun. I miss the old Rhett. Life is too short to be all work and no play."

Clearly, they had some type of history. How much, I wasn't sure, but we would be having a conversation later.

Rhett cleared his throat and motioned for me to come over and rescue him. "There is someone I want you to meet." His shoulders relaxed slightly when I stepped up to him. "Claire, this is Natalie, Natalie, this is Claire. She's a family friend."

Her face contorted into something sour at that introduction. "I'm also an old friend of Rhett's too, isn't that right?" She reached out and pulled on his tie so she could run her fingers through it. "And let's not forget the benefits part."

Rhett's eyes met mine, silently pleading for patience.

I took a deep breath, doing my best to stay composed. I couldn't stake any type of claim on him without causing a scene, but seeing her openly flirt with him and not being able to say anything was driving me crazy.

"Is that so?" I stepped closer, feeling my disdain for the woman override my common sense. I plucked her hand off him. "Funny, he's never mentioned you before."

She pursed her lips, her eyes narrowing slightly. "Aren't you the worker who knocked me over earlier?"

"You mean, am I the one you bumped into, causing me to drop everything and pick it all up by myself? Yes. That was me."

Her smile tightened. Oh, she didn't like that very much.

She let out a light laugh that didn't reach her eyes. "Right. I'm sure you have work to do, so if you wouldn't mind giving us a minute alone, that would be great." She drained the rest of her champagne and held it out for me to take. "I could use another glass. Would you mind running to the bar and grabbing me a refill?"

Thankfully, Rhett stepped in, saving me from causing a scene.

"Claire." He sighed, running a hand through his hair. "I'm going to be honest with you for a second. I know you are hoping for something more between us, but that's not going to happen. I've tried to be polite, but it seems that hasn't been clear enough. You need to stop letting my mother plant ideas in your head."

She blinked, clearly thrown off. "Do you really think this is an appropriate conversation we should be having in front of one of your employees?"

Ouch!

I cleared my throat. "Technically, Rhett isn't my boss. I work for the Arrows, but it's my job to stay by his side and make sure he stays on task tonight." I smiled sweetly, but my tone was icy enough to warn her not to mess with me.

Her eyes narrowed. "So, what are you? His personal manager?"

"Among other things, yes," I replied with a forced smile.

Rhett glanced toward the door to make sure no one

was paying attention. "I don't want to make things more awkward, but I hope I made myself clear on where I stand." He motioned for me to start walking toward the main ballroom. "Now, if you'll excuse us, we need to get ready for the auction. I hope you enjoy the evening, and thanks again for your support."

Rhett guided me down the hallway to a small room away from the noise and prying eyes. "I'm sorry about that. She just wouldn't take a hint."

"I know," I said, softly noticing how tired he looked. "But you were honest. That's all that matters."

He nodded, his gaze softening. "I needed her to understand that there was no chance. Not now, and not ever."

I shook my head. "I think you made your point. You handled it perfectly. I'm the one who lost my shit."

He chuckled, keeping his voice low. "This is getting harder, and I think we are both getting sick of pretending, so I'm ready to quit playing games when you are."

"This isn't a game to me." I sighed heavily. Didn't he realize that I was already feeling too much too quickly? That I was so damn scared that I couldn't see straight.

"Then why are we putting ourselves through this?" he asked, searching my eyes for an answer.

"Because I'm scared of getting hurt again and I'm trying to be smart about how we move forward."

His expression softened, and he grabbed my hand. "I get it, but being afraid doesn't mean you have to let the fear control you. We're in this together, remember?"

The faint sound of voices started seeping through the doors, breaking through our little bubble.

I sighed. "We need to get back out there before people come looking for us."

He kissed my lips gently. "Fine, but this conversation isn't over."

———

I stepped into the main ballroom, where the auction was in full swing. Everywhere I looked, legendary players and coaches from all the different teams filled the room. The sound of hushed whispers and occasional bursts of laughter filled my ears. If it weren't for Rylee talking nonstop about how they were "some of the greatest players of all time" I never would have known who half of these people were.

"Our first item up for bid is a signed helmet by a nine-time pro bowler, three-time Super Bowl champ, and five-time most valuable player, Maverick Cross."

Applause erupted, and I spotted two eager bidders with their paddles shaking in their hands. There was going to be so much money raised tonight from all the signed helmets, jerseys, and exclusive meet-and-greet packages. Rhett could downplay his role all he wanted, but the truth was, he was making a real difference in the community.

"Let's kick off the bidding at one thousand dollars." Paddles were thrust in the air, each one a challenge to the previous bid. The auction was swiftly turning into a fierce contest.

"Going once, twice, three times." The auctioneer pounded the gravel. "Sold for fifteen thousand dollars to the man in the third row. Congratulations." The crowd clapped, and my eyes caught Rhett's from across the room. A smile lit up his entire face as he sipped his champagne.

The sports world might have painted him as a carefree party boy, but beneath that image was a man of substance.

Everywhere I looked, people were smiling and enjoying

themselves. Rhett poured his heart and soul into this charity, and it was touching to see his NFL family show up to support him.

The next item up for bid was a beautiful gold necklace with an opal pendant donated by a local jeweler. I was tempted to join the bidding war, but with my new car payments and trying to save up for my own place, I needed to be responsible with my cash.

Rhett walked over to a silver-haired man sitting on an aisle seat in the second row and whispered in his ear. They spoke briefly while the man nodded, keeping his gaze fixed on the stage. My brows squinted together, but I didn't have time to dwell on it as I made my rounds around the room, snapping pictures while trying to stay out of the way. I needed to make sure I had enough photos and video content to put together later.

It wasn't until I turned my attention back to the stage that I realized the necklace went for ten thousand dollars to the man Rhett had just spoken to.

My eyes went to my sneaky husband, who simply winked back at me.

The crowd applauded before a hush fell over the room as the final item of the evening arrived on stage.

"Ladies and gentlemen, we have a special treat for you. Our final item up for bid is an exclusive date with Atlanta's most eligible bachelor, star tight end, six-time pro bowler, and four-time all-pro Rhett Daniels from the Atlanta Arrows. He holds the most receiving yards in the league and would be a great catch for a local hometown girl."

Rhett sauntered across the stage with a playful grin as he waved to the crowd.

My stomach dropped when I spotted Claire. I tried to focus on taking pictures, but the worry was eating away at me. I knew I couldn't afford to bid on him myself, and if I did, it would only cause a scene.

The bidding started at five thousand dollars and quickly rose to twenty, with Claire having the last active bid. A lump started to grow in my throat, and I had to remind myself that this was for charity.

I stood back, fully prepared for Claire to win, but at the last second, Rylee stood up and raised her paddle. "Fifty thousand dollars."

I turned sharply, my eyes locking onto hers. What the hell was she doing, and why was JP not stopping her?

"Sold!" Rylee gave me a triumphant smile. It was so big, it practically split her cheeks.

Claire, on the other hand, dropped in her seat, crossed her arms, and glared at everyone around her.

Guess she wasn't used to things not going her way. Welcome to the real world, *sweetheart.*

Rhett exited the stage, and my head spun.

I waited until most of the people started to disperse before I walked across the room and stepped into his personal space. "What is going on?"

He pulled on his tie and looked around, playing stupid. "I have no idea what you mean?"

I whacked him on the shoulder. "I have so many questions, but let's start with the big one. Why did Rylee bid on a date with you?"

He motioned for me to follow him backstage, which was more private, and watched as the guests started to depart and head back toward the bar.

"I paid her so I wouldn't have to worry about being auctioned off."

"You did?" I blinked, trying to make sense of this. "Wasn't that the whole point?"

He rubbed the back of his neck. "If I'm going on a

date with anyone, it's going to be with you. I didn't want to leave it up to chance and end up with Claire."

I looked up at him with wide eyes. "So, you donated your own money to keep yourself from being bought?"

"I did. I also got you something." He reached into his pocket, pulled out a tiny object, and handed it to me.

As soon as he placed it in my hand, I already knew what it was.

Tears pricked my eyes. "You bought this for me?"

I held up the gold chain and admired the opal pendant. The chain was delicate, like it could break easily, but I knew, based on what he paid for it, that it was solid gold. My thumb rubbed circles around the opal as it dangled in the air.

"I saw you eyeing it from across the room, so I had to get it for you."

There was a lump in my throat, making it hard to speak. "It's too much."

He squeezed my hand. "I disagree. It's not enough."

"Why did you buy this for me?" I stammered, feeling my thoughts scatter like a pile of leaves blowing in the wind. I had no idea what was happening, all I could do was stand still and try to keep my brain from short-circuiting.

"Because I feel something for you, and I know you feel it too." He said, and lifted my hair up so he could fasten the necklace around my neck. "And there is nothing I won't do to show you how serious I am about you."

I couldn't focus. His words wrapped around me like a vise, suffocating me and taking away my ability to breathe. He was right; I felt it, too, but I was terrified to admit it.

My vision blurred with tears as I played with the pendant around my neck. At that moment, I realized that I had just fallen head over heels in love with my husband.

CHAPTER 15

NATALIE

"Tell me again why we're driving to Texas instead of flying?" I asked, looking away from the winding country road and toward Rhett.

"Because I've been running on a schedule for months. I want to take advantage of my freedom and not have to be held hostage to anyone's timeline."

I leaned back in my seat. "I still can't believe Tracy asked me to accompany you to this ad shoot."

He turned to me with a smile. "She was obviously impressed with the work you did for the charity last week."

My cheeks flushed with pride at being recognized for my efforts. She said as much when she presented me with this opportunity. However, in the back of my mind, I wondered if putting us together so frequently was a recipe for disaster. Was it foolish to think we could keep our professional lives separate? I guess time will tell.

The drive was spent alternating between mindless conversations and listening to the radio. There were times when it was quiet, and other times, we laughed so hard our stomachs hurt.

As the day went on, the clouds became dark, and droplets of rain started hitting the windshield. A loud crack of thunder had me jumping in my seat.

Rhett swirled his head in my direction. "Not a fan of storms?"

"I don't mind them as long as I'm indoors. I actually find the sound of rain to be relaxing. Lightning isn't my favorite, especially when a tree can fall down on this truck at any second."

"We're running a little low on gas, and I need to stretch my back. My body was not made for these long car rides. Can you look up and see if there is anything nearby?"

"Sure."

I pulled my phone out and searched for a rest stop. There were nothing but endless fields filled with farm animals and little roadside stands selling produce in the area. Trackers with barrels of hay routinely passed us by. I'd seen enough cows to last me a lifetime.

We pulled into a convenience store a few miles up the road. The lot looked shady, like something you would see on a Netflix documentary about a missing person.

Rhett pulled a baseball cap out of the glove box. "Why don't you use the restroom first and grab a few snacks while I pump gas?"

"Do you want anything specific?" I opened the door and slowly climbed out of the car. My body was stiff from sitting for so long.

"Just a Gatorade and maybe some trail mix or chips, and don't forget a bag of Skittles."

"You got it." I walked over to the bathrooms on the side of the building and they were as gross as I thought they would be. After washing my hands and trying not to touch anything, I walked to the front. Rhett was standing by his truck, taking pictures with two guys who were smiling and chatting with him. I stood and watched him for a moment. He was kind and gracious and even clapped them on their backs when they walked away.

The girl behind the counter was typing on her phone. She didn't even look up when I set my things down in front of her. "Do you want a receipt?" she asked as I swiped my card.

"Just a bag, please." I looked out the window. The sky was getting darker. The weather app called for light rain, not a downpour.

She handed me a bag, and I loaded it with our drinks and snacks. As I was making my way across the parking lot, the sky flashed with lightning, and almost immediately after, there was a clap of thunder.

When I slid inside the car, Rhett was staring at his phone. "I think we should find a place to sleep tonight. It looks like it's only going to get worse."

A warm bed and a pillow sounded good to me. "Why don't you drive, and I'll look online and try to find a place."

I tapped away at my screen, searching for a place for us to seek shelter for the night. There weren't many options, so I clicked on the first suggestion that popped up and entered the address into the GPS. The rain was coming down hard, and Rhett was inching his head as close to the windshield as his seat would allow. If I hadn't been so focused on making it safely through the storm, I might have admired the little town we traveled through.

Pretty brick buildings lined the quiet, rain-soaked streets. An American flag flapped in the wind outside the post office. There was a general store that looked deserted and a cute bookstore with overturned flower baskets dangling from its wooden porch.

We turned down a side street, and the truck slowed as

we approached a motel that looked like something out of an old movie. It was probably charming back in the day, but time had certainly taken a toll.

Thankfully, an awning at the front entrance shielded us from the downpour. Rhett parked the car and pressed the button to open the trunk. "Home sweet home."

I followed him into the lobby and was surprised to find it so quaint and charming. It was nothing like what I pictured. We were greeted with antique lamps, vintage photos lining the walls, and plush armchairs arranged around a cozy fireplace.

An older woman with white hair sat behind the counter, sipping a cup of coffee and engrossed in a paperback.

Her head lifted, and she pushed her black glasses up to the bridge of her nose. "Well, hello there. Welcome to the Amber Inn. Are you checking in today?"

Rhett leaned his arm along the counter and flashed her a smile. "Good evening, ma'am. Unfortunately, we don't have a reservation, but we were hoping you had a room available for tonight. The storm doesn't appear to be letting up, so we are looking for a place to stay until it passes."

She sighed happily. "Let's see if I can find you something." She tapped away on her computer. Unlike the young teenager at the convenience store, this woman looked excited to see us. "We're under renovation, so rooms are limited. Plus, there is a car show this weekend, and we are booked at capacity. We have one queen room available."

He turned to me, a smile playing on his lips that he had no intention of hiding. "Well, I'd prefer a king, but beggars can't be choosers, can they?"

"Does the room at least have a pull-out couch?" I

asked, wondering how the hell I was supposed to relax sleeping in the same bed as him.

She shook her head. "I'm afraid not. It's a basic room with a queen bed and a chair. It does have a coffee maker and a mini fridge, though."

"What about a rollaway bed?" I pressed while trying to think of alternative options.

"Sweetheart." He sighed while running a hand through his hair. "I can't sleep on those. My back will go out."

I crossed my arms. "Well, then maybe we could order some extra blankets and pillows, and you can sleep on the floor."

He looked amused at my discomfort. "Or maybe *you* could sleep on the floor."

I placed my hands on my hips. "Giving me the bed would be the gentleman thing to do."

The poor lady watched our exchange, looking unsure how to intervene.

"Listen, kids," she sounded annoyed with our bickering, "I need to know if you would like the room or not?"

"We'll take it." Rhett pulled out his card and slid it across the counter.

We shared a glance, and I willed myself to calm down. This was not the ideal setup, but we would have to work with what we had.

After grabbing the room key and our bags, we walked up the stairs and down the hall, following the numbers to our room.

Once we stepped through the doorway, my brows furrowed. It was even smaller than I imagined, and sitting in the center was a single bed that looked more like a double than a queen. My heart sank because the room felt more cramped than I imagined. The realization that we would be sharing a bed created a level of anxiety that I wasn't prepared for.

We still hadn't talked about the past two times when we almost crossed a line. The avoidance has been eating me up inside. I've replayed those moments in my head, and all I seem to do is overanalyze his words and try to make sense of these feelings. It wasn't healthy, and I was scared to bring it up, but I didn't know how much longer I could keep pretending.

Tonight was going to be a test. Things were going to either be really awkward, or we would finally clear the air and come to some type of understanding.

"Hungry?" Rhett asked, dropping his duffel bag on the floor. He didn't seem all that upset over our tight accommodations. In fact, he looked as happy as a dog with two tails.

"I could eat," I lied. I was too nervous to think about food, but I knew he had to be starving.

He pulled out his phone. "Let's see what our options are?" He bent his head and started tapping on the screen. "The Wi-Fi sucks."

"Maybe they have snacks in the lobby," I said, sticking my nose in the bathroom. It was basic but clean.

"I doubt it." He yawned, sounding exhausted.

"You've been driving all day. Why don't I go out and try to find us something?"

"Absolutely not." He stood to stretch his arms over his head. The hem of his shirt slid up his stomach. It was going to be a long damn night. "Stay here, relax, and pick out a movie. I'll check and see if that diner we drove by when we were getting off the highway is open. Relax? Was he insane? I wasn't sure I was going to be able to survive this—the two of us alone, with one bed. Lord, help me. Although a few minutes to myself sounded like a good idea, I needed to get myself together.

Once he left to search for food, I took a quick shower and changed into my pajamas. It felt good to wash my body after traveling all day. After brushing my hair and organizing my clothes for tomorrow, I plugged my phone into my charger and pulled up my social media. Out of curiosity, I clicked on Rhett's public profile.

A majority of the images were taken from the social media team and included numerous pictures of him in his uniform. The ones that stood out to me the most were the photos of him on game day, arriving at the stadium dressed in a perfectly tailored suit. You could feel his confidence and excitement in every picture.

I took a calming breath, wishing I had a cup of herbal tea to help ease my nerves. Getting through these next few days without losing my mind and possibly my heart was almost impossible. It was hard to believe that I didn't even know who he was a few weeks ago. Last month, I had a life in Boston, a long-term boyfriend, a townhouse, and friends nearby. Now? I had a new job and a husband I was planning on divorcing.

I leaned up against the headboard, allowing my mind to replay the events of the last few weeks. There was something calming and equally disturbing about how I felt.

Before I could dig deeper, the door swung open, and Rhett stepped into the room, drenched but smiling while holding two plastic bags. "I hope you like turkey sandwiches because that's all I could find."

I jumped off the bed to help him with the bags. "Sandwiches work for me," I said, taking the food from his hands. The poor guy was soaked. "It's still coming down hard, huh?"

He shrugged his jacket off and shook out his hair. "It's

a complete downpour. I'm going to shower and change real quick."

I waved him off. "Go ahead, I'll get everything ready."

He walked into the bathroom, and I pulled out the food and brought everything over to the bed. I arranged everything in the middle, trying to make it as presentable as possible. Thankfully, he remembered paper plates and silverware.

Ten minutes later, Rhett stepped out of the bathroom. Droplets of water dripped down his stomach and disappeared into his cotton athletic shorts.

I shifted my eyes up to his face and swallowed. "Um, I unwrapped your sandwich." I held up the plate. "I figured we could eat together."

Jesus. I sounded like an idiot.

"You didn't have to wait for me," he said, running his fingers through his damp hair, which was sticking up in places that only made me want to ogle him more.

"I don't mind," I told him, moving to the side to make room.

Tension strained between us, or maybe I was the only one feeling it. Rhett stretched out on the bed and placed his dinner on his lap.

"What are we watching?" He pointed to the TV.

I cleared my throat and pressed play. Rhett howled in laughter when he saw the movie on the screen.

"*The Hangover*, huh?"

It was a struggle to keep a straight face. "When it came up as a movie option, I couldn't resist."

He bumped my shoulder with a grin. "It's one of my favorites."

I feigned interest in the movie, and tried to ignore how quickly my willpower was slipping with each passing second.

It was going to be a long night.

———

"What are you doing?" I asked, watching him slide his gym shorts down his muscular thighs. They were toned and tan and way too sexy for a pair of legs. It was so unfair.

His smile was slow, trying to act innocent. "I'm getting ready for bed."

"Do you have something against sleeping in shorts?"

"Yeah, actually, I do. I get hot at night." He stretched his arms out over his head and flexed his muscles on purpose.

I looked around the room, searching for someplace else to sleep, but there were no other options.

"What's the matter?" He smiled. "Are you afraid you won't be able to keep your hands to yourself?"

I flashed him a smile back. "You snore, and you're going to keep me up all night."

He swaggered forward, knowing exactly what he was doing. He wasn't going to make this easy on me. "Yeah, well, you talk in your sleep, so we're even."

My mouth popped open. "What? Please tell me you're joking?"

He squinted his eyes. "Has no one told you that before?"

I rolled my lips together. "I haven't had a roommate since college."

The expression on his face was priceless. "What about Levi?"

"We didn't sleep together." I looked away and cleared my throat, trying to get rid of the awkwardness. "I mean, we had sex, but he didn't like sharing a bed at night, so I would sleep in the other bedroom."

His eyes widened. "That's fucked up."

My fingers played with the ends of the white comforter. "It's not as uncommon as you think. Our schedules didn't always line up, and he needed sleep. Besides, a majority of our relationship was long-distance, so we were used to sleeping apart."

He shook his head. "I can't believe you wasted so much time with that douche. Just so we are clear, if you were really mine, there would be no way in hell you would sleep anywhere but in my bed, and that would be after I made you come at least twice."

My cheeks heated. "Don't say stuff like that."

"It's the truth." He shrugged and went into the bathroom to brush his teeth.

I walked to the left side of the bed and repositioned the additional hotel pillows I had requested for the room in the middle. These pillows would be the only barrier between us tonight.

I pulled the comforter down and grabbed my travel pillow from my suitcase. I climbed in, pulled the sheet under my arms, and stared at the ceiling, willing my heart rate to slow down.

Rhett walked to his side of the bed, slid under the covers, and turned off the light. The mattress shifted from his weight, so I moved as far to the left as I could without falling off.

"You better stay on your side of the bed," I warned, keeping my eyes trained on the window. I knew if I looked at him, I would cave.

He scooted closer, clearly enjoying my discomfort. "You don't look like you have much room. Why don't you come a little closer?" There was a hint of teasing in his tone.

"I'm fine," I said, bringing the sheet up to my chin.

He slid his leg against mine. "I promise, I will only bite if you ask me to."

"Why are you so close? Did you just say not too long ago that you were hot?"

"I was, but they must have fixed the thermostat, because now I'm freezing and need a little warmth."

My body moved away from his, and like a practiced dance, he shifted toward me. His arm slipped underneath me, eliminating whatever space was left.

When I tried to pull away, he huffed out a laugh. "I didn't realize I married a porcupine."

"That's what you get for marrying a complete stranger off the street… Wait, what did you just call me?" I scowled as his comment finally registered in my ears.

"A porcupine. It fits you perfectly. Maybe that's what I'll start calling you."

"You better not, considering it resembles a mole with beady little eyes. I wouldn't consider that very flattering."

His gaze slid to mine. "Think about it. Porcupines can be cute from afar, but they get very protective when you get too close. They are pointy and sharp on the outside but soft and vulnerable on the inside."

"Don't forget they are painful to touch too."

"Maybe they just need a little comfort." He reached for me when I tried to pull away again. "Come here, my little porcupine."

"Stop calling me a damn porcupine." I giggled as his giant body trapped mine. God, why did he have to smell so good? I just wanted to breathe him in.

I stopped moving when he lifted me up so he could watch me. His gaze dropped to my lips.

I swallowed, daring him to kiss me. I was such a walking, talking contradiction.

"I want you so bad right now." His voice was gruff, almost pained.

I pressed my hands to the scruff on his cheek. "I want you too, but this would change things."

"Would that really be a bad thing?"

"It will be when this marriage ends."

He slid his hands along my arms. "Who says it has to end?"

CHAPTER 16

NATALIE

I couldn't tell you which one of us moved first. All I knew was his hands were in my hair and my mouth was on his. There was no hesitation in our kiss, no more holding back. I was going all in.

He shifted his weight above me as I sank into the kiss. His stubble scraped against my mouth as he continued stroking his tongue deliberately against mine. I allowed him to take control and quiet all the doubts in my head. Weeks of wondering and wanting all led up to this moment.

His lips skimmed down my neck, teasing and nipping while my fingernails dragged along his shoulders. My breath was erratic, and I found myself drifting into a place I never wanted to come back from.

"Are you sure you're ready? Once we do this, there is no going back," he asked, patiently waiting for my answer.

I allowed his words to hang in the air for a minute. This wasn't just about tonight. It was about everything that would come after—the feelings, the commitment, crossing this line with him would change everything.

I looked into his eyes and saw the vulnerability as he silently pleaded with me to take the leap with him.

"I'm ready."

He reached out and cupped my face gently. "No more going back and forth, promise?"

I realized at that moment that I didn't want to. "I promise."

His thumb traced gentle circles along my cheek. "Are you sure? I don't want you to feel pressured. I want this to be your choice."

All I could think about was how much I wanted this. "I'm not going to change my mind. I'm sure."

With that, he captured my mouth and kissed me. It was soft but quickly deepened, becoming more urgent. "I've thought about our night together a lot. I might not remember much, but I remember enough." His hands slid down my waist, anchoring me to him as if he were afraid I would change my mind.

I wrapped my arms around his neck, pulling him closer. "I've thought about that night too, but this is going to be different, there were no feelings attached."

"You're right, which is going to make this even better."

I closed my eyes, because there was something so raw and honest in his expression and it was too much to acknowledge. I just wanted to lose myself in his touch and block out his words.

His hand moved up underneath my top, and he paused. "Look at me, Natalie. I don't want you hiding from me or trying to pretend this isn't happening." My eyes fluttered open as his hand moved to my breast. His thumb rolled against my nipple before giving it a tug. I moaned in pleasure as his mouth met mine in a hot and greedy kiss. His lips sucked and teased; every inch of me was on fire. He might not remember everything, but I sure as hell did.

It was the most intense encounter I ever had. That's why adding feelings to this was risky. But he was worth it, and I was pretty certain I wouldn't be able to stop this right now, even if I wanted to, which I didn't.

Rhett nudged my legs apart and crawled over the top of me with a devilish grin. With one swift movement, my shirt was tugged off, and his mouth was on my breast.

"I've missed these tits." He sucked one nipple into his mouth while palming the other one in his hand. "I've been dreaming about them," he whispered, pressing his cock in between my thighs. "Every time I close my eyes, I see them."

"I've been having a few dreams myself." I groaned while he slid my shorts off.

"Yeah?" He lifted his head, a slow smile crawling on his mouth. "Tell me."

"How about I show you instead." I ran my hands along my breast, loving the way he watched me. Everything was sensitive, so I tried easing some tension by bucking my hips forward and sliding myself along his cock. The build was soft and slow, and I was on the brink of losing my sanity. I've never gotten this close so fast.

He brought his mouth to my ear. "I swear to God, Natalie. You're like an addiction that consumes my every thought."

I knew the feeling. He was on my mind every second of the day. He had no idea how much space he took up in my head.

His mouth found mine as I continued to push my hips against his. This kiss was all tongue and teeth. I never wanted it to stop. I arched off the bed as he continued to suck and nip in places that were already sensitive. I spread my legs wider, encouraging him to keep going.

"Jesus. Look at you. I want to touch you, everywhere. I want to watch you. I want to feel everything." He lifted me up and turned on his back, never once taking his eyes off mine.

I leaned over the top of him and pushed my hands onto his strong shoulders. There was nothing between us but bated breaths and hungry pants.

I wrapped my legs tightly around his thighs. "You're talking too much."

He laughed and opened his mouth to suck on my finger. "Just trying to convince you to give me a real shot."

"You know the rules. One month. That's all I can promise." It was a reminder to me more than him.

"I told you before. Your rules suck."

A breath shuddered out of me when he grabbed the base of his cock and dragged it along my opening. The back-and-forth movement along with the deliberate pressure had me whimpering in pleasure.

"And for the record, every line you draw, I plan to cross, and every rule you make, I plan on breaking, so do your best sweetheart."

"You need to stop saying things like that." I threw my head back when he rubbed the tip of his cock in slow circles along my folds.

I gasped when he shoved two fingers inside. My body tightened around his hand while he rubbed and pressed, searching for that bundle of nerves that would send me over the edge. "It's the truth, and the sooner you stop fighting this, the quicker I can convince you to take a real chance on us."

"What do you think I'm doing right now?" I moaned at the sensation that was filling me all over.

He cursed under his breath and buried his finger

deeper. "I told you before, I want more than just your body."

His fingers moved in and out while his tongue devoured mine. He was a man possessed, and all I wanted to do, was hold on for dear life and never let go.

"You're so fucking wet." His finger slid in and out. "Stop denying yourself this. I can give you whatever you want. Just say the word."

I gasped out when he pressed his thumb against my clit. Holy fuck. I was coming from his hand alone—in a matter of seconds. He continued gliding in and out as I squirmed against him. What the hell was he doing to me?

"Are you on the pill?"

I opened my eyes, feeling my heartbeat pound in my ears. "Yes."

He touched my face. "I went to the doctor when I got back from Vegas and haven't been with anyone since you. I don't want to stop to grab a condom, especially if I don't need one."

My mind buzzed with so many questions. I never had sex without protection, and despite only knowing him for a short period of time, I trusted him more than anyone. Maybe I had lost all common sense, and maybe I would regret this, but I wanted him so badly that I would have to deal with the consequences later if I had to. I needed him inside me.

"Okay."

"Okay what?" He dipped his head forward, his eyes searching mine. "I need you to tell me what you want me to do."

"I want you to fuck me. Right here. Right now. You don't need to leave this bed. I trust you. The question is, do you trust me?"

His eyes flashed with something I couldn't quite

explain, and in the next second, he flipped me over, lined himself up, and thrust inside. There was no resistance on my end as he slowly moved in and out. My body welcomed every inch he was giving me. I was taking it all as he filled me over and over again. I wrapped my legs around his back at the same time he buried his head in the crook of my neck. He swirled his hips, finding a different angle, making me arch into him.

Each stroke was harder. Each thrust was deeper. The bed banged rhythmically against the wall. The mattress squeaked. Rhett was wild and untamed. He wasn't being gentle or sweet; he was wound too tight and was one second away from unraveling inside me. My body tightened around his. Each fingernail was leaving an imprint on his back. The sensations inside me were on the verge of pouring out. I called out his name as he thrust faster. He was driving me out of my mind, making it impossible to think about anything else.

His hands dug into my hips as he increased his rhythm. Jesus Christ. He was not letting up. My vision blurred, and everything tingled. He pushed inside one last time, and I threw my hands around his neck, needing something to hold on to.

He rocked himself against me. So many promises and unspoken words hung in the air. I was close and ready to give him anything. He adjusted his hips and started picking up the pace.

"Oh, God." I sunk my teeth into his shoulder to stifle my scream. The strongest orgasm I'd ever had in my life came spiraling through me.

"That's it, baby." He braced the weight of his forearm beside my head. "I'm going to make you feel so good. You will never want to leave me. I will ruin you for anyone else. In the end, there will only be me."

My name was on his lips as he followed me over the edge. I could feel his warmth spread inside me. Wave after wave rippled out of him. His body shuttered before it went completely still. His eyes were closed, and his mouth was open. He was the most beautiful man I had ever seen.

He pulled out, rolled on his back, and threw an arm over his eyes. Heavy breaths came from his mouth as we both lay there for a moment.

My fingers ran lazily up and down his arm, silently reflecting on what just happened and what this would mean.

He pulled me toward him and played with the opal pendant hanging from my neck. "I don't want this to have an expiration date, Natalie, so I'm laying all my cards on the table. I want you. I want this. I'm going to fight for us, so be warned because I don't plan on losing."

I wanted to tell him that he didn't have to fight for me, because he had already won, but I knew that would change everything and I wasn't ready to admit that yet.

Instead, I tucked myself into his side, listening to the steady beat of his heart. "I want to try and see where this goes, but I can't commit to anything more than this right now."

He twisted a strand of hair around his finger. "Tell me what's stopping you from taking the next step? Even though you don't say it, I know you have feelings for me."

Tears welled up in my eyes. "I do have feelings for you. They're the type of feelings that can do damage to my already fragile heart."

He cupped my face. "You don't think I'm scared?"

"You're scared of me?"

"I'm scared that once you get those divorce papers, you're going to leave me. And it terrifies the hell out of me that I might never feel this way again."

I rested my head on his chest. "Let's take things one day at a time," I said, entwining his fingers with mine.

I wasn't going to allow myself to think about anything else tonight. Instead, I curled into his side and allowed him to pull me closer and forget about the world around us.

CHAPTER 17
NATALIE

WE PULLED UP TO A BIG WOODEN SIGN THAT SAID, "Welcome to Galloway Distillery." It was a massive property offering something for everyone: hayrides, live music, food, and drinks. There were also adorable little shops scattered around that I wished I had time to explore.

"This looks like a place I'd like to come back and visit someday," I said as we passed by a restaurant called Whiskey Bites. The front porch was adorned with rocking chairs, and there was a giant stone-walled fire pit off to the side, surrounded by traditional wooden picnic tables.

"We can come back later when everything is open if you want."

I picked up my coffee from the cupholder and took a sip. "I wish I could, but with me leaving at the end of the week, I can't afford to miss any more work."

"Oh, that's right. You have to fly to Boston for Gina's bridal shower on Friday." He rubbed his hand along his jaw. "You really trust me alone, unsupervised?"

I shook my head. "Try not to get arrested or burn the place down while I'm away."

He grinned. "Does that mean I have to cancel the keg and the strippers?"

"No, you can keep them."

He reached over and squeezed my leg. "Best wife ever."

This was the first conversation we had since we left the hotel this morning.

On the drive over, we were both quiet, which worked for me. When I woke up this morning, I might have freaked out with all the thoughts running through my head. At first, I smiled at the comfort of waking up in his arms. It was a feeling I could get used to. Then reality set in, and my mind started buzzing, contemplating the long list of complications that we still needed to work through. This photo shoot would be a good distraction.

We stepped out of the truck and were greeted by a man wearing Wrangler jeans and a flannel shirt. "Hello. Welcome to Galloway Distillery. I'm Joe, the general manager. Zoe is waiting for you in the main room."

Rhett introduced me as we walked by the barrels of whiskey and bourbon that led to the tasting room. The place resembled a mixture of old country western and hipster-chic with its tall ceilings, rich brown walls, and knotty wood floors.

"Rhett Daniels, it's such a pleasure to meet you." A woman in tight jeans, brown cowboy boots, and a short black sweater approached us. She was stunning and carried herself with an air of confidence that I admired.

He held out his hand. "You too. I believe you spoke to my manager on the phone."

"We truly appreciate you coming here," she said with a bright smile. "Do you have any questions for me?"

"None at all. This is my assistant for the day, Natalie." He smiled smugly.

Assistant, my ass.

"Wonderful." She glanced at me before turning back to Rhett. "I'm the one that will be taking the photos; I can't wait to get started." Her deep brown eyes peered up at him. I didn't like the vibe I was getting, so I inched my body closer to his.

"I'm sure you have done a million of these shoots before, but I would be happy to walk you through whatever you need me to."

"You're the boss today, so I'm just going to follow your lead." He winked and rewarded her with a smile that caused his dimples to pop out. My eyes narrowed, and jealousy started licking its way up my bones. I didn't trust her as far as I could throw her, but I needed to tame the green-eyed monster in me and remind myself that the smile and the wink didn't mean anything. He made his feelings quite clear to me last night.

Zoe directed us down the hallway to a room on the right. I tried to push my growing suspicions about her aside because it wasn't going to do me any good.

Joe came strolling back in. "Can I get you anything? Water, coffee, or a glass of whiskey."

Rhett laughed. "I might take you up on the whiskey offer once we're finished. I'll have water for now. Thanks." He turned to me. "How about you?"

"Water is fine."

"So, Rhett, how does it feel to have another Super Bowl win under your belt?" Zoe asked while taking a few things out of her bag.

"It feels out of this world. We worked our asses off."

"Well, congratulations. I'm happy for you. You looked great all season, so I'm not surprised." Her dreamy smile intensified as she stared up at him and then glanced at me. "Would you mind if I stole him for a minute and brought him to the makeup room we have set up next door?"

"Go ahead, I need to return a few emails. I'll be right here if you need anything."

I sipped my water and watched them walk out together, wondering what he thought of her. Could he tell she was flirting? Or that she was interested? Everything from her striking features, generous curves, and sultry voice was intimidating to me. He dealt with women like her every day. Why on earth would he want just me when he could have a variety to pick from whenever the mood struck?

Normally, I wasn't easily intimidated, but when it came to matters of the heart, I wasn't as strong as I'd like to be. I'd been hurt and lied to, and thanks to my ex, my confidence had taken a beating. Just when I felt like I was bouncing back, I was hit with another level of uncertainty. Would I be enough for him? Would he truly be happy settling down with one person? The truth was, I didn't know him well enough to answer those questions.

Instead of letting my doubts fester, I opened my iPad and went through my inbox to keep myself busy. When they returned to the room, Rhett was dressed in a black shirt with snaps for buttons, a pair of heavy-looking tight jeans, a gold belt buckle, a cowboy hat, and boots that had me salivating at the mouth. Holy fuck, did he look hot. I was never into cowboys until now.

"What do you think?" He turned around and stuck his butt out. "Does my ass look good in these jeans or what?"

Never in my life have I seen a sexier man until that moment.

"You look all right. You're just missing the bandana and the leather chaps." I shrugged, trying to play it off. I took a sip of my water because, holy hell, this Texas heat was getting to me.

Rhett's lips curled up to the side. He knew I was full of shit.

Zoe walked over and started playing with the collar of his shirt. "Can you undo the top buttons?"

"Sure." He handed me his water bottle.

I was becoming irritated with how she kept touching him—a little brush of the shoulder here, a light arm squeeze there. If that wasn't enough, she kept batting her eyelashes and biting down on her lip, trying to get his attention. Rhett was used to this type of behavior, but that didn't make it any easier for me to watch.

Joe and another man popped their heads in. "You guys ready?"

The three of us made our way into the main tasting room, where all the equipment was set up. Rhett confidently walked up to the bar. I couldn't help but notice Zoe's intense gaze. Her eyes seemed to devour him with a hunger that was hard to ignore.

"We're going to do a couple shots here where we can get the best close-ups, then we'll move out back and put you on the tractor." Her voice was low and husky as she directed him into a pose, making sure to capture the best angles.

Rhett placed his hands in the front pocket of his jeans as she instructed. "I'm ready when you are."

Everyone got in position while I stood back and took out the camera. My job was to take a few shots for the Arrows' social media pages, although the pictures I was capturing didn't feel like work. Rhett was the epitome of Southern charm, with his chiseled jawline and captivating eyes—eyes that were on me, sparkling and teasing.

I adjusted my lens, feeling a flutter in my stomach. I had to compose myself. I had a job to do, but all I could think about was how those lips felt against my skin and how capable those strong hands were.

God, the things that man could do should be illegal.

Zoe placed her hand on his forearm and whispered something in his ear. He looked up at me and cleared his throat. Unease gripped me as I observed their exchange. He murmured something back to her, and I felt my anxiety grow with each passing second. I couldn't hear what was said, but that knot of insecurity in my chest started to tighten.

She brought the camera to her face and started snapping away. "Lean back against the bar. That's great." She beamed at him as he held the glass of whiskey in his hand. "Flex those muscles, handsome," she called out. Her voice was full of suggestion. I couldn't have been the only one who picked up on it.

My eyes stayed on them as the photographer continued to flirt and make passes at him. With each click and shutter of the camera, she became bolder.

"Let's try something a little more intimate," she said, trying to guide him out of the room. "I have a mattress in the back. I'm thinking you can strip down to your boxers, and I'll prep your skin with some oil to give it a shiny look."

You've got to be kidding me.

His eyes met mine in a rush of panic. Couldn't she tell he was uncomfortable?

"I think you have enough images," I snapped, causing the room to go silent. "Mr. Daniel's time is limited, so I think it's best that we move this outside so we can wrap this up and be on our way."

She looked taken aback by my bluntness. "Oh, okay. Sure."

This was the second time in a row that I had to step in

and intervene when a woman started getting too handsy. I couldn't believe he had to deal with situations like this all the time. He obviously could take care of himself, but he shouldn't have to.

Once the shoot was moved outside, I tried to be less standoffish. It was hard to ignore how she was throwing herself at him. To Rhett's credit, he wasn't doing anything to encourage her interest.

That should have made me happy, but I almost lost it when she leaned in and slipped him her number at the end. I didn't want to feel vulnerable and insecure. He's given me no reason to doubt him, but those old wounds started to fester and chip away at me.

I hung off to the side, unsure how I was going to act with him without sounding irrational. Logically, I knew I had nothing to worry about. These were the types of challenges we would face. Even if the world knew he was married, the fangirls would still flirt, not giving a damn that he was in a committed relationship or not. I had to have faith in him, no matter how tempting some of these women could be.

Once the shoot was wrapped up, Rhett and I said our goodbyes and walked to his truck. All the while, his hand stayed on my back. I opened my door, and he helped me in, and I couldn't help but feel relieved that we were leaving.

"Are you going to talk to me or give me the silent treatment the entire way, like you did earlier?"

I sighed, feeling like my emotions were hanging in the balance. It didn't feel like I was going to be getting a handle on my state of mind anytime soon, so I figured it was best to be honest with him.

"I didn't know how to bring this up."

"Bring what up?"

"Today was hard for me. Watching Zoe hit on you was a wake-up call."

He scrubbed a hand down his face. "I don't know what to do or say to make you understand that you are the only woman I want. And at the same time, I am second-guessing myself, wondering if I'll ever be able to earn your trust."

"It's not that I don't trust you," I quickly added. "I don't know how to compete with all these women. I was never an insecure person before, but after dating a player and being cheated on, it's hard to silence the doubts in my head sometimes."

With an exasperated sigh, he smacked his palm on the steering wheel. "Don't compare me to that jackass. It's not fair that I'm paying the price for his fuckups."

"You're right; it's not fair, and I'm sorry, but I can't ignore the fact that you have a reputation." I squeezed my eyes shut and shook my head. This was wrong. I was lashing out, and he didn't deserve it. But at the same time, I was dealing with a lot of insecurities, and they only seemed to continue to pile up.

"Natalie, how I've lived my life is no secret. Women know who I am and think because of my reputation that they have a shot with me." He shoved a hand through his hair. "I can't rewrite the past, and I wish I could. But I thought after last night that you were finally giving me a chance to prove myself."

This was so unfair to him because last night, I did give in. I woke up in his arms and convinced myself we could do this. Then, seeing Zoe flirt with him was a reality check. I was letting that fear of never being enough to keep a man like him satisfied ruin all the progress we've made.

"You shouldn't have to prove yourself. You shouldn't have to change who you are."

"Don't you get it? I want to. I want to be a better man. That man with the reputation, that's not me anymore."

I folded my arms across my middle, feeling the need to apologize. "I shouldn't have thrown your past in your face. That was unfair. These are my insecurities. Feelings I need to deal with. I'm not putting space between us." I swiped a tear. "I'm just trying to find a way to keep my heart safe."

Rhett cursed under his breath and pulled down a side street. We turned into an empty parking lot of an auto repair shop. He unbuckled his seat belt and leaned against the console.

"Look at me." He cupped my cheek, forcing me to look his way. "It's okay to be scared." His eyes tracked over my face. "I'm scared too, but we will figure this out together."

Now, I felt embarrassed about making such a big deal out of something that didn't need to be. "For a guy who has never had a relationship before, you sure know the right words to say."

Tenderness swam in his eyes. "I've just never had the right person to say them to." He skimmed his knuckles across my cheeks. "I'm glad that the paperwork was stalled. It's given us a chance to take a step back and gain some clarity. I know you're not all the way there yet, but when you're ready to move forward, I'll be right by your side."

The idea of putting my heart on the line again was terrifying, but Rhett wasn't Levi. He deserved at least the benefit of the doubt. For him, I would try.

"Can we take it slow?"

"We can." His mouth quirked. "As long as I get to kiss you."

My face brightened, and I seriously questioned how I would survive, taking things slow and steady. "What kind of kiss are we talking about?"

He gripped my chin. "This kind." His mouth met mine

in a gentle, soft kiss. I sighed into him, feeling exhausted from fighting these feelings. No one but Rhett has ever been able to make me feel so weak yet so alive at the same time.

The noises from the cars whipping by in the distance faded away. Rhett sunk his fingers into my hair, angling my head exactly where he wanted me. My feelings for this man were so strong that they scared the living daylights out of me. Maybe that was a sign that what we had was worth fighting for.

"Let's talk this through," he said, tracing his thumb along my lips. "Tell me what I can do to help you move past these fears you have."

"I don't want you to think that I'm comparing you because nothing could be further than the truth. I know what it feels like to make someone your whole world, just like I know what it's like to lose it."

While Rhett wasn't Levi, it was hard to break down the walls I carefully built to protect myself. I couldn't just jump head first and put all my hopes and dreams into a future with him until I was one hundred percent positive that we were strong enough to survive long-term and that I wouldn't end up broken in the end.

"Have you ever considered that maybe you and Levi didn't work out because you weren't meant for each other? You might find some peace if you acknowledge that."

"Oh, trust me, I have accepted that."

"I would also like to add that you might not have been right for him, but you're perfect for me."

I shook my head and questioned how I got lucky enough to find someone so remarkable. "There you go again, saying all the right things. You make it sound so easy."

"It won't be easy, but I'd rather try to have something real with you than fake it with someone else."

"I don't like to think about you with anyone else," I said, going for honesty.

A ghost of a smile appeared on his lips. "I told you before, there is no one else. When are you going to get that through your thick head?"

I nudged his shoulder. "Just when I was going to apologize again."

"I don't want your apology," he said, linking his fingers with mine. "I want you to go on a date with me."

My eyes burned with tears. I just laid out all my insecurities for him to pick apart, and instead of scaring him away, he accepted me for who I was and still wanted to move forward with me.

I squeezed his hand. "I would love to go on a date with you."

"Good." His smile was so genuine that I couldn't help but smile back. "I know just where I'm going to take you when we get back to Atlanta."

CHAPTER 18

NATALIE

"Roller skating?" I laughed as we walked into the building, which looked like something out of a 1970s movie set. "This is your idea of a date?"

"Did you think we would do something generic like go to a movie?"

"With you, I never know what to expect."

"Are you complaining?" he asked as he walked by a small arcade with a concession stand in the back that was closed for the night. It looked like Rhett had rented the place out just for our date.

"Not at all. I'm just curious, why roller skating?"

His hand was now on my back as we walked further into the building. "My mom would pick up Ford, Reagan, and me every Tuesday after school. It was the one day a week where she would leave work early so she could spend time with us."

"That is so sweet." I spun around, taking it all in. My eyes caught on a disco ball hanging in the middle of the rink. I pictured a young Rhett taking his dates here as a teenager.

"Was this your hangout spot in high school, too?" I sat down on the bench to lace up my skates.

He coughed into his hand. "Uh, no. I was too cool for roller skating by then."

"Doing what?"

"Going to parties and playing seven minutes in heaven."

I laughed. "I bet you've seen your fair share of dark closets back in the day. What other fun things did you do at these parties?"

He shook his head. "You sure do ask a lot of questions."

"I'm just trying to get to know my husband a little bit better," I said, playfully batting my eyelashes.

"We've got all the time in the world to get to know each other," he said, kicking his shoes off. "Do you at least know how to rollerblade?"

"Nope," I said, tightening the laces on my skates.

He scratched his chin. "Ice-skate?"

"I tried once and hated it."

I left out the fact that Levi tried to teach me once. It was a disaster, and I ended up colliding with a group of young kids. When I crashed into one, it was like a domino effect as the parents watched in slow motion as their children tumbled down one by one. Some were crying so hard it was a miracle I didn't get sued. That was my first and last time.

"Well, this is going to be fun." He chuckled and stood up. It was hard to miss his sarcasm.

"For you, not for me. I'll be on my ass most of the time."

When I attempted to stand up, my legs wobbled. Rhett extended a steady hand. "I won't let you fall. I promise."

Too late for that. I thought as he guided me out to the

center of the rink. He held on to my waist, guiding me from behind.

I hesitated at first, trying to keep my balance, but when I felt my limbs flailing, I tightened my grip on his fingers.

He laughed beside me as if he found this whole thing amusing. There was a reason I didn't play sports in high school: I had zero coordination.

"Bend your knees a little bit." He let go of my hand for a minute, and I felt myself falling backward. He chuckled. "Okay, this is going to be tougher than I thought. Hold on to the railing and watch me."

He skated off, doing lap after lap, striding across the rink like he was an Olympic roller skater. A laugh bubbled out of me because he was such a damn showoff. He twirled and spun with such confidence that I wouldn't be surprised if he pulled out a retro headband and started leaping through the air. The man was too damn cute for his own good.

He was crossing his skates at the ankles, doing zigzags, and skating backward with an impressive burst of speed.

I was smiling harder than I ever have in my life.

After he was done, he tentatively came to a stop in front of me. "Are you ready?"

"Don't they have a practice area like they do on the ski slopes?" I asked and looked up to see him smiling.

"You don't need a practice area."

"You are really enjoying this, aren't you."

I might have been complaining left and right because the thought of falling and breaking my leg was terrifying, but I was still having fun.

His eyes were sparkling. "I always enjoy spending quality time with my wife."

I took his hand as he guided me through the proper techniques, trying to hide how much I liked it when he called me 'his wife'. "Just bend your knees and find your balance," he explained gently.

"I don't feel like I have any control," I said as he squatted next to me.

"It's all about your posture, babe. Just move slowly."

"Like this?" I asked, feeling like I was walking like a damn duck.

His eyes were twinkling. "Just like that, but maybe a little faster."

The second I glided my foot forward, I lost my balance and fell on my ass. Instead of helping me up right away, what did he do? He pulled out his phone and took a picture, that's what.

"You told me you wouldn't let me fall," I grumbled as he finally helped me up. He was laughing so hard I wouldn't be surprised if he peed his pants.

"I didn't let you fall. You wiped out; there is a difference."

"I hate you," I said, standing on shaky legs.

"Whatever you say." He led me over to the railing. "Remember, practice makes perfect. Try holding on to this."

I gripped onto the railing for dear life, determined not to give up. As I took tentative steps, I noticed my movements got less wobbly. Rhett was giving me words of encouragement, but all I could focus on was staying upright on my feet. After a few minutes, I attempted to glide without holding on. Every little movement forward gave me more confidence.

"I think you're ready to be my skating partner." Rhett's eyes lit up with pride.

I grabbed his hand for support as we slowly skated in a circle along the rink. Each time we went around, I glided a little bit faster.

Skating wasn't that bad. It was kind of fun, actually. We continued skating hand in hand until I eventually found my groove.

"Ready to race me yet?"

I laughed. "Not yet. I feel comfortable at this speed."

"Party pooper." He sank his fingers into my waist and stared into my eyes. He leaned forward very carefully and gently kissed my lips. It was sweet but powerful enough to pack a punch.

"Do you want to do a couple more laps or get on with the second part of our date?" He leaned back and rolled up the sleeves of his shirt. The fabric strained as he pushed them up to his elbows. Those muscular arms had no business being so distracting.

I dragged my eyes up to his face. "There's more?"

"Yeah." There was amusement in his eyes as he darted his tongue out to wet his bottom lip. "But you might want to get your mind out of the gutter first. You look like you want to lick me from head to toe."

I shook my head and did my best to deny it. "You think that's what I was doing?" I waved my hand in the air like that was the most ridiculous thing I'd ever heard. "I was just wondering why you don't have tattoos like most guys on the team."

Jesus, that was so random. Could I be any more obvious?

He laughed and cupped my face, running the pad of his thumb along my cheek. "So, you're not just a snoop, but a little liar too."

"I'm not lying." A guilty blush darkened my cheeks.

He raised an eyebrow with a knowing smile. "You're a horrible liar, but okay. The reason why I don't have any tattoos is because my parents would disown me if I did."

"I hope you're exaggerating."

The thought of meeting his parents someday was nerve-wracking. He's mentioned on multiple occasions about how strict they were. Despite what he said before about not caring what other people thought, I knew how much he longed for their approval. Deep down, I wondered if their opinion of me would make or break our relationship.

"Not completely." He helped me over to the bench so we could slip our skates off. "Are you ready for part two now?"

I smiled up at him. "I can't wait."

———

"Wow, I had no idea you were such a big deal here," I exclaimed as the hostess guided us through one of the coziest restaurants I'd ever seen. Rhett beamed, waved, and even chatted with a few customers as we passed their tables.

A crackling fireplace sat in the middle of the wall, creating a welcoming vibe. As we walked further into the room, my attention was drawn to the flickering candles on each of the dark, rustic wood tables. It was so charming and inviting. I hoped the food would be just as good as the atmosphere.

"When are you going to realize that your husband is a pretty big deal?" He laughed and pulled my chair out for me. "People love me, and this is one of the few places where I can come and actually enjoy a meal in peace."

"What's so special about this place?"

"Remember, I told you about our housekeeper, Cruze? This is her son Luis's place."

"Ah, so it's not your celebrity status that's earning you such special treatment?"

"Baby, I'm a celebrity everywhere." His comment caused me to laugh. One of the things I loved about Rhett was that he never took life too seriously.

"What would you like to start with?" he asked as I looked over the menu. "It's kind of a foodie place, but the food isn't pretentious."

"Everything looks interesting." I smiled as the hostess set our waters on the table. "I feel like loading up on carbs after that workout."

Rhett smirked and leaned his elbows on the table. "It's adorable that you considered that working out."

"Excuse you, Mr. I'm-The-Best-Tight End-In-The-League. My muscles ache because my legs aren't used to exercise."

"What do you have against fitness?" He took a sip of his water; amusement filled his eyes.

"Well, first of all, I don't like to sweat."

"I hate to break it to you, sweetheart, but you moved to the wrong state. There is a reason why they call it Hot-Lanta."

"I am aware, but thankfully, most places have A/C."

A basket of assorted rolls was placed in front of us. "Sorry to interrupt, but I wanted to stop by and say hi."

I glanced at the handsome man in a dark suit. He had an easygoing smile and a friendly demeanor.

"Luis, my man." Rhett stood up to greet him with enthusiasm. "How's it goin', dude?"

"Going great, but it's been too long, my friend." His attention turned to me. "You must be Natalie. I'm Luis, it's great to meet you."

"Likewise."

Rhett threw his arm around his friend's shoulder. "Luis here is also my personal chef."

"Oh, you're the one who left the delicious Chicken Florentine in the fridge."

Luis smiled. "That's me." He patted Rhett's stomach. "Somebody needs to make sure this guy eats something other than pizza and fried chicken."

"Hey, don't go hating on pizza, man. After all, that red sauce is from a tomato, which is technically a vegetable."

"Actually, a tomato is considered a fruit, and the reason why you love that red sauce so much is because it's loaded with sodium." Luis rolled his eyes and looked at me. "Your man here is a picky eater. He eats like a ten-year-old."

"I'm surprised he picked this place. The menu is a big step above his typical bar food," I teased because if there is one thing I learned about Rhett, it is that his go-to food was burgers and pizza, and he always seemed to have a pack of Skittles on him. "Your food must be really good."

Luis shook his head with a boyish grin. "He's just here to help secure his investment."

"Investment?" I blinked in confusion.

Luis squeezed Rhett's shoulder. "Your guy here is a silent partner. If it wasn't for him, I never would have secured the loan and gotten this off the ground."

I glimpsed at Rhett, who looked away sheepishly. He was just full of surprises, and every time I discovered a new layer, I found myself falling deeper in love with him.

"I've got to get back to the kitchen, but I wanted to apologize for having to miss the Born to Love event. Mom was in bed all day. She could barely move and the stubborn woman refused to go to the doctor."

Rhett shook his head. "You were where you needed to be. She's more important."

Luis gave him a quick nod. "I still feel terrible, and I just wanted to thank you again. You're helping out a lot of families."

Rhett looked uncomfortable. "Of course, it's the least I could do. Seeing her struggle and working tirelessly, made me realize how tough it can be."

"You know it means a lot to her." He looked over his shoulder and then back to Rhett.

"Your mom is an amazing woman. We are all lucky to have her in our lives."

Luis smiled. "Thanks for coming tonight. It was great seeing you. I hope you both enjoy your meal and if you need anything, let me know."

The two men shook hands, and I waited for Luis to leave. I couldn't believe I never connected the dots until now. Rhett had one of the biggest hearts of anyone I'd ever known.

"I didn't realize that Born to Love was so personal to you. I think what you're doing is amazing."

He sat back down and took a sip of his water. "I really don't want to make a big deal out of it."

I nudged him with my foot. "Stop being so modest."

He rolled his eyes. "I'm not being modest. I meant what I said, so let's not make a big fuss over it."

I leaned back in my chair and studied him. "Rhett Daniels, you are a big old softie."

He paused as his water reached his lips. "As my wife, you should know there is nothing soft about me."

We were interrupted when the server came over to take our orders. We both ended up getting one of the specials. I ordered a glass of wine while Rhett ordered a beer.

We finished our appetizers and continued to talk, only to be interrupted a few times by friends coming over to say hello. I could see why women were so taken with him, and guys wanted to be friends with him.

He had charisma and charm and had a way of looking people in the eye and making them feel special.

"Talk to me about football. Are you the fastest guy on the team?" I asked, digging my fork into the salad once our food arrived.

"You know absolutely nothing about my position, do you?" he asked, taking a bite of his steak.

"Don't judge me. I'm learning, and I've been doing research."

"Oh, yeah?" He leaned back and wiped his mouth with a napkin. "Let's hear it."

I rolled my tongue around in my cheek. I knew much more than I was letting on but couldn't resist the urge to toy with him. It was only payback, after all, for him letting me fall on my ass so many times today.

"I've been watching Travis Kelce on Instagram. He plays the same position as you, and he seems to run pretty fast."

Rhett barked out a laugh. "Yeah, my man is a beast, but tight ends aren't the fastest positions. That title goes to running backs and wide receivers and sometimes cornerbacks and safeties."

"Makes sense," I said, taking a bite of my sea bass. "Tell me more about the position you and Travis play?"

His eyes narrowed. "Travis? Why are you so interested in Travis?"

I pushed my hair behind my ear. He was so fun to rile up. "He seems pretty hot right now, so I figured he would be a good place to start."

It was taking everything I had not to burst out laughing from the look on his face.

He set his elbows on the table and angled his head to the side. "He doesn't play for the Arrows. And just so you know, he has a girlfriend."

"I know that, but he's very popular, so I figured I could

learn more about the sport by looking at his socials," I teased, batting my eyelashes playfully.

"I'm pretty popular too." He raised an eyebrow at me like he was trying to figure out if I was serious or just yanking his chain. "My jersey outsells his, and if you are going to stalk any athletes on social media, you should start with mine."

"Whatever." I shrugged my shoulders like that idea bored me to death and continued with my teasing. "Tell me about Travis."

He draped his arm along the back of the booth. "I'd rather not."

"Have you ever met him?"

His jaw worked back and forth. "Yes, and now that I know how infatuated you are with him, I'll make sure you never do."

"Harsh." I reached for my water, trying to hide the smile lifting the corners of my mouth. I was so proud of myself for keeping up with this charade.

"Right, so back to me. What do you want to know?"

Everything.

"Seeing that it's the offseason, what do you usually do in your downtime?"

"I like to keep busy, so I play a lot of golf, attend a few sponsorship meetings, and shoot a few commercials." He smirked, and I scowled. "I also attend a few fundraisers and volunteer at my organization, but you already know all that."

"I want to know what you do for fun besides golf?"

"Well, I like to drink, sleep, eat, and play video games."

"What are your hobbies?"

He ran a hand through his hair. "I don't have any hobbies."

I leaned back in my chair, not buying these short,

generic answers. "Why are you avoiding answering my questions?"

He stared at me for a moment, and I didn't miss the way he shifted in his chair or the shadow that crossed his face.

He exhaled loudly. "What I used to consider fun are things you aren't going to want to hear."

"Oh." I slumped back in my seat. I mentally kicked myself for even going there. Rhett, the party boy, was known to have a girl or two on his arm.

He eyed me cautiously. "That was all before you."

I reached out and placed my hand over his. "Hey, it's all good. It's in the past. We promised each other we would try, right?"

"Yeah, we did." He took a sip of his beer. "Speaking of the past, how are you feeling about the wedding next week? Are you nervous about seeing Levi?"

"A little," I said, tucking a strand of hair behind my ear. "But not because I still have feelings for him. I'm worried about how awkward it will be."

He squeezed my hand. "I get it, but I'll be right there with you. You won't have to face him alone."

His words were meant to comfort me, but they had the opposite effect. I was worried about how Levi would react when he saw that I had moved on.

Chances are, it wasn't going to be good.

CHAPTER 19

NATALIE

"I can't tell you how happy I am that you were able to fly in for the bridal shower," Gina said, placing the last gift on the floor.

She acted like there was a chance I wouldn't come. I knew she didn't mean anything by it, but isn't that what friends do? They make time for each other and support one another.

"I wouldn't miss it," I told her while unbuttoning my jacket. I didn't mention that there were a few times where I was uncomfortable during the shower.

Most of the people were friendly, and maybe I was being paranoid, but I thought I heard a few whispers from the wives and girlfriends of the players, commenting on how they couldn't believe I was still in the wedding party. They didn't understand how Gina and Hudson could allow me to be a part of their lives now that I was no longer dating Hudson's best friend.

"We haven't talked much since you moved. How's Atlanta? Meet any hot football players?" Claudia wiggled her eyebrows playfully.

I wasn't sure how I was supposed to answer that. We didn't keep secrets from each other. We'd been friends for years, and in all that time, never once did I go out of my way to hide something so significant from them.

"Atlanta is great. I love my job." I followed her and Claudia into the living room and flopped onto one of the recliners.

"Is there a reason why you didn't answer the second part of that question?" Gina's eyes met mine as if she could see right through me. I wiped my hands down my dress, deciding it was finally time to come clean. "I need to tell you both something, but you have to swear that this stays between us."

"You know you can tell us anything," Claudia said gently.

It didn't feel that way for some reason, but these two were my best friends. If I couldn't confide in them, then who could I trust?

I took a deep breath and met their eyes. "Remember my one-night stand in Vegas?"

Claudia stared at me, blinking. "You're pregnant?"

"Nope." I would have laughed at the expression on her face if the truth wasn't just as crazy. "I married him."

There was a moment of stunned silence. Gina's mouth fell open while Claudia's wineglass froze midway to her lips.

"Wait, what did you just say?" Gina asked, covering her heart with her hands.

"I know this is a shock, but I didn't know how to tell you guys," I said quickly. "And I know this sounds insane, and it's unexpected, but there is something about him that just feels right."

Claudia sat forward. "What the fuck possessed you to

get married to a stranger? Were you even in the right state of mind?"

This was where I was torn. While my marriage might not have started out with the best of intentions, I felt guilty admitting that. It wasn't something I wanted to acknowledge or accept. Rhett and I have come a long way since that night.

I scratched my head, pausing for time. "I don't know how to explain it to where it will make sense. Things happened so fast. Neither one of us was thinking clearly. There are circumstances, and I don't want to get into too much detail, but just trust me when I tell you I know what I'm doing."

"Why didn't you tell us?" Gina asked. Now that the initial shock had worn off, hopefully, they would ease up a bit with the interrogation.

"It's really complicated," I said, hoping they would both understand. I knew they probably wouldn't. They'd been disconnected from my life for a while, and they had no idea how much progress I'd made over the last month.

Gina lifted a brow. "This is pretty fast, don't you think? You just broke up with Levi two months ago."

I couldn't even be mad at the comment. I was a rule follower. I did things by the book. I stayed in my lane and usually approached things with caution. This was completely out of character for me.

"It was unexpected, but that's not even the worst part."

"And now I'm confused." Gina frowned. "How can this possibly get any worse?"

Taking a deep breath, I placed my nervous hands on my lap. "It turns out he plays on my uncle's team."

"I fucking knew it," Claudia shouted, and my head snapped to hers because there was no way I heard her right.

"If that was the case, then why didn't you say anything to me?"

My mind went back to that night and how she pointed him out to me. She knew exactly who he was when she dared me to flirt with him. I wasn't sure if I should be pissed or grateful.

She had the decency to look guilty. "Because I knew you wouldn't have gone after him."

"Wait, who is it?" Gina asked.

I curled my hands around the arm of the chair and cleared my throat. "Rhett Daniels. He's a tight end for the Atlanta Arrows."

Gina blinked. Her eyes narrowed as she studied me. "Rhett Daniels? I thought his name was Theo?"

"Theo is his real name, but he never uses it. He gave me that name when I didn't recognize him."

"I recognized him." Claudia smiled from ear to ear.

Gina shot her sister a dirty look before turning her attention back to me. "Let's circle back to what happened that night."

I sighed. "After we left the club, we ended up having a few drinks in a lounge at one of the casinos. We ended up talking about Levi and our breakup. He took pity on me when I told him about your wedding and how I was going to be uncomfortable. After a few shots of tequila, he suggested we get married, and I take him as my plus one. But now everything is a mess because Beau still has no idea."

"So, this is some type of arrangement, and it's all pretend?" Gina's eyes bent together as if she were trying to understand this better.

I sighed, breathing a bit easier now that the truth was out. "It started out that way, but now that I've gotten to know him, I want more."

"So, what's stopping you?" Claudia's voice was filled with concern.

That was such a loaded question. I wasn't sure how to answer that because I was still trying to understand it myself. "Uncle Beau made it clear that there was no mixing business with pleasure. I'm terrified of how he would react. He's always been supportive of me, but he will be furious if he finds out."

There was a sense of unease gnawing at my insides. I wasn't even worried about myself at this point. Rhett had more to lose than I did. I would never be able to forgive myself if he got traded to another team because of me.

"I can't believe you felt like you had to keep this from us." Gina looked hurt.

"Did you honestly think we would judge you?" Claudia asked, coming over to sit beside me.

My mouth opened and closed. Did I tell them that, yes that's exactly what I thought? I loved them, but for some reason, things have felt different since Levi and I split. I couldn't shake the feeling that our friendship was on the verge of falling apart.

Since Vegas, the only time they have reached out to me was if it was about the wedding. Not once had they checked in to see how I was doing. Not a phone call or a text, just emails about dress fittings and wedding accommodations.

Granted, the phone worked both ways, and I was just as guilty for not reaching out. In my defense, my silence had more to do with keeping my marriage a secret than anything else.

"I didn't want you to worry about any more drama before the wedding."

Gina's shoulders sagged with relief. "Thank you. There is already enough going on as it is. You're not seriously still thinking about bringing him to the wedding, are you? That would only make things worse."

My throat felt dry, so I picked up my wine, feeling the need to do something with my mouth before I said something I'd regret. That wasn't the reaction I was hoping for. "Actually." I set my glass down; my frustration had reached its maximum capacity. I was sick of biting my tongue and worrying about avoiding a confrontation. "I am planning on bringing him. I assumed if Levi got to bring a plus one, it would only be fair that I was awarded the same courtesy."

Gina leaned forward and frantically started playing with her engagement ring. "Yes, but Levi is a mutual friend. We don't even know this guy."

I wasn't trying to be insensitive to her feelings, but the fact that she would even say that to me made me angry.

"I'm sorry you feel that way. You must have forgotten that Levi knocked up another woman while we were together," I said harshly. "So, explain to me why he's allowed to bring a guest and I'm not?"

I had no idea how this escalated so quickly. Gina was supposed to be my friend, and it was the first time I felt like she didn't value our friendship as much as I did.

Claudia leaned forward and put her hands out. "Okay, Natalie has a point. It's not fair. We're all adults here. Everyone can just stay in their corner and behave. It's one night."

Gina pointed a finger at me in warning. "Fine, but please, no drama."

"I'm not the one you need to worry about," I reminded her.

Once everyone calmed down, we took out the wedding planner and started going through what was left to do. Gina's lack of approval was casting a shadow on my newfound happiness, and I was growing sick and tired of sacrificing my own voice just to appease her. Claudia did her best to steer the conversations into lighter topics, but I could still feel Gina's judgment weighing me down.

I had the seating chart spread out in front of me when my phone buzzed with a new text.

A smile split my cheeks when I opened it.

Rhett
Just wanted to let you know that the strippers just left, and the keg is almost gone.

Me
Damn, sounds like I missed all the fun.

Rhett
How's the wedding madness going?

Me
It's insane.

Rhett
See, getting married in Vegas is so much easier.

Me
You're not wrong. I think Gina is pissed at me because I bailed on drinks last night.

There was a happy hour for the wedding party at a local pub, but I skipped it. Instead I lied and said I had work to catch up on. I knew Levi would be there and I didn't want to risk it.

Rhett
She seriously expected you to sip drinks with Mr. I'm A Cheating Asshole?

I laughed.

> **Me**
> Crazy right?

> **Rhett**
> Just try to keep busy until I get there.

> **Me**
> Five days feels like forever. I wish you could skip your golf tournament and get here sooner.

He was playing in a celebrity tournament, so I wouldn't see him until the big day.

> **Rhett**
> Are you missing your husband, wife?

> **Me**
> I'm counting down the days.

> **Rhett**
> What's the plan? Are you going to hide away in your hotel room every night until I get there?

> **Me**
> Well, I am working remotely this week, so at least I have a valid excuse.

> **Rhett**
> Try to have a little fun. But if you get bored and need me to send you a dick pic, or something like that, I would be happy to send one.

A laugh sprang free when another text came through.

I closed out the chat with a renewed sense of calm. Rhett always knew how to make me feel better. If he expected me to freak out about him moving my stuff into his bedroom, he was going to be in for a pleasant surprise.

Being away from him had provided me with some clarity. And I couldn't wait to see the look on his face when I told him that I was ready to take the next step with him.

CHAPTER 20

RHETT

I GLANCED AROUND THE BALLROOM OF THE SWANKY country club in downtown Boston. I spent enough time in these places to know that this little shebang cost a mint. There were candles and flowers everywhere. If you asked me, it was borderline obnoxious, just like the people at my table.

Somehow, I was seated next to a few guys from the hockey team. Their loud voices made it impossible to hear anything else. I was used to loud, crude-talking athletes, but these guys thought they were all that and a bag of chips. Their dates were already tipsy, and I wondered if that was the only way they could tolerate being around them.

"Hey, are you Rhett Daniels?" one of the hockey players asked.

"Yep," I grumbled because I couldn't take my eyes off my wife or the nightmare playing out in front of me. Everyone clapped and smiled as the newly married couple finished their first dance. When the rest of the wedding party joined in, my hands squeezed my tumbler so hard I thought it would shatter.

He held out his hand. "Jake Sletcher, I'm a huge fan."

I shook his hand firmly. "Thanks, man, I appreciate it."

"Are you a friend of the bride or the groom?" He seemed unfazed by my grumpy attitude as I watched Natalie and the way she swayed in her ex-boyfriend's arms.

"Neither." I turned to him, needing to get my eyes off the two of them dancing. I swear, this was the longest, slowest song I'd ever heard. "I'm here with a friend."

He sipped his beer. "Nice. I wanted to congratulate you on winning the big game. That was epic."

I sighed heavily through my nose as Levi pulled Natalie closer. I was begging for trouble, but I couldn't look away, no matter how hard I tried. "Thanks. It was a battle making it through the playoffs, but the team managed to pull it off."

The DJ tapped the mic to get everyone's attention. Jake clapped me on the shoulder. "I'm heading back to my seat. Enjoy the offseason. I look forward to watching you kick ass in the fall."

"You too. Maybe I'll see you in the finals in June."

I shook his hand one last time before taking my seat. Jake seemed like a decent guy, unlike his asshole teammate.

Levi walked up to grab the microphone. "Hello, everyone." He smiled, and I couldn't help but study him. I could see how some women could find him attractive. He had shoulder-length hair that he kept tucked neatly behind his ears. He was all fake charm with an exaggerated smile.

"First, I'd like to thank my best friend and teammate for scheduling his wedding during one of my days off." Laughter sprang out through the crowd. I must have been the only one not to find him funny. "And second, Gina, it's a nice change to see you in a dress, considering you're the one always wearing the pants in the relationship." More laughter sounded throughout the room. "With all seriousness, I'm just upset that I was asked not to share any embarrassing stories about the groom, so if my speech is lacking, it's because those are the only stories I know." He looked at Hudson, who was shaking his head.

My heart pounded in my chest when his eyes turned toward Natalie. "Witnessing your love for Gina is a bittersweet reminder of what I once had. And while I want to be envious, you both deserve all the happiness in the world. If I could share one piece of advice with my best friend, it would be that life is too short, so don't let anyone or anything come between you. And finally, never lose sight of what brought you together in the first place."

"Cheers to the bride and groom."

As the music floated around the reception hall, I kept glancing at Natalie, who was noticeably unsettled. I wanted to go to her and see if she was okay after that speech, because let's be honest here, every single person in the room knew he was talking about her. Instead, I sipped my drink and watched her laugh with one of the bridesmaids. When she caught my eye, she excused herself and walked toward me. I took a few breaths to collect myself.

"Hi." She smiled when I handed her my whiskey and Coke. She looked like she needed it more than I did.

"Are you having fun?" I asked.

I sure as fuck wasn't, but I couldn't tell her that, could I?

She sipped my drink. "I've been too busy with bridesmaid duties to enjoy myself. How about you?"

"It's not the worst wedding I've ever been to, so I'll survive."

My prime rib was overcooked, the potatoes were

bland, and the salad had blue cheese crumbles. I fucking hated blue cheese. Thank God my appetite was shit; the portions were so small even a bird would starve. The open bar was the only thing filling up my stomach at the moment.

"I'm sorry about Levi's speech." She rested a gentle hand on my shoulder.

I kissed the side of her head. "Don't worry about it."

Her brow raised. "You don't have to pretend that you're not upset. I would be if the shoe was on the other foot."

There was no sense in denying it. "I'm not upset with you. I'm pissed about the situation. I'm sick of hiding who you are to me."

Natalie set the drink on the table and flung an arm around my neck. "Dance with me."

I looked around for any prying eyes. "Natalie. You're a little close, don't you think? People are going to start drawing conclusions."

She shrugged. "Let them."

That earned a laugh. "What are you doing?"

"I'm asking you to dance. Come on." She grabbed my hand as I followed her to the dance floor.

As soon as the next song started, I pulled her close. We swayed together, getting lost in our own little world. My eyes traveled down the length of her.

"You look stunning," I said, brushing her long blond hair off her shoulder. Her blue dress matched her eyes, and the silky fabric draped gracefully along her curves. Natalie was the epitome of class and elegance, and when you paired that with her down-to-earth personality, I felt like the luckiest guy in the room.

"Thank you. Did you notice I'm taller too." She kicked her foot out to show me her hot as fuck heels.

"And yet I still tower over you." My eyes dipped down to hers teasingly.

She laughed and swatted my arm playfully. "Watch it, big guy. These heels are sharp enough to be used as weapons."

I spun her around to the lyrics of Luke Combs "Better Together" before bringing her back to me.

"I was hoping you would be using them for something else later." I wiggled my eyebrows as we glided across the dance floor. I pulled her closer to avoid the couple dancing next to us who were about to bump into her.

A blush crept up her neck. "Maybe I just might do that."

My grip tightened on her waist. "You have no idea how badly I want to kiss you right now."

Hell, I wanted to do a hell of a lot more than kiss her. Just having her in my arms, touching me, awakened things in me that I couldn't control.

She ran her hands up along my chest, never breaking eye contact. "I was hoping you would. So, what are you waiting for?"

Was she serious or still teasing me?

I looked down at her, feeling my pulse race. "I was letting you take the lead tonight. I wasn't sure how much PDA you were comfortable with."

Her hand rested on my chest, right over my beating heart. "I'm sick of hiding my feelings for you and always looking over my shoulder. I don't want to do that anymore."

It took a minute for her words to catch up to me.

I tilted her chin up. "What are you saying, Natalie? I'm going to need you to spell it out for me."

I held my breath, feeling my blood pumping harder and harder through my veins. I was suddenly aware of how much I needed those words to be true because, in a short amount of time, this woman has owned every single part of me.

"You asked me to give you a chance, and you have been patient with me and given me time to figure out my feelings. Never once have you complained or given up. But I don't need any more time because I know with everything I have that I want to be with you. For real. No more hiding, no more lying, and no more excuses." She shifted her weight from one foot to the other. Her blue eyes were soft and warm and a little unsure. "So, if you still want me, I'm all yours."

Without replying, I grabbed her by the elbow and led her off the dance floor. "Where are we going?" She chuckled, doing her best to keep up with me.

"Someplace where we can be alone." People were clapping and cheering, and out of the corner of my eye, I saw Gina and Hudson cutting into the cake. We weaved through the people and rounded the tables like we were on a mission. I guess I was because I needed her in a place where no one could bother us.

There was an exit door to the left, so we made our way downstairs without breaking our stride. The pro shop was my first stop, but the door was locked. Thankfully, there was an empty storage room with the door slightly open where we could slip into without being noticed. We stepped inside the dimly lit room. It was cluttered with golf clubs, towels, and various equipment.

I closed the door and quickly secured the lock. She gasped when I spun her around and pinned her against the wall.

"It looks like I have you right where I want you, Mrs. Daniels." My hand gripped the back of her neck, my fingers threading through her hair.

"What do you plan on doing with me, husband?" Her voice was low and seductive, and just thinking about all the things I wanted to do to her lit a match inside me.

I gave her an arrogant smile. "I should make you pay for all the weeks you've tortured me."

"Tortured?" She laughed. "That's a stretch, don't you think?"

I dropped my mouth to her neck and dragged my tongue over her collarbone. "No, but I do have plans to stretch something right now."

She glanced around the small room, double-checking the lock on the door.

"Aren't you afraid someone could walk by and hear us?"

"Does it look like I give a fuck?" I moved my hand over her breast, kneading and squeezing it through the fabric of her dress. I could feel the heat coming from her body, making me grip her nipple tighter.

Her head fell back against the wall, and she let out a whimper. "God, Rhett."

I trailed my lips along the side of her neck, nipping the skin with my teeth, making her yelp. "I love knowing that you're mine."

She made me feel things I didn't know I was missing from my life. From the moment I first kissed her on the dance floor, I wanted to know everything about her. And I've loved every damned minute I got to spend with her.

I lifted the hem of her dress and dragged my hand up her thighs. I could feel her wetness through her lace thong.

She pulled my mouth to hers and kissed me forcefully. "Please hurry up."

I rolled my thumb along her clit, toying with her for a minute. "Patience, wife."

She let out a frustrated growl and started rocking her

hips against me. "I can't control what happens if you take your time."

I pulled back and started stroking her. "Is that a challenge?"

"I'm just stating facts." She pressed the heel of my palm against her clit. "So don't tease me."

I cocked my head to the side. "You think you're the boss of me now?"

"I am your wife; it's my job to boss you around."

I withdrew my fingers that were coated with her wetness. "Do you want me to stop?"

"If you ever want to fuck me again, you better put those fingers back in and finish the job."

I grinned. "That's my girl. Now, hold on to your dress, or you're going to have a mess on your hands."

I kneeled on the floor and looked up at her. I pushed her panties to the side, groaning at the sight. "Fuck, Natalie. You are so ready for me."

"I'm always ready for you. Now, do your worst because it won't take much right now."

I hissed in a breath, trying to keep myself from losing control. I flicked my tongue against her core and licked at her insides. She was warm and perfect and the sexiest thing I'd ever seen. And without sounding arrogant, I'd seen a lot, but nothing, and I mean nothing, compared to her.

Knowing she was mine and that I got to worship and touch her every day made me feel like the luckiest son of a bitch alive.

I could feel her swell against my mouth as I licked and sucked while holding her legs open. My fingers dug into her hip, holding her in place and letting her know who was in control this time. I dipped a finger inside and flicked at her clit with my tongue. She encouraged me to keep going with her hands and tiny whimpers. I was taking my time. My only focus was making her feel good. I added another finger and spread her open wider so I could go deeper. Her legs began to shake, so I arched my fingers around her insides, knowing she was seconds away from falling apart on my tongue.

"Rhett," she cried out while tugging on my hair. "I'm going to come."

"Damn fucking right you are." I clamped my mouth down on her clit when I felt a burst of pleasure come tearing through her. Her eyes closed, her mouth fell open, and all I could think of was—*Mine. Mine. Mine.*

Natalie came apart on my tongue, and I kept my face rooted there, not wanting to miss out on a drop of her pleasure.

I eased back, pressing a kiss to the inside of her thigh before lifting my head. Her cheeks were flushed, her eyes were still hooded over, and her body looked thoroughly satisfied.

She gently ran her fingers along my face and then leaned in to kiss me softly. When I noticed a tear slip down her cheek, I looked up at her with concern.

"Why are you crying?"

She sniffed, and her eyes filled with more tears. "I don't know how to say this."

"You can tell me anything."

She wiped another tear away and took a deep breath. "I'm crying because I love you."

Time stood still as her words hung in the air. For a moment, I couldn't breathe. I'd imagined her saying that to me countless times, but coming from her lips was almost too much to take in. I could see it in the way she looked at me. I could feel it in every kiss, touch, and conversation.

But to hear her utter those three little words solidified what I already knew.

I placed my hands on her thighs, feeling my heartbeat in my chest. I'd spent my entire life feeling lost and searching for something I couldn't explain. Now I had my answers. I knew where I belonged.

With her.

"You're crying because you love me?"

I could see the vulnerability in her eyes, the fear that I might not feel the same way.

She nodded with a shaky smile on her lips. "I know it's too soon, and you're probably not…"

I stood up before she could get another word in and brought her mouth to mine. "I love you too. I've been wanting to tell you for a while, but I wasn't sure how you would react."

She grinned. "I didn't want to let another day go by without telling you how I felt."

"I'm glad you did, because I'm not sure I would have had the balls to say it first."

She chuckled. "You're ridiculous."

I pressed my lips to hers. "Ridiculous and in love. That's a great combination."

I held her face in my hands and planted one last kiss. When I pulled back, the biggest smile I'd ever seen split her cheeks.

"We should probably get back upstairs before Bridezilla comes looking for me."

A chuckle rumbled out of me. I loved these moments with her when we both seemed perfectly content. I didn't know much about being in love, but I'd never been this happy in my life and never wanted this feeling to end.

———

Natalie and I had just reached the last step and were about to enter the ballroom when I pulled her back. "One more kiss." I nuzzled that sweet spot behind her ear that drove her crazy.

She giggled in my arms. "You're insatiable."

My hands went to her ass. "What do you expect? One taste of that sweet pussy is not nearly enough."

"Ahem." The clearing of a throat had me looking over my shoulder. My eyes met Levi James, who was giving me a full-on-glare, like he was trying to burn a hole right through me.

I stood straighter, smoothing a hand over my rumpled tie. "Can I help you?"

"I need to speak to Natalie for a moment, please?" His eyes were narrowed and the dent between his eyebrows was so deep, I wondered if it was permanent.

"That's up to Natalie," I said, smoothing my thumb along her hip. He took in my hand, and I watched his face twist into a scowl. Seeing us together definitely had him riled up.

Natalie folded her arms across her chest. "I'm sorry, Levi. But I don't think that's a good idea."

He kept his gaze trained on me like he knew he had an advantage. This was his crowd, his town, his friends.

I wish I could say I was enjoying every second of this, but Natalie was uneasy, and I didn't want to add to that, so I held out my free hand, the one that was just inside my wife. "Rhett Daniels, I don't believe we've met before."

"I know who you are." His grip on my hand was tight. He was strong, but I was stronger.

"Ah, are you a fan?"

Asshole cleared his throat. "I just know who you are. Do you mind letting Natalie and I have a private moment?"

"Actually, I do." My voice was tight, not leaving it up for discussion. "Whatever you have to say, you can say in front of me."

He looked at Natalie. "Since when do you let other people talk for you?"

I stepped forward, steeling myself for a confrontation that I knew was inevitable. "The lady has already told you it's not a good idea."

He glowered at me. "I'd appreciate it if you get the fuck out of my face."

Was he serious?

Natalie came up and touched my back gently. I had my body positioned in front of hers, blocking his view, so she had to peer at him over my shoulder. "Levi, you are causing a scene. Stop it."

"Five minutes. That's all I need. Then I will leave you alone." He kept his steely gaze on hers, and my protective instincts kicked in. I would rather she not give him the time of day, but I would not be that guy. I trusted her. She chose me, but the thought of the two of them alone together left a bitter taste in my mouth.

She glanced between us, torn between telling him to fuck off or giving in to his request so she could finally be done with him.

"Fine." She huffed. "Five minutes and not a second more."

I swallowed hard, feeling the weight of his stare bearing down on me, but I refused to allow him to think that he had the upper hand. I squared my shoulders and met his gaze. "You do anything to upset her and we're going to have a problem."

Natalie wrapped her hand around my biceps. I could tell she hated this as much as I did. "Rhett, please don't worry. I just want this over with. I'll be right back."

I squeezed her hand and let her go, even if that was the last thing I wanted to do.

She looked over her shoulder and glanced at me before disappearing through a doorway. I was left standing there, hoping I didn't just make a mistake.

CHAPTER 21

NATALIE

LEVI WALKED OVER TO THE SMALL WINDOW IN THE conference room that overlooked the Boston Harbor. "You look beautiful, Natalie."

I closed my eyes and reminded myself he was only doing this because I was with somebody else. He could have tried to talk to me weeks ago. Instead, he waited until I had moved on. I was finally happy, and I would never forgive him for pulling this stunt.

I turned to face him, unsure how I was going to keep my temper in check. I wanted to lay into him but that would only waste time. "The clock is ticking," I reminded him.

He observed me carefully, waiting to figure out which direction he wanted to take this conversation.

"So, Rhett Daniels is the guy you've been dating? Is it serious?"

"You could say that." I wasn't sure what he wanted me to say, because if I told him the truth, he wasn't going to like my answer.

He shifted on his weight and ran a frustrated hand down his face. "I wasn't expecting you to look so happy."

Of course he wasn't.

"Were you hoping I would be lovesick and miserable?" I spat with enough hostility for him to get the hint.

He rested his hand on my arm, and when he saw my eyes narrow, he pulled it away quickly.

"Of course not. Regardless of what has happened, we share a history. I only want what's best for you."

If that were the case, we wouldn't be having this conversation.

"Maybe you should be more concerned about Brittany and your baby."

He huffed. "I don't want a life with her."

I arched an eyebrow. "Well, too bad; you're having a baby together. She's going to be in your life whether you like it or not."

"But we're not together." His voice sounded frustrated. "Did you notice that she isn't here? I broke things off with her so I can fix things with you."

"That doesn't change anything for me because there is no fixing us. Not now. Not ever."

His body tensed. "When did you become so cold and detached?"

"Maybe I'm just sick of playing your games."

He looked at me with a bewildered look in his eyes. He wasn't used to seeing this side of me. This was all new to me, too.

After spending so many years trying to balance my relationship and my studies so I could be there for him and his career, all the sacrifices, plane rides, tears, and heartache were all for what? So that he could toss me aside because he wasn't getting enough attention? He thought that I would just walk right back into his arms like nothing ever happened.

Sorry, buddy, I don't think so.

"I'm not playing games. The only person I want to settle down and have a family with is you. This baby doesn't change that. If you give me another chance, we can find a way to make it work."

I shook my head. "You're too late."

"Why?" he asked, narrowing his eyes. "Why does it have to be too late?"

"Your five minutes are up. I'm sorry." I started to walk away, but he grabbed my arm.

"Natalie, wait." He reached into his pocket and pulled out a small black box. He flipped it open to reveal a round, enormous solitaire diamond on a platinum band.

I would have thought I'd imagined this if I weren't staring at it with my own eyes. "Why are you showing me this now?"

I truly had no idea why he was doing this. There was no way this was my life.

"Because it's yours." He dropped down on one knee. "It was always meant to be yours. You are the only woman I would ever want to settle down with."

"What the hell am I supposed to do with that?" I managed to stammer out.

Slowly, he rose to his feet, the ring box clutched tightly in his fingers. He wrapped his arms around my shoulders, pulling me into him. I stood there, stunned. My mind raced, searching for words.

"I was hoping you would put it on your finger where it belongs."

"That's not going to happen," said the familiar voice coming from the front of the room. I glanced over to see

Rhett standing in the doorway with a murderous expression on his face.

Levi squared his shoulders. "I know you came with her, but this is none of your business."

Rhett stepped forward; his hands were clenched into fists. He looked like he wanted to tear Levi apart, from limb to limb. "I beg to differ."

"You can beg all you want. You're just wasting your time, man. You don't stand a chance. She still loves me."

Levi clearly had no clue how wrong he was.

"You think so?" Rhett cocked his head to the side and I bristled at the vein popping out of his neck. Agreeing to hear Levi out was turning into one big mistake. I should have said no and walked away. I should have listened to my gut because deep down, I knew this would only end badly.

"Yeah, so why don't you go back and enjoy the open bar." He sneered. "Maybe find someone to take home. There are plenty of single ladies to choose from."

"Sorry, I can't do that." His deep brown eyes locked on Levi's. "Because Natalie is my wife, and unlike you, I'm not a cheater."

His face fell. "What?"

I swallowed, noticing the genuine confusion on his face. This wasn't what I had in mind when I said I was ready to stop hiding. We haven't had a chance to tell our families yet, and the last thing I needed was Levi running his mouth.

"Rhett is my husband," I said, taking a step back because, Jesus Christ, the testosterone in the room was off the charts.

"No." He shook his head; his face was still full of shock.

"Yes." I swallowed. "We got married in Vegas a little

over a month ago. We haven't announced it yet because we're taking some time to ourselves."

That wasn't a complete lie.

"How the fuck is that possible?" He looked between us, shoving his hands through his hair. "Were you cheating on me with him?"

I cringed. I knew this looked bad, but he had a lot of nerve making an accusation like that after what he did. "I can't believe you would ask me that."

"I'm so confused. There is no way you moved on that quickly. I don't believe it."

"Believe it." Rhett came and stood at my side.

Levi stepped closer. "Tell me this is some kind of mistake that we can fix. Just say the word, Nat, and I'll get you out of this. Just give me a second chance, and I'll make it all go away."

I could feel Rhett's body shaking with anger. "I'm going to say this one more time. Natalie is my wife. You don't get to plead and beg for a second chance, especially when I'm standing right fucking here. You had her. You lost her. Time to move the fuck on, dude."

Levi seemed unfazed by Rhett's threat. "Get an annulment, please, Nat. We spent years together. You barely know this guy."

Rhett shoved him back. "You seem to have a hearing problem, so let me spell it out for you. You and Natalie are finished. She is my wife. One more word out of your mouth and I'll knock out whatever real teeth you have left in it. Only a piece of shit would hit on another man's woman while he's standing right there."

Levi held his arms out. "Go ahead, asshole, I fucking dare you."

Rhett's arm flew back and connected with Levi's lip. Blood seeped from the corner of his mouth and dripped down along his chin. Levi has had his share of fights, but Rhett was bigger and stronger. I didn't even want to think about the damage these two could do to each other.

Levi wiped the blood off his mouth and shook his head. "There is a reason why I'm known to spend more time in the penalty box than on the ice, you motherfucker. And I promise there ain't no ref in sight with a little yellow flag to toss in the air to save your ass when things get too rough."

Rhett grabbed Levi by the throat and shoved him against the wall. "I could squeeze the living daylights out of you if I wanted to. Instead I'm going to give you one last warning. This ends today. Stay away from my wife. Do we have an understanding?"

Levi twisted his way out of Rhett's grasp. "You want to fight me? Let's fucking go." He rolled his sleeves and lunged at Rhett. I screamed over the top of them as they tumbled to the ground, punching and kicking the shit out of each other.

The door to the room banged open. Gina's eyes were wide with disbelief while Hudson raced across the room. "Hey, break this shit up right fucking now."

Hudson's arm came around Rhett, who was on top of Levi, and pulled him off his friend.

"What the fuck is going on?" Hudson's face twisted in anger as he used all his strength to keep his body wedged between the two men.

Levi staggered back, breathing heavily. "He fucking started it, that's what."

Rhett swiped a spot of blood off his lip. "That's what happens when you start shit-talking and don't know how to shut up."

Hudson stood between them, holding both arms out to keep them separate. "What the hell, man?" He turned to

Rhett. "I don't give a fuck what he said. This is my wedding, and I think it's best if you leave."

Gina stood in the middle of the room, frozen in shock. My body filled with regret. This was exactly what she feared, and while it wasn't all my fault, I still felt the need to apologize.

"Gina." I approached her tentatively. "I am so sorry."

"I warned you." The hurt in her voice didn't surprise me. A part of me hated that she was right, but when I looked at Levi, he wasn't Mr. Innocent—far from it.

"You did warn me, and if there was a way I could have avoided this, I would have."

She glared at me. "I told you not to bring him."

"And you know why he's here," I said, trying to defend myself. There was so much about this that was fucked up. I didn't even know where to start. Not that an explanation would do any good.

"What I know is that you're selfish. This was my wedding, my one special day. And you had to ruin it all because you were afraid to show up alone."

She had every reason to be upset, and I wanted to cut her some slack, but I just couldn't find it in me to do so. She had it all wrong.

Rhett's hand settled against my back. "I think you made your point, Gina. But if you're looking to blame someone, you're looking in the wrong direction. I could have handled myself better and for that, I apologize. But that's the only apology you will get from me. Maybe someday you'll realize what a mistake you made by treating a girl who was supposed to be one of your closest friends like a second-class citizen. If you asked me, you didn't deserve to call her a friend."

No matter how hard I wanted to salvage what we had, I needed to accept that things would never be the same again. With a heavy heart, I allowed Rhett to lead me to the door. When he saw the tears slip from my eyes, he tucked me against his side.

"Are you okay?" he asked, rubbing my arm.

My body leaned into his for comfort. "I will be once we get home."

I knew people drifted apart, and as heartbroken as I was, our friendship was turning into something unhealthy. It was no longer the safe haven it once was.

It was time for new beginnings and to start focusing on people who lifted me up and accepted me for who I was.

CHAPTER 22

RHETT

"I'm sorry about Gina," I said, while handing Natalie a glass of wine. After the reception, we went back to the hotel and packed up our shit. We lucked out and caught a late flight home, because I could sense that Natalie didn't want to spend a second longer in that city than she needed to.

"You don't need to apologize. I know you wouldn't have gone after Levi if he hadn't provoked you."

My fingers ran up and down her arm. "Yeah, but you and Gina were close. Maybe once she calms down, she'll reach out."

Hopefully, she'll have a better attitude.

It's only been a day, but I was still holding out hope that Gina would come to her senses. Her anger might have been justified, but if she was going to be pissed at someone, it should have been me. I might have thought Gina was a selfish bitch, but she was still somebody important to Natalie. It made me angry at how loyal my wife was to her friends, especially when they didn't deserve it.

"Maybe." She sighed. "At least we don't have to hide anymore. We don't have to pretend that we barely know each other. Once we talk to our families, we can just be Rhett and Natalie."

"Do you really think Levi is going to keep this news to himself?" I asked, kicking my feet up on the coffee table. I didn't see how this was going to be good for us.

She sipped her wine. "Probably not. That's why the sooner we get this out in the open, the better. I meant what I said, Rhett. I love you. No matter what happens, that's not going to change."

I leaned forward to press a kiss to the side of her head. "What do you think is going to happen?"

"Well, for one, your family will likely hate me. And Beau, I don't want to even think about what he'll do. Hell, the whole world might have an issue with us being together, but I don't care. I'm committed to making this work."

She had no idea what those words did to me. Every second we were together, I fell harder and harder.

I threw an arm around her shoulder. "You know I don't care what people think, right?"

She rested her head on my arm. "Yes. I wish I could be more like you. I wish I didn't care so much."

She obviously was thinking about Gina.

I tugged her against my chest. "You're perfect just the way you are."

"You think I'm perfect, huh?"

I smirked, running my hand up along her cheek. "I know so, and I'm never wrong."

She shook her head. "You're crazy."

I stared into those baby blue eyes that I loved so much. "Crazy for you."

She snorted. "And cheesy."

I tightened my arms around her. "I like holding you. It makes me feel useful."

She cried all the way back to the hotel yesterday. Never in my life have I felt so helpless. I was a guy, and I was used to fixing things. If my tire was low, I put air in it. If the TV wasn't working, I could figure out why. Hell, I could even hang drywall if someone asked me to. If there was a problem and I didn't know what to do, I could write a check to someone who did. But this wasn't something I couldn't solve or fix.

She lifted her head. "I know we still have to deal with our families. But oddly enough, I'm looking at the bigger picture."

I kissed the top of her head. "Speaking of families. How do you feel about meeting mine?"

She closed her eyes. "I'm dreading the thought of it."

I laughed. "I promise, they're not that bad."

"Somehow, I find that hard to believe."

I leaned in, my mouth fighting a smile. "I think I'm going to have to loosen you up a bit before you meet them. You are way too tense."

Gently, she pulled on my shirt. "What did you have in mind?"

I darted my tongue out and teased her lips before she opened for me. My hands coasted up and down her arms. Our lips met, soft and gentle at first, but when Natalie moaned into my mouth, I gripped the back of her head, making her squirm. I wanted her to keep making those noises. It spurred me on, knowing I could do this to her, and it sucked that I had to stop.

I slowed the kiss and backed away from her mouth. "There is a lot more where that came from, but first, I want to feed you. You've barely eaten anything since yesterday."

She threw her head back against the couch. "You're seriously thinking about food right now?"

I pulled on her bottom lip. "Don't pout. It's my job to take care of you now. If I have to withhold sex from you, I will. So, please eat something so I don't have to do that because I really like having sex with you."

"Fine," she grumbled. The woman was absolutely adorable. "But you better make it worth my while later."

———

"You are a big fat cheater!" she yelled, looking at the dice. "I know for a fact that you flipped it over when I went to get a glass of water."

Maybe if she had eaten more of her dinner, I would have played by the rules. Honestly, though, this was a hell of a lot more fun, so I didn't feel an ounce of guilt.

"How dare you accuse me of cheating. You're just jealous because I got a Yahtzee three times now, and you had to cross it off your list." I gave her a shit-eating grin, not bothering to mention that she also had to cross off four of a kind. "Now, lose the pants, sweetheart."

She huffed. "No."

She had already shed her socks, shirt, and sweatshirt. I thought playing Yahtzee with a twist would help her relax a bit. Whenever we crossed something out, we had to remove an article of clothing.

"Those are the rules you agreed to."

She crossed her arms. "I should have said no to this stupid idea when you proposed it."

I rubbed at my jaw, keeping my gaze fixed on her lace bra that hid absolutely nothing. "Can you prove I cheated?"

She held my gaze. "You are an asshole."

I leaned forward. "Drop. The. Pants."

She took a deep breath and skimmed her eyes over my chest. She had no idea the level of self-control I was exercising at that moment.

Natalie glanced away, biting her bottom lip. Something in her expression caused me to pause.

I pushed the game aside and reached for her. "What's that look for?"

She looked away. "Nothing."

Bullshit! Why the hell was she so nervous all of a sudden?

"Look me in the eye and tell me it's nothing."

"It's stupid."

I pulled her down in my lap, hoping she would tell me what was going on in that pretty little head of hers. "Why don't you let me be the judge of that."

She rolled her lips together and took a deep breath. "This is humiliating, and I can't believe I'm actually admitting this out loud, but you're Mr. Perfect without a flaw on his body, and I'm just me, with dimpled thighs and a soft stomach."

What the hell? I had no idea how to respond, so I cracked a joke because she was crazy if she believed that.

"You think I'm perfect?"

She smacked my chest. "You know damn well that you don't have to worry about how you look."

My face turned hard. "That's what this is about?"

"You date models or women who don't have a single flaw on their body."

I leaned forward and ran my hands along her thighs. "Let's get something straight right here and right now. I don't give a fuck about anyone else. I couldn't even tell you the names of those women you see on my Instagram. They were nothing to me but a way to pass the time. You have no reason to be self-conscious, not with me or anyone." She started to pull away, but I gripped her legs, stopping her. "You're not going anywhere until you admit that I'm right."

She looked down at her lap. "I know you mean that, but I hate feeling that if I wasn't enough for Levi, how am I supposed to believe that I'll ever be enough for you?"

"This is crazy. I'm the one who should be worried. When I look at you, I don't just see a beautiful woman with a great figure. I see your kindness, and I feel your empathy. Your ambition is sexy as fuck, and your sense of humor puts a smile on my face every God damned day." I cupped her face in my hands, wiping away a tear that leaked from her eye. "Up until you, nothing in my life mattered. Maybe that's why I never took it so seriously. There have been lots of people who have come and gone, and you are the only one I can't live without."

She rested her head on my shoulder. "You always know how to make me feel better. You make everything okay."

I kissed the top of her head. "I'll always remind you of how amazing you are."

She leaned closer, and her eyes softened. "Thank you for loving me."

"Always." I winked.

Her fingers slid into my hair, pulling me closer and taking my lips with hers. Natalie's hands started moving over my chest and arms, like she was exploring every inch of me. I hoped to God I put whatever fears and doubts she had to rest. The woman was my reason for breathing. She was my everything.

She pulled back and brushed her fingers across my face. "Do you still want me to strip for you?"

My eyebrows bent in confusion. "Hell, yeah, I do."

She stood up and slowly started sliding her leggings off.

My jaw ticked when she lifted her knee to pull the fabric past her feet. This playfulness was such a contradiction to how she was a few minutes ago. She was giving me whiplash, but there was no doubt in my mind that she was absolutely perfect for me. Life with her would never be boring, that was for sure.

"Natalie, please tell me this is going where I think it's going. I'm so turned on right now that if I don't get to touch you in the next second, I might die."

My chest rose and fell, watching her slip her hands inside the waistband of her panties and slide them off, completely exposing herself to me.

"Here you go." She held out the thong and dangled it along her fingers. "I'm going to bed, and I really hope you'll join me." She threw them in my lap and sauntered away.

I chased her into the bedroom. She squealed when I lifted her up and threw her over my shoulder.

"Put me down. You're going to throw your back out."

"Please." I rolled my eyes and dropped her on our mattress. "My gym bag weighs more than you." She grinned while I took another step forward. "And to be clear." I pulled my shirt over my head and started removing the rest of my clothes. "I totally cheated at Yahtzee."

"I like a man who is honest." She licked her lips with a hungry look in her eyes.

I moved over the top of her and ran my stubble over her soft cheeks. "I'll always be honest with you, baby."

I crashed my lips down to hers, gripping the sides of her face. I needed to touch her everywhere. I couldn't stop. The woman was gorgeous, and the fact that she was questioning it was mind-blowing. I never understood why women put so much pressure on themselves to look perfect.

Sure, I had a six-pack and was blessed with good DNA, but those features didn't make me any different from millions of other guys.

I moved my hands slowly over every dip and curve, loving how she felt under my palms. I wanted to take my time and appreciate all of her. My lips were everywhere. My hands went to her exposed breast. She moaned when I sucked a nipple in my mouth. "You are perfect, Natalie. You are beautiful way beyond your physical appearance." I glided my hands down her sides, and I threw a leg over my back. "Don't ever question that again." I slid my finger in and out of her while her hand gripped my cock. We were both drawing pleasure from each other, but I needed to be inside her.

She smiled up at me. "You really do have a big, soft heart."

I braced my tip at her entrance and filled her completely. "I told you before, there is nothing soft about me." I moved, keeping my eyes on her the entire time. I've had my fair share of sexual encounters, but this felt different. It felt like I was making love. There was no other way to describe it. I had no idea it could feel this way.

Natalie grabbed on to my arms as I continued to rock inside her with this insane need to send her over the edge. I gently pulled back and kissed her slowly. I wanted her to feel everything. I wanted her to watch me move over the top of her and love every single second of it.

I was giving her a piece of myself that I'd never given anyone before. It made me question how I had been able to live all these years without her.

My jaw tightened as I pushed deeper. We both came together. Neither one of us spoke. We allowed our emotions to do all the talking.

I tucked her against my side, giving in to the

exhaustion. My heart felt lighter, but my mind was still racing with worry. Tonight felt like the calm before the storm.

Our families would have to accept this because I would not allow their disapproval to tear us apart.

CHAPTER 23
RHETT

"Are you sure I look okay?" Natalie asked, smoothing her hands down her pale pink dress.

"You look like a cute little Barbie Doll." I bopped her on the nose, but she didn't look amused.

"I knew I should have worn the black dress." She swatted my hand away.

Natalie tried on ten different outfits before deciding on which one to wear. She was afraid of being over the top or too casual. If you asked me, she could have worn a plain white T-shirt and baggy jeans, and she still would have looked beautiful.

"I don't want to screw this up."

"You won't." I brought her hand to my mouth and kissed her knuckles.

"So, what did you tell them? How much do they know?"

"I haven't told them a thing."

She looked ready to kill me. "Why would you spring this on them like this?"

I tucked a piece of hair behind her ear. "I didn't know

how to tell them. I figured they would go easier on me if you were there."

She rolled her eyes. "They are going to think you knocked me up and I'm trapping you for a paycheck."

My hand paused on the door. "That's actually not a bad idea. Wanna ditch this place and go make a baby."

"If I thought you were joking, I would laugh. But you will use whatever excuse you can if you think it will lead to sex."

"Look at you." I smirked. "You can already read my mind. We are officially a married couple."

She swatted my shoulder and straightened her dress. "You should have told them."

I pushed the door open, not bothering to ring the bell. As soon as we stepped inside, loud voices and laughter filtered throughout the house. But conversations came to a screeching halt when I entered the kitchen.

My mom's eyes went to mine and Natalie's linked hands.

Cruze, our housekeeper and childhood nanny, broke the silence. "Rhett, my beautiful boy. It's good to see you." She closed the oven and walked over. I noticed her limping on her left side. She'd been slowing down over the years, and my parents had been struggling with how to handle the situation. She refused to retire, but sadly, we all knew that day was slowly approaching.

Her wrinkled hands cupped both sides of my cheeks. "I miss you. You never come to see me anymore."

"Now that the season is over, I have more time for visits." I smiled into her brown eyes, which held so much warmth and fond memories.

She clucked her tongue and shook her finger in my face. "Like I haven't heard that before. You don't fool me. You're lucky I'm sending you home with some food."

"Oh, yeah. What did you make?" I peered over at the stove.

"I made a tray of enchiladas and tamales. I also wrapped up some churros for you to take."

"You rock! This is why you're my favorite," I whispered in her ear so my mother couldn't hear me. Her homemade churros were the best.

She kissed my cheek and pulled back. "And who is this beautiful lady?"

My hand went to Natalie's back. "Everyone, this is Natalie."

Cruze pulled her into a hug while my mom politely shook her hand. My dad stepped forward in a blue suit. His hair had more gray now than black, but he was tall and built for a man in his early sixties.

"Clayton Daniels. It's a pleasure to meet you."

She returned his handshake, her nerves visible in her wobbly smile. "Thank you. It's great to finally meet all of you."

My brother, Ford, waved and eyed me firmly over the rim of his glass while my sister looped her arm through my brother-in-law's.

"I'm Reagan, and this is my husband, Wess." He was blond and skinny and stood out like a sore thumb compared to the rest of the family.

"Uncle Rhett," my niece, Saylor, screeched and ran toward me. Her blond curls bounced as she leaped into my arms.

"What's up, Say? How are you doing, baby girl?" I spun her around like an airplane.

Her sweet little laughter floated through the kitchen. "Uncle Rhett, put me down so I can show you my new gymnastics flip."

"Gymnastics, huh?" I smiled while sliding her down my chest.

Just then, Violet came wobbling forward, holding on to a stuffed lamb while smiling beneath her pacifier. Their kid was always happy.

"There's my girl, baby V." I held my hands out so she could run into them. The back of her diaper bounced, looking like it weighed ten pounds.

"I gots something for you, Uncle Rhett." Saylor held out a small beaded bracelet. "It's a friendship bracelet in your team colors, orange and blue." I spun the tiny block of letters that spelled out *Daniels#89*. "I want you to have it."

I balanced Violet on my hip and grinned down at the little cutie. "I love it, baby girl." I held my wrist out. "You want to put it on me?"

Saylor eagerly slipped it over my wrist. It was tight and barely fit, but she was so excited to see me wear it I didn't want to take it off.

"How's it look?" I held my arm out so Natalie could see.

She smiled at Saylor. "It's the prettiest bracelet I've ever seen."

Saylor grinned up at the woman at my side. "I can make you a friendship bracelet too. I have a brand-new bead making kit."

My sister took a sip of her wine and set it down. She walked over, placing her hands on Saylor's shoulders. "I need you to help Cruze find a pair of clean clothes for baby V first."

"Come on, girls," Cruz said as they both started jumping up and down. She picked up Violet and held her hand out for Saylor, and we watched them disappear down the hall together.

My heart hammered in my chest as my eyes moved across every one of my family members. The thought of breaking the news to them like this was unsettling. They might drive me crazy sometimes, but I loved this stuffy little bunch.

I fidgeted with the collar of my dress shirt. Despite my attempts to reassure Natalie that things would be fine, my stomach was suffering from a sudden bout of nerves.

"I have some news, and I figured I would share it while we are all here together."

I took Natalie's hand in mine, her fingers still as a statue, and met my mothers' eyes. She was going to be the toughest one to convince. "Natalie and I got married."

My mom's eyes widened, and her jaw slacked open before forming into a frown. No doubt this news caught her off guard and messed up her plans for me to marry Claire.

"Wait, did you say you're married?" My dad was the first to speak. His voice was tight as Ford and Reagan exchanged glances. I knew they would have a hard time accepting this. That's why I wanted to tackle it head-on and get it over with.

My parents might have been a little too buttoned-up for my tastes, but they were everything to me. They loved their kids unconditionally and were devoted to their family. Guilt was coming at me from every angle, twisting my insides up.

"Am I missing something here?" My sister, always the drama queen, crossed her arms and glared at me. Her husband sat beside her, looking too scared to speak.

The tension in the room was mounting by the second.

"This can't be right," my brother said while pouring himself a generous glass of bourbon.

My mom stared at me, her mouth open and closed as if she were searching for the right words. I felt a knot form in my stomach. "How could you do this without telling us? What am I supposed to tell the Settlers? What about Claire?"

I shifted uncomfortably and glanced at Natalie beside me. I couldn't believe I was stupid enough to think this would be a good idea. I was hoping my family would give her a warmer reception.

"Mom, I was never going to marry Claire. I don't have any romantic feelings for her. That was always your idea, not mine," I explained, trying to keep my tone gentle.

She wrung her hands in front of her. "But you two were together…"

"Mom, listen to me. Claire and I were never together in that sense. She either misread things or she lied to you. Regardless, it was never going to happen."

She nodded and looked at Natalie. "I'm sorry. That was very disrespectful of me. I'm just in shock. Please forgive me."

Natalie gave my mom a warm smile. "It's okay. I understand."

My mom picked up her wineglass and turned her attention back to me. "Tell me you at least got married in a church."

My family had always been traditional and set in their ways. My free-spirit and easygoing personality was a far cry from the life I was born into.

"No, but we did get married by Elvis. Isn't he one of your favorites?" I smiled at her, hoping she would go easy on me. She folded her arms and stared me down, letting me know my little grin wasn't working on her.

I walked over to place my hands on her shoulders,

hoping to put whatever reservations she had to rest. "Mom, look at me," I said gently, hoping to appeal to that soft spot that she had for me. She could be overbearing and critical at times, but at the end of the day, I was her son. "I'm sorry. It was a quick ceremony. We wanted to keep things simple."

Her eyes darted from me to Natalie, curiosity evident in her expression. "Can you tell us how you guys met?"

"Sure," I said. "We met in Vegas right after the Super Bowl."

"Why the rush?" My sister's voice was laced with skepticism.

I knew my family would have questions and think this was impulsive, but I hoped they would eventually support my decision. Maybe I was wrong.

"I didn't rush into anything. I knew right from the start that Natalie was different and marrying her just felt right." I took a deep breath, trying to steady my nerves. "I know this is a lot to take in, but I was hoping you guys would support my decision and welcome Natalie into the family."

I wasn't going to get into too much detail. How Natalie and I got here wasn't any of their business. They didn't need to know the specifics. The only thing that should matter to them was my happiness.

"I apologize for being blunt," Reagan said to Natalie. "This is odd, even for Rhett."

"Reagan, let's not make things more awkward," I said, not appreciating her jab. Normally, I could handle my sister's sarcasm, but I was feeling protective of my wife and trying to ease her discomfort.

Ford set his glass down. "Rhett, a word please."

Reagan shared a look with the rest of my family. "We'll go take the girls out on the swing set. Natalie, would you like to come see the playground out back?"

"I would love to." Her smile softened slightly, but I could still see the worry in her expression. Despite how we got together, she was the best thing that's ever happened to me. If my family had an issue with my marriage, that was tough shit.

I turned to my wife. "You sure?"

"It's okay. Go." Natalie placed her hand on my arm. I found it ironic that she was offering me comfort when it should have been the other way around.

I kissed her on the head. "I'll only be a few minutes."

Dad held up his hand when his cell phone rang. "I've been waiting for this call. It won't be long. You guys head into my study. I'll take this in the parlor."

Ford and I walked over to the set of doors that led to my dad's study. I took a seat across from him and prepared myself for the interrogation.

"Rhett, you've always been a little wild, but this is crazy, even for you. Marrying someone you barely know. Come on. Something about this isn't adding up."

I shifted uncomfortably in my seat. "Why can't you just be happy for me?"

He scoffed, crossing his arms across his chest. "Not only is this sudden, but you always said you never wanted to get married. Now, you're going to commit your life to a complete stranger?"

His words stung; she might have been a stranger when we first met, but things had changed. "I understand your concerns, but you'll have to trust me on this."

"That line might work with everyone else, but it doesn't work with me." His eyes narrowed. "Are you sure this doesn't have anything to do with Mom shoving Claire down your throat?"

My brother was way too smart for his own good. I fully expected him to demand a further explanation, yet I was hesitant to give him the full story. The truth was buried beneath layers of judgment and insecurities. He would see me as weak and desperate, a man who succumbed to fear and pressure.

This arrangement might have started out as a way to get everyone off my back, but Natalie and I ended up connecting on a level that I never anticipated. I might have married her out of desperation, but I was staying with her out of love.

"Why are you probing so hard? What are you trying to accomplish, exactly?" If his intent was to get under my skin, it was working.

Ford steepled his fingers together, contemplating me. "If that isn't a politely scripted answer, I don't know what is. You might be the black sheep in the family, but you still know how to avoid answering questions."

I glanced down at my watch, noticing it was only six thirty. "I'm not avoiding anything. It's actually quite simple. Natalie is my wife. End of story. Why I married her is nobody's business."

Did I expect my marriage to raise a few red flags? Yes. Did I expect this level of scrutiny? No, but I should have.

"Oh, so you're keeping your personal life personal now, huh?" His tone was colored in disbelief.

All I could do was laugh. "What is your problem?"

He leaned back in his chair. "This seems pretty fast, so I'm not buying it."

My jaw tightened. "I don't care, and just because you're forced to sit behind a desk and work for Daddy doesn't give you the right to question the decisions that I make in my personal life."

He narrowed his eyes, not liking being called out. "Did you ever stop to think about what this would do to the family?"

"See, that's where you and I are different." I pointed my finger at him. "Every decision you make, from your color-coordinated socks to who you marry, revolves around how it impacts the family. Your happiness is secondary. I'm just not made that way."

His nostrils flared, telling me I hit the nail on the motherfuckin' head. Ford married Bailey straight out of college. She was pretty, sweet, and well pedigreed, but she wasn't the love of his life. No, that title belonged to Savannah Mills. She was a caring waitress who waited tables at the local country club. She was also a single mother with a dad in prison. Not exactly "marriage material." My parents gave him a choice, and he chose Bailey. She wasn't horrible, and he could do much worse, but if he could go back, I think he would choose differently.

He held onto the sides of his chair in a death grip. "You're an asshole."

"What can I say, brother." I bent my knee and dusted off my leg. "You bring out the best of me."

I got off on screwing with him, especially when he was in a mood. Ford wasn't always this uptight, but I guess living a life full of resentment would drain all the fun out of a guy.

"You're just jealous because I inherited the brains in the family." He tugged on his wool sweater vest and crossed his legs. I wanted to make fun of his pleated slacks and leather loafers but figured I'd already said enough.

"Yep, that title goes to you, but I'm okay with being the better-looking one."

He exhaled loudly and leaned back in his chair. "Listen, I know I'm being a dick, but you blindsided us. Do you know anything about this woman? This is strange, even for you. I want to know what we're dealing with here in case she's some gold digger with a dark past. All it takes is one little Google search to find out everything you need to know."

"She doesn't have a shady past, and she's not a fucking gold digger."

"Did she sign a prenup?"

"My managers are handling everything on my end." I was hoping my answer would satisfy him. If he found out the truth, he would flip.

"Has she ever been arrested?" He reached into the desk and pulled out a notepad from the top middle drawer.

"Not that I know of?"

"What is her financial status? Any outstanding debt? Does she work?" He started scribbling things down.

"She has a job."

"What does she do?"

"She works in the public relations department for the Arrows."

He lifted his head. "I thought you met in Vegas?"

"We did. She was hired before we met."

His gaze bore into mine; his expression was unreadable. "What does management think about this?"

I tapped my fingers against the armrest. "I haven't informed them yet."

"Don't tell me you would be stupid enough to violate a no-fraternizing policy."

My lip tightened. "It's a little more complicated than that."

He dropped his pen on the desk and pushed the notepad aside. "How complicated?"

I hesitated for a minute. "She's Beau Landers' niece."

There was a moment of stunned silence before he started swearing under his breath. "Please tell me you're joking."

"Even I wouldn't joke about something like this."

"Seriously, Rhett. What on earth would possess you to marry Beau Landers' niece? That's just asking for trouble."

"I'm pretty sure it had something to do with the tequila I was drinking that night."

He looked at me like I had sprouted a third head.

"Jesus Christ." He plowed a hand through his hair. "So, you were shitfaced out of your mind."

"You know how Vegas is," I joked, but the dude didn't crack a smile.

"No, actually, I don't know because I'm not fucking crazy like you. How do you think Beau will react to this news?"

I hesitated, my gaze drifting over to the bookshelves on the wall. "I'll find out soon enough. We plan on telling him as soon as he gets back from Africa."

His expression softened. "Do you want me to fix this? I could have this gone by morning. Just say the word."

That was the last thing I wanted.

I sighed, trying to get him to understand. "This isn't a mistake that needs to be fixed. I love her and want to stay married to her."

"I don't know, brother, you hardly know this woman. Maybe you should think this through before making any final decisions."

I coughed into my hand. "My mind is already made up. This is what I want. We just need to get her uncle on board."

Ford leaned forward, resting his arms on the desk. "Do you think that's going to be a problem?"

I scratched my head. "He might've told Natalie that he wouldn't approve of her dating anyone on the team and wouldn't hesitate to trade anyone who tried to get close to her."

Ford inhaled sharply. "Rhett, only fucking you."

My dad walked through the door, pocketing his phone. "What did I miss?"

CHAPTER 24

RHETT

There was a loud knock at the door. I scrambled off the couch when the knock turned into a bang.

I yanked the door open to find Beau Landers in a suit so wrinkled it looked like he just walked through an automated car wash. I don't think I'd ever seen him look so disheveled or angry in my life.

"Sir?" I said, feeling my heart skip a beat at the sight of him.

He was breathing heavily and seemed visually upset. "Are you going to invite me in?"

"Is everything okay?" I looked over my shoulder, feeling a growing pit in my stomach.

I didn't know what to expect, but my guess was that he wasn't here to give me a raise or talk about plays and touchdowns.

He ignored my question and pushed past me.

Fuck! Fuck! Fuck!

He knew.

"Is my coffee ready yet?" Natalie called from around the corner. The pads of her bare feet hitting the floor. She stopped short when she saw her uncle standing in the middle of our living room.

Beau's eyes widened when he spotted Natalie in nothing but my jersey. The one I had her wear when I fucked her for the fifth time last night.

"Well, it looks like the rumors are true." His eyes challenged mine, but I didn't dare move. "You've both been lying to me."

There were so many things I planned on saying. I spent hours practicing a speech that I hoped would be good enough, but somehow, all thoughts and words died on my tongue.

"Uncle Beau." Natalie's voice was barely above a whisper as she moved toward him. "This is not how we wanted you to find out. Please let us explain."

"I think this explains it all." He pushed an iPad in front of me. I glanced at the screen. There was an article from a tabloid with a bold headline.

NFL Star Marries Team Owner's Niece in Secret Vegas Wedding, Keeps Marriage Hidden.

My pulse immediately quickened while I silently read the words.

Rhett Daniels, the star tight end for the Atlanta Arrows and son of Senator Clayton Daniels, recently married Natalie Evans, the niece of Beau Landers, the team's owner, in a drive-thru chapel off the Vegas Strip. While Daniels is well-liked for his charismatic personality, his secret marriage has caused a stir among fans and the NFL community. Not only did he keep the marriage under wraps, but reports suggest that Miss Evans was in a relationship with Levi James, the Center for the Fenway Falcons, at the time of her marriage to Daniels.

The drama doesn't end there, as James confronted the newlyweds at a friend's wedding, alleging that Daniels assaulted him in an unprovoked attack. James intends to press charges. Despite this, there has been no response from Daniels or the Arrows, leaving many wondering what the future holds for the NFL's newest controversial figure.

"What the hell?" My eyes darted to Natalie and then back to the pictures. There were endless photos of the two of us standing at the altar at the chapel in Vegas, kissing and smiling from different angles. My stomach felt like it bottomed out.

That motherfucker! I should have kicked his ass when I had the chance.

"Good news travels fast, huh?" Beau's hand trembled at his side. "Did you honestly think you could keep this from me?"

I ran a hand through my hair, trying to figure out how those pictures got leaked. My lawyer and agent were supposed to take care of it, so how the hell did Levi get his hands on them? Somebody was getting fucking fired.

"Beau." I shook my head, feeling stupid for turning my damn phone off. "We were planning on telling you. You were not supposed to find out like this."

"How convenient." He stepped forward. "How long has this been going on?"

Beau Landers was a good man. He was a forgiving man, but he was also a man you didn't fuck with. He was not someone you lied to.

"Sir, let me explain, please."

He looked at his watch. "I've got all fucking day, Rhett, so start talking."

"Okay, let's sit down." I started moving toward the

couch, preparing for what I knew would be an uncomfortable conversation.

When I turned, Beau stood in the same spot with his arms crossed over his chest. "I'd prefer to stand. I'd also like an explanation, so let's cut right through the bullshit. How did this happen?"

I glanced at Natalie, who looked absolutely terrified, before settling my gaze back on the man who had the ability to end my entire career in a single heartbeat.

I couldn't shake the feeling of dread that settled in my gut. "Natalie and I met in Vegas. Neither of us knew who the other was. We didn't realize the connection before…" I swallowed, feeling my breath lodge in the back of my throat. "Until it was too late. I swear to you. I had no idea she was your niece."

His eyes were hard. "As angry as I am for being blindsided and publicly humiliated, I am more disappointed in both of you more than anything."

I swallowed down a big ball of regret for letting this go on for so long. "I understand, and for what it's worth, I'm really sorry that you had to find out like that."

"You're sorry?" His hands went to his hips, and he leaned forward. "You're only sorry you got caught."

I shook my head. "That's not true." As bad as this sucked, I was relieved that he finally knew. I've been carrying this secret around for weeks. I knew it would eventually blow up, but at the same time, I didn't care.

"Do you have any idea what kind of mess this will cause? You can apologize and explain all you want, but you lied to me, you destroyed my trust. You went behind my back, married my niece, kept it from me, and instead of coming to me the second you both realized what you had done, you tried to cover it up. I had to find out like this?"

He pointed to Natalie in nothing but my jersey. I

cringed and wished I could sink into the floor. I wanted to justify things by pointing out that Natalie was my wife and what we did was none of his damn business, but I was smart enough to know that would only make the situation worse.

Natalie approached him carefully. "Please don't be mad at Rhett. He wanted to tell you, but I asked him to wait."

"Tell me what exactly?" His eyes sharpened. "Because from reading this article, it looks like two drunken fools made a stupid, impulsive decision to get married. It doesn't get more 'Vegas' than that."

I hung my head. I've spent years building a relationship with the man, and I'd like to think we'd formed a level of trust and respect. It was painful to think it was destroyed all in one night. Clearly, I underestimated the situation.

"Beau, if you're going to take your anger out on someone, take it out on me, not her."

I couldn't let Natalie take the blame for this mess. Hell, I couldn't even blame Levi. This was all my own doing.

His spine straightened. "You think you can tell me what to say to my niece now?"

Her hands shook as she pulled on the hem of my jersey. "Uncle Beau. We didn't want to keep this a secret from you, but we were afraid of how you would react." She was trying her best to reason with him, but I think we were past that point.

"Natalie, what you both did was wrong. I would expect something like this from him, not you," he snapped.

"Sir." I clenched and unclenched my fists at my side, trying to break up the tension I had building up inside. "I'm going to ask you one more time to please not speak to her like that."

"Oh, I'm sorry." He unbuttoned his jacket like he was

getting ready to use me as a punching bag. The guy was older, so he didn't physically stand a chance against me, and I really hoped it didn't come to that. "But you are not in control of this situation right now, young man."

"She's my wife."

"You're not good enough for her."

I stared at him. Every muscle in my body tensed. "With all due respect, that's not for you to decide."

"We are going to have to agree to disagree, my friend." He spun around to face Natalie. His entire face was pulled tight in frustration. "What in the ever-loving hell were you thinking, child?"

Natalie's chin wobbled. Silent tears streaked along her cheeks. "I know this is a shock, and this marriage might not have started out under the best of circumstances, but since then, we've developed real feelings for each other."

He turned his angry eyes to me. "How could you do this, Rhett? And before you start, don't insult me by feeding me some cock and bull story. Commitment has never been your strong suit when it comes to women, and while you may care for her, I will never accept this."

Talk about a hit to my ego.

"Look, Beau. No one is disputing that it was wrong to keep this from you. Natalie and I have lived with the guilt for the past six weeks. But I'm not walking away from her."

He moved forward, forcing me to retreat. "She's pregnant, isn't she?"

My eyes widened. "No."

Even if she was, it shouldn't matter.

He scrubbed an angry hand down his face. "What a fucking mess. Do you two have any idea what kind of position I am in? You didn't even warn me. There is no way we can get in front of this now. This is a PR nightmare."

"Beau, I swear to God, we were planning on telling you when you got back from Africa," I said, struggling to find the right words. I knew winning him over would be tough, if not impossible, but I was determined to prove to be good enough for her.

He looked up at the ceiling and then leveled his gaze on Natalie. "I've done nothing but look out for you since your mother passed away. You don't lie to the people you love. I deserved better, and I expected more from you."

She squeezed her eyes shut as more tears spilled down her cheeks. I walked over and put my arm around her shoulders. I could see how much his words were tearing her apart.

"Listen, Rhett. You're not a bad guy, you just make shitty decisions. You are a talented athlete with a lot of playing time left in your career, but you won't be playing on my team. You've proven that you can't be trusted, and that is everything. You need to start looking at trade options, because I'm cutting you loose."

Natalie gasped. "You can't do that."

"I can and I fucking will," he shouted.

His words hit me harder than being tackled by a three-hundred-pound linebacker. After all the blood, sweat, and tears I've put into his organization, he was just going to cast me aside. My heart started racing at the thought of playing for another team.

"Beau, I know this is a shock, but you can't mean that," I managed to choke out, even though I knew he was dead serious. He didn't use scare tactics and threaten for no good reason. He didn't have to. "I'm one of your best players. I've worked my ass off. I'm at the top of my game." My words came tumbling out in a rush.

He held his hand out, cutting me off. "This isn't just about you, Rhett. This is about your teammates, your fans, and everyone who ever believed in you. The last thing we need coming off a championship is a distraction to the team. It's one we can't afford, nor will I tolerate."

My stomach roiled, and I felt like I was going to puke. "What the hell am I supposed to do now? The teams already have their rosters lined up for next season. Do you have any idea how hard it will be for me to try to find someone who will take me at the last minute?"

Beau's expression softened. There was a hint of sympathy in his eyes. "Call your agent. Take some time to regroup. I'm sure you will have no trouble finding another team to give you a chance."

I hung my head, feeling absolutely fucking crushed. After all the years of giving it my all, sacrificing everything, and spending years trying to prove myself, I was being kicked to the curb like yesterday's trash.

"Uncle Beau." Natalie's voice trembled. "What if we get a divorce?"

My head whipped to hers. "Natalie, we are not ending this marriage."

I fought for her and fell in love, knowing the consequences. I was not giving her up. Not now. Not ever.

Beau sighed heavily. "It's too late for that, everyone knows."

"Okay." She rubbed her hands nervously. "What if I quit?"

Beau scrubbed a hand over his chin. "Natalie, this scandal has nothing to do with your job. It's about who you are and the integrity of my football organization."

"Beau, is there anything I can do to change your mind?" I asked, pulling on the back of my neck. I was freaking the fuck out. This was an absolute nightmare.

"Rhett, as much as it pains me to say this, I don't see

this working out. As far as I'm concerned, what you did was unforgivable, and I don't give second chances."

My heart raced at the thought of being traded and sent away from my teammates and the only woman I had ever loved. Our life was just starting. I didn't want to move away. I didn't want to play for anyone else. I didn't want any of this.

Everything I worked hard to achieve just went up in fucking smoke.

"Uncle Beau, can you please give us some time to talk through this?" Natalie's eyes were on mine while I stared blankly across the room.

Beau ran his hand through his wavy white hair and glanced at me. "Rhett, I am sorry that it came to this. I spent my entire life building this team. My reputation is what made me millions. But more importantly, Natalie is family. It's my job to look out for her. She deserves better than this. Deep down, you know that's true. Now, if you'll excuse me, I need to call my legal team."

With that, he blew past us and stormed out the door.

I slumped down on the edge of my sofa, staring at the wall.

"Rhett." Natalie kneeled in front of me. "I am so sorry."

"It's not your fault." I knew she was only trying to make me feel better, but there wasn't anything she could say or do to make me okay with this.

"What can I do?" she asked softly, sitting down beside me and placing a gentle hand on my back.

"Nothing." I offered her a weak smile. "I just need a minute or two to process this. I knew this could potentially happen, but I honestly never thought it would get this far."

Never in my life did I ever recall being more frustrated or scared shitless at the same time.

I just fucked up my relationship with Beau. My teammates were going to be upset. My family was going to be disappointed, and my fans were going to feel let down.

Her hand rubbed small circles on my back. "We'll get through this, okay? I'll talk to him. Maybe I can convince him to change his mind."

While I was grateful for her being here, I couldn't shake the disappointment that settled deep inside me.

I stood up. "I need to call my agent. I need to know what my options are."

"I hate this." She cried and started pacing the room. "And I hate Levi for doing this "

I blew out a breath. "As much as I hate the guy, we can't lay all the blame at his feet. Do I want to hunt his ass down and finish what I started? Absolutely. But that doesn't change the fact that I'll probably have to leave the only home I've ever known. And I can't even think about what that's going to mean for us. We were just starting to get our shit together, and now we have to face long-distance. I mean, I know it's not the end of the world, and people do it all the time, but it just sucks. Everything fucking sucks."

Her eyes were filled with tears. I wanted to comfort her, but I had other important things to do.

Like finding a new team and a city to play for.

CHAPTER 25

NATALIE

I took a sip of my coffee and glanced at my phone, which was charging on the counter. I fell asleep while reading last night and was too tired to plug it in. I reached over to see if there were any updates from Rhett. Last night, he flew to New York to meet with his agent and attorney.

Every time I thought about him being traded to another team, a wave of guilt washed over me. Beau warned me that this could happen, but I still didn't believe it would get this far. It was stupid of me to think it wouldn't escalate to this.

I refreshed the screen, hoping for a sign of life. A dozen notifications started popping up. Five missed calls from an unknown number and a string of text messages from my aunt Suzie.

Aunt Suzie
We've been trying to reach you.

Beau had a heart attack.

"Oh, my God." I clicked on her number and brought the phone to my ear.

The phone rang, and I closed my eyes and started pacing the room.

"Natalie," Suzie answered, her voice barely a whisper. I heard her moving across a room and a door closing behind her.

"I'm so sorry," I rushed out. "I just saw the messages."

"Beau is okay. No need to beat yourself up."

A puff of air rushed from my lungs. "How bad was it?"

Uncle Beau was only sixty-one. He was still young, and he still had so much life ahead of him. I couldn't believe this was happening. Had he been sick all this time? Had he had symptoms? I had so many questions.

"He was having his breakfast with his friends at the country club when he started feeling some sharp pains in his chest. They called nine-one-one and brought him to the hospital. They found a clogged artery and put a stent in."

"So, he's okay?" My hands were trembling as tears spilled down my cheeks. I should have been there sooner. I shouldn't have fought with him. God, I will live with that guilt for the rest of my life.

"He's going to be fine. The hard part is going to be keeping him away from the cheeseburgers and french fries."

"Thank God." I dropped into the chair and breathed out a sigh of relief.

"He's in intensive care," she said. "They are going to be waking him up in a few minutes."

My feet started moving across the room. "I'm on my way."

I hung up, grabbed my things, and jogged toward the elevators. I pulled up my Uber app and ordered a ride. There was no way I was going to be able to drive myself.

Thankfully, by the time I made it outside, a car was already idling at the curb. Once I hopped in, I rested my head against the seat. Our relationship might have hit a rough patch yesterday, but he was the only family I had left.

I pulled out my phone and shot a text to Rhett.

> **Me**
> Uncle Beau had a heart attack. He's fine, but I'm on my way to the hospital now.

> **Rhett**
> Holy Shit! Where are you? Can you talk?

My knees bounced with nerves.

> **Me**
> I'm in the back of an Uber. I don't have much to report. You have a full day of meetings, so please don't worry. I will be fine.

> **Rhett**
> Nothing is more important than you. Things got a little heated yesterday, but I still care about the guy. I'm going to cancel my meetings.

A lump formed in my throat. I was so glad we were texting because I wasn't sure if I could even talk.

> **Me**
> Please don't do anything until I know what we're dealing with. I'll call once I know more.

> **Rhett**
> I'll keep my phone on and wait for your call. I love you.

> **Me**
> I love you, too. Good luck with your meetings. We'll talk soon.

I slipped my phone back into the bag as we approached the hospital. I rushed through the sliding glass doors and made my way over to the check-in desk. My heart was pounding while I waited for them to print out my visitor badge.

Tears welled in my eyes as I made my way through the maze of corridors. I stepped off the elevator, trying to read the room numbers. The antiseptic smell, bright lights, and muffled voices of doctors and nurses brought me back to a time I never wanted to visit again. For some people, a hospital was associated with a place of healing. For me, it was a reminder of pain and loss.

My stomach twisted in knots as I entered Beau's private room. He was lying in a hospital bed, with an IV bag in his arm and a monitor beeping in the background. He was completely still and had lost all color from his face. He looked nothing like the man who stormed out of Rhett's condo yesterday.

Aunt Suzie was sitting in a chair. She glanced up and quickly came over, wrapping her arms around me. She searched my face in concern. "Everything is going to be fine. He's a tough old bird. He isn't close to being done yet."

I sagged against her. "I was so scared," I said, wrapping my arms around her and trying not to cry.

"That's why I told you not to worry." She sniffed and patted my back. "Thanks for coming."

"Of course." I let her go and wiped under my eyes.

"He's barely been able to stay awake. He wakes up and goes back to sleep." Her eyes were red-rimmed as she stared at him. My heart broke for her. They've been together for over thirty years. They didn't have any kids. All they had was each other. I had no idea how she was holding it all together.

"I'm so sorry, Aunt Suzie."

She patted my shoulder. "It's fine. Try not to beat yourself up though, okay. It's not going to do anybody any good. I'm glad you're here."

"There is nowhere else I'd rather be," I said, trying to get my shit together. She already had enough on her plate. She didn't need to worry about me, too.

She walked to the nearest chair and pulled it out. "Have a seat. I'm going to go make a few calls and stop by the cafeteria. Can I get you anything?"

I slumped into the chair and leaned forward. "I'm all set."

She gave me a sad smile, squeezed my shoulder, and left the room. Sitting around and waiting was driving her crazy, so I could understand why she needed a break.

I looked up at Beau's heartbeat on the monitor, feeling my mind race with guilt and regret. Tears stung my eyes, and I berated myself for causing him so much stress. I know Beau was only acting out of concern and was doing what was best for his business. If only I could turn the clock back, I would have handled things differently.

There was a soft knock on the door. "Natalie."

I turned to see Rylee and Kinley standing in the doorway.

"Rhett called," Rylee said as I got to my feet. "He didn't want you to be alone. He's worried about you."

I gave them both a hug and sniffed back my tears. God, I wished he were here right now. I needed him in ways I didn't even understand.

"How's Beau doing?" Kinley reached for my hand.

"He's going to be okay." I explained what the doctors said as a nurse came in to take his vitals.

Rylee's phone vibrated in her purse. She pulled it out, glanced at it quickly, and silenced it before shoving it back into her bag. "Rhett is going out of his mind with worry. He was in the process of booking a flight and skipping his meeting, but JP talked him out of it."

I was afraid he would try to do something like that. "Thank JP for me."

"There's a waiting room at the end of the hall. Do you have a few minutes?" Rylee asked.

"Sure." I ran my hand down my pants, grabbed my purse off the back of the chair, and followed them out the door.

I sat in one of the chairs and folded my legs underneath me. "Thank you both for coming and checking on me."

"How are you holding up?" Rylee asked, taking a sip of her coffee.

I leaned my head back. Should I tell them that I felt responsible for Beau's heart attack? That I felt awful that Rhett was losing his spot on the team? That I was questioning every single one of my life choices right now?

"I'm hanging in there," I muttered. I didn't want to burden them, but I suspected they could tell I was choosing my words carefully.

"Rhett told us what happened yesterday." Kinley squeezed my hand. I rolled my lips together, tasting my salty tears.

For the first time since I agreed to give this marriage a fighting chance, I was questioning if it was all for nothing. Rhett could be living his life without a care in the world. My uncle might not have had a heart attack, and I wouldn't feel so helpless right now.

I thought about the last time I saw Beau. He was so mad at me. I shouldn't have let him leave like that. Maybe I could have talked to him and gotten him to cool down a bit. Instead, I was scared, and now I was beating myself up, feeling like I was on an endless loop of self-destruction.

I dropped my head in my hands. "I made a mess of everything, and I have no idea what to do."

Rylee grabbed my arm. "You can talk to us, you know. About anything. We might be friends of Rhett's, but we're here for you too."

I wasn't an emotional person, but those words did me in. They had no idea how much that meant to me, especially after everything that happened at Gina's wedding.

I smiled, feeling a lump in my throat. "Can I ask you both something?"

This situation had been weighing on me, tearing me apart from the inside out. Maybe they could help me gain some perspective.

They both leaned forward and nodded.

"Do you think Rhett will truly be happy playing for another team?"

It killed me that I was responsible for this. He loved Atlanta and his teammates, and I had a feeling he would be settling anywhere he went.

Kinley looked down at her water bottle. "When

Maverick found out I was pregnant, and he made the decision to retire, I thought he was going to regret it. But life works in mysterious ways. I believe he was meant to be a father more than he was meant to play football. I know it sounds crazy, but from what I see, Rhett is happier with you than when he's on the field. A career in the NFL doesn't last forever, but your marriage can. I think he will be happy as long as he has you."

I gave her a small smile. "Yeah, but this is different. This isn't Rhett's decision. He's being forced."

"I think Rhett will end up where he is meant to be." Rylee squeezed my hand. "Does he love it here? Yes. Do we wish he could stay and retire as an Arrow? Absolutely. But in all the time I've known him, I've never seen him so stupid over a girl. You mean the world to him, and I have no doubt you feel the same way. I know you're in a tough spot right now, but your love is stronger than you think. You'll get through this."

Their words should have made me feel better, but all I wanted to do was cry. I wanted to believe that Rhett and I could have it all like they did.

I shook my head and looked away. "You are both forgetting that Rhett has never had a serious relationship before. We're just starting to get to know each other. We haven't talked about a future or if he wants kids someday. What if he ends up miserable and resentful and ends up hating me?" I sniffed. "Let's be honest. This is all my fault."

Kinley set her water down. "Rhett is a big boy, and I know for a fact that he does not blame you for the situation he is in. You both have plenty of time to talk about what you want out of life. He might joke and act like an idiot most of the time, but he is sweet and kind, and he is head over heels in love with you."

My chest tightened. "But that could change."

Rylee leaned forward. "Natalie, what's going on? Why are you trying to talk yourself out of being with him?"

I wiped at my cheeks. "How is this all supposed to work? Do I give up my job and my relationship with my uncle to have a life with him? Or do I give up Rhett and free him from this mess?" I stared at them, hoping they could give me the right answer. "No matter which way you slice it, it feels like I will have to choose. I know you probably think I'm crazy because his career is so much bigger than mine, but I'm just finding my footing after having the rug pulled out from under me. I spent four years with a man that I planned on building a future with. What if this all blows up in my face and I end up losing twice?"

Kinley reached into her purse and handed me a napkin. "Breathe." Her expression was a mixture of empathy and concern. "I know this is a lot, but don't think of it as choosing one relationship over the other. Think of it as following your heart."

"But what if my heart leads me down the wrong path? It wouldn't be the first time."

They both exchanged sympathetic glances.

Rylee squeezed my knee gently. "There is no such thing as a wrong path. Each path teaches us valuable lessons in life. There is no right or wrong choice to be made. You just have to follow your instincts and have faith that no matter what direction you choose, you'll be okay."

While I appreciated their words of comfort and support, my reality was the same. No matter which direction I chose, a piece of my heart was going to be broken forever.

CHAPTER 26
NATALIE

I checked my phone for the hundredth time and sipped my coffee. According to the link tracking his flight, Rhett should have been home by now. I glanced out the window, noticing the sun was casting an orange and pink glow across the sky. My head was a chaotic mess of emotions, each one pulling me in a different direction.

I clutched my mug and settled into the cushion. The minutes ticked by slowly as I waited for him to walk through the door.

I ran through every scenario in my head and knew deep in my soul that this was the right decision. Maybe I was reacting out of panic and desperation, but the more I sat alone in silence, the more I tried to steady my racing heart.

I heard the rattle of keys as he slid them into the lock. He pushed the door open, and my heart leaped into my throat as familiar footsteps echoed through the hallway.

His smile faltered when he caught sight of my tears.

"Hey, what's wrong?"

He was wearing a black suit with a blue dress shirt. I wanted to weep at the sight of him.

"Can we talk?" I asked, moving to the edge of the couch.

His brows turned down when he spotted my suitcase. "Is it Beau? Is he okay?"

My nervous fingers were twisting the hem of my shirt. I swallowed hard, feeling tears start to form. "He's making progress."

He threw his keys on the table and took his suit coat off. "Then why do you look so sad?"

I turned away, unable to meet his eyes. Instead, I focused on the frayed edge of the area rug underneath my feet and the hum of the dishwasher running in the kitchen.

"Because I'm afraid of how you will react."

His strong shoulders slumped in defeat. "You're leaving me, aren't you?"

I took a deep breath and finally looked up. "No, it's not that." I shook my head quickly. "I'm feeling overwhelmed and don't know which way to turn. Everything is happening so fast, and I can't keep up."

His eyes held mine. "Does this have anything to do with the suitcase by the door? And I'm not talking about mine."

I moved my eyes around the room, trying to avoid his gaze. "I just need a little space and some time to think."

His laugh was filled with anger. "I just met with another team. I'm willing to have you in my life any way I can, but you're not willing to do the same."

He was only a few feet away. I wanted to reach out and touch and reassure him, but I knew it wouldn't do any good.

"That's not true. Look at where we are." I pointed to

where our suitcases sat by the door, each one headed in a different direction. "I'm a huge distraction to you, and you don't need that right now. Everything feels like it's falling apart. Beau is in the hospital, and you're being traded to a new team. There is just too much happening at once."

"So, you're just going to give up." He flexed his hands at his sides and shook his head in disbelief.

"I'm not giving up. I'm just asking for a little bit of space." I wrapped my arms around my stomach, trying to hold myself together. "You need to focus on your career, and I need to make sure he's okay. We need to take a step back and get our shit together if we want this to work."

He growled with frustration. "We do work, don't you see that? What we have is the only thing in my life that makes sense. I finally found a person who I want to be with, and she doesn't fucking want me."

"That's not true. I do want you. This is only temporary. I just need time."

"Time for what?" he snapped. "Time to figure out if you want me or not?"

I stood up and reached for him, but he took a step back. "Rhett, I know you're angry, but please don't do this. All I'm saying is you need to focus on your career without worrying about me, and Beau needs to focus on his recovery without worrying about us."

He turned away, running a hand through his hair. "How much time are we talking about?"

"I don't know." This conversation was going all wrong. I could see the tension in his shoulders. All I did was cause him stress. Couldn't he see that?

I wiped the tears with the back of my hand and patted the seat next to me. "Please sit and calm down."

He sighed and collapsed onto the couch. I leaned my

head against his shoulder, feeling that ache in my chest consume me.

He wrapped his arm around me. "Talk to me, Natalie."

I buried my head in his chest. "Beau is in the hospital, and you're on the verge of being traded and uprooting your life to a new city. Everything is a mess and it's entirely my doing."

No matter how hard he tried to convince me otherwise, I knew in my heart that I had failed the two people I loved the most in the worst possible way.

"Natalie, I say this with all sincerity, but don't you think you're being a little dramatic here? I'm not trying to be a dick, and I want nothing more than to make this better for you. But leaving me isn't the answer."

"Then what is?"

"How about sticking by me. I know life sucks right now, but I firmly believe we will get through this."

The hurt in his voice broke me, and I had to force myself to follow through with this. "I want you to focus on your career. I don't want to be a burden on you."

"Burden?" He paused. "Don't you fucking get it? I would trade everything for a life with you. So why the hell am I the only one fighting for us here?"

The emotion spilling out of him pulled at my heartstrings. My resolve waived slightly, but that pit in my stomach and the sense of unrest were too big to ignore.

I placed my hand over his, trying to steady my voice. "There is a part of me that is selfish and wants to say the hell with it. If you go, I go. We'll fight the world together. But I know that there is a good chance that you will resent me in the end. Maybe not today or tomorrow, but one day, you will wake up and regret it all."

"You are wrong. I've spent my entire life chasing titles

and winning awards. And you know what? None of that means shit to me right now. You're all that matters."

I shook my head as another tear slid down my cheek. "You're just saying that because you've lived most of your adult life alone, but you don't have to be alone. You have a family that loves you, friends that adore you, and—"

"A wife who doesn't think I'm worth the risk."

I swallowed down the lump in my throat. "Nothing could be further from the truth, which is why I can't do this. I would feel differently if I thought we could simply outrun all our problems without suffering the consequences. But it's not that simple, Rhett." I moved so I could sit on the table in front of him. "This isn't what I want. It isn't just about you and me. I know at the end of the day, Beau will be fine. But there is also a chance that he will cut me out of his life if we stay together. I need to work on repairing that relationship first before I move forward with you. And you need time to make sure this is what you want."

His expression hardened. "So, you're just going to push me away?"

I shook my head, never hating myself more than I did at that moment. "I'm not pushing you away. I'm asking for time and understanding. Have you looked online lately? I've done nothing but bring chaos to your doorstep. Sometimes, we need to do what's best instead of what we want."

"You can spin it any way you want to make yourself feel better, but just be honest, you're acting out of fear, and instead of leaning on me, you're turning your back on me. That tells me you don't believe in us."

He was angry and had every right to be. I took his hand and squeezed it. "Listen to me. I'm not leaving you. This isn't the end. It's just one chapter of our lives. I am doing what I think is best for you. I know it doesn't feel like it right now, but I'm doing this for us because I feel like it's the right thing to do."

"What about what I want? Do I get a say in any of this?"

My lower lip quivered. "Of course you do. That's why it's important for both of us to give each other space to figure things out."

"I don't want space, and I sure as fuck don't need to figure anything out. Unlike you, I know what I want. I don't need a day, a week, or an inch of space to know that I love you and want to spend my life with you. I've spent the last six weeks fighting for you, trying to get us both on the same page. I have done nothing but put you first. I don't know what else I can say or do to stop making you doubt us. Maybe I should stop trying. Maybe you'll never get there."

"Don't say that." I cried, tears blurring my vision. "I'm doing this because I love you."

"You love me, huh?" He laughed bitterly. "Do you believe it's that simple? That we can just hit pause and pick up where we left off whenever you decide you're ready? I thought we were in this together, but I guess I was wrong. Instead of standing by my side, you're choosing to walk away. You know what? Maybe Beau was right. Maybe I'm not the right guy for you."

My eyes slammed shut, and it felt like I was breaking apart at the seams.

"You can't believe that."

"I don't know what to believe right now."

I clutched his hands in mine. "I don't have all the answers, but I know I have to do this."

His jaw worked back and forth as he tried to keep his emotions in check. "I understand why you need to be there for your uncle. What I don't understand is why you can't be there for me too."

"I swear to you. I'm not choosing him over you. That's not what this is about."

"It sure feels like it."

He looked at me with tears in his eyes, and I couldn't take it. No matter how much it hurt, the road ahead was too uncertain. It would be so easy to stay. Maybe I would have felt differently if our relationship hadn't been so new and fragile. But everything was falling apart, and I didn't know which way to turn.

I stepped forward, needing to be close to him. "I need you to understand that this is only temporary."

He crossed his arms. "So, what am I supposed to do in the meantime? Pretend you don't exist?"

My face paled. "Of course not."

"This is ridiculous. You really don't see how fucked up this is?"

His hands were balled into fists. He was taking this the wrong way. I was doing this all wrong. I was hurting him. I needed to stop this and make him understand.

"Please, just listen to me."

"If the next words out of your mouth aren't, 'I love you, Rhett, and I'm not leaving,' then I don't want to hear it."

I covered my mouth, fighting back a sob. "You have worked so hard to get to where you are. I don't want to be the reason you can't give it your all. I've already cost you too much."

His face was a mixture of anger and pain. "You don't get to make those decisions for me."

"I promise, this isn't the end, okay?"

I walked into the bedroom and retrieved the other suitcase I hadn't finished packing earlier. I started shoving things inside. Nothing was neatly folded or organized. It was a mess, just like my life.

I walked over and pulled my phone charger out of the outlet. I stared at the picture of us at the gala with tears blurring my eyes. Every inch of space in this room held so many memories: late nights of spilled popcorn during movie nights, mornings with coffee and so much laughter, tender kisses and gentle touches, and love. So much love. It all stared back at me, making this moment even harder.

"I'm begging you not to do this." He stood in the doorway, his eyes red-rimmed, and just the sight of him made my throat tighten. "You told me you would try."

I closed my eyes, praying for strength. "You have no idea how badly I want to stay, but I'm tired, Rhett."

He gripped the doorframe. "Have you once stopped to consider that I might need you right now? More than ever."

My heart was breaking as I struggled to find the words to make all the pain go away, but I couldn't think of a single thing.

"I love you, Rhett, more than anything. This hurts like hell, but all I know is I'm the reason you're going through this. All I'm doing is hurting you. I don't even know why you would even want to be with me. I want to be the best version of myself for you, and I want you to be absolutely sure that I'm what you want. You need to focus on your career without me complicating things."

"You're going to regret this, Natalie. And when you finally come to your senses, just remember that you're the one who did this, not me. All in some misguided attempt to do the right thing."

When he turned his back and walked away, I sank to the floor. The weight of my decision pressed down on me, and I wondered if I had made the right decision. He thought I was giving up on us when all I was doing was making sure we were right for each other before we went any further. Our relationship had been a whirlwind, and if we didn't press the brakes now, we would eventually crash.

This break was either going to solidify our commitment or be the crack that tore us apart permanently.

CHAPTER 27

NATALIE

It's been five days since Uncle Beau's heart attack. Three days since I moved my things out of Rhett's apartment. I've done nothing but cry and try not to read the awful things people were saying about me on social media.

His fans were filled with hate and resentment, and they were blaming me for everything. Levi had painted himself as the victim, and the fans were eating it up.

Rhett's PR team put out a statement, saying that this was a personal matter, and they had no comment at this time.

I hated this, but at the same time, I knew it would happen.

I've been running on four hours of sleep everyday and doing whatever I could to distract myself. My brain was a mess, my stomach hurt, and I've done nothing but settle in my feelings and feel sorry for myself.

I had no one to call. No friends and no family other than my uncle, who was lying next to me in his hospital bed. The only person I wanted to call, I couldn't. My heart hurt.

There was a tap on the door. A woman walked in, holding another flower delivery. As soon as the news spread about my uncle's heart attack, there was overwhelming support from the NFL community. The room was filled with gift baskets, cards, and so many flowers that we were running out of places to put them.

"I'll take that." I stood up to grab the vase from her hands.

Uncle Beau's eyes popped open. He rolled them when he saw what I was holding. "This is all too much. I don't like people fussing over me."

"Stop being so grumpy," I said, rearranging the roses in the vase. "You have people who care about you. You should be grateful. They just want you to feel better."

"If they wanted to make me feel better, they would send me a bacon, egg, and cheese breakfast sandwich with a side of hash browns, instead of all this," he muttered under his breath. "Prisoners get better food than this crap."

I sighed while running a hand through my hair. "Don't be ungrateful, old man. And the food isn't that bad. You have to remember, you're on the cardiac floor, and bacon isn't the ideal choice for someone who just had a heart attack."

He grumbled another response while I rearranged his pillows.

"You've been spending too much time here."

I smiled while adjusting his blanket. "Are you sick of me already?"

He studied my face. "I'm trying to figure out what's going on with you. We haven't talked about well, you know." He looked away, and I couldn't tell if he really wanted to talk about it or if he was just curious about the status of my relationship.

I've been here every day. Not once has Rhett's name come up.

Beau's mood hasn't been that great, so I've been avoiding this conversation. He wasn't a fan of being cooped up in a hospital bed without his laptop. Aunt Suzie finally gave in yesterday and allowed him to use his cell phone, but she took it away when he ordered a pepperoni pizza and had it delivered to his room. I haven't wanted to say or do anything to rile him up any more than he already was.

I patted his arm. "Don't worry about any of that. We can discuss all that when you're feeling better."

He turned his head when Dr. Powers came in with a nurse and a rolling cart.

"Mr. Landers. It's great to see you're awake. How are you feeling?"

He scooted forward. "Feeling better already, Doc."

She put her hands under the hand sanitizer dispenser and grabbed her tablet. "That's great to hear," she said with a reassuring smile as she approached the side of the hospital bed. "I've looked over your recent scans. The cardiac MRI showed minimal scarring, your ejection fraction numbers look great, and your blood pressure seems to be responding well to your new medication."

I folded my hands together. "That all sounds promising."

She slid her glasses down. "It is very promising. It helped that he got here as early as he did. Some people ignore their symptoms, and by then, it's too late. This is the best outcome possible."

She put her stethoscope up to his chest and proceeded to do a physical exam. I pulled my phone out and gave my aunt an update. We put a schedule in place to ensure that someone was here at all times. She'd been spending the night, and I'd been taking the morning shift.

"Your vitals look great, your oxygen is slightly low, but nothing too concerning. You're showing great signs of improvement."

He sat up. "Fantastic. When can I get out of here?"

"Hopefully, tomorrow. You will need to continue taking your medications and follow up with your cardiologist. I cannot stress enough how important it is to follow a healthy diet, exercise every day, and avoid stress."

He laughed. "Have you ever tried running a football team with fifty-three active players? All they do is create stress."

She folded her arms and stared down at him. "This heart attack was a wake-up call, Mr. Landers. I understand that you have a very demanding job, but in order to prevent another heart attack, you need to make some lifestyle changes."

He didn't look very thrilled with that advice. "What are you suggesting?"

"Number one, lay off the saltshaker. Number two, you need to make positive changes in your life. Perhaps you can delegate some of your job duties, at least for now, so you can focus on your health."

Her words were clear, but we both knew that wouldn't happen.

I moved closer to the bed. "Uncle Beau, just promise to take it easy, at least for the time being," I said gently, trying to reason with him.

He waved off my concern. "I can't just drop everything. You know how busy I am, but I will do my best."

I sighed, feeling frustrated because I wasn't convinced

he was taking her advice seriously. "Your health is important right now. Please know your limits and not push yourself."

Dr Powers shook her head. "Your niece is right. You need to eliminate stress."

He folded his hands in his lap. "I'll do my best."

Uncle Beau was a proud and stubborn man. Trying to get him to change his ways would be like redirecting the Mississippi River.

"Okay," she said, not looking convinced. "I'll just remind you one last time that you need to prioritize your health. I'll check back in with you before I leave."

She squeezed my arm and walked out the door. I picked up the pamphlet and started looking over the menu, trying to find a food option for lunch that he would be happy with.

"They have chicken noodle soup. It doesn't sound that bad. They also have a create your own sandwich option."

"I don't want to talk about food."

"Okay." I set the menu down. "What do you want to talk about?"

"I'd like to address the elephant in the room," he said, causing me to look up into his eyes. "You've been by my side every day, and I know you are hesitant to broach the subject due to my health, but we need to address it. It's more stressful watching you pretend that you're okay. I can tell you're upset, so don't lie. Talk to me."

I avoided his eyes, knowing if I met his gaze, I might break down. "I don't want to upset you. Please don't make me do this. You heard the doctor. Plus, I've already caused you enough stress. You might not even be here if it weren't for me."

He squeezed my hand. His grip was gentle but firm.

"Natalie, you are not to blame for my health. I was upset because I was concerned. You can't control that."

Tears stung my eyes as I internally berated myself. "I know you only wanted what was best for me. I'm sorry for letting you down. If I could go back and do things differently, I would."

"Sweetheart, we all make mistakes. What's important is that we learn from them. I'll do whatever I can to get you out of this mess."

I was trying to apologize for hurting him, but he assumed I was referring to my marriage. I wanted to correct him, but there was a nagging voice in the back of my mind, reminding me that his health was too fragile.

"Right." I swallowed. I needed to choose my words carefully. He wasn't stupid, and I had already lied to him enough.

I avoided his eyes and started organizing the table near his bed. I picked up a few stray napkins and started straightening a few get well cards. I had too much nervous energy flowing through me, so I needed to keep busy. Maybe, if I kept moving, we could avoid this uncomfortable conversation.

He moved the water jug out of my reach when I went to grab it. "Marrying Rhett was a mistake, right?"

He could never be a mistake. The only mistake I made was making him feel second-best.

I started fussing with the blanket on his bed. "You're not ready to hear the answer to that question."

Uncle Beau studied me. "Natalie, are you in love with him?"

I closed my eyes, wishing we could postpone this conversation, but he wasn't going to let it go. "I love him with all my heart."

He sighed. "Does he make you happy?"

"He does." I licked my dry lips and focused on the potted plant in the window. "I know you don't approve of our relationship, but I can't give him up. We both deserve a chance at happiness, and I would like your support. I know you're not ready to give it to us now, but I hope someday you will."

The room went silent other than the beeping of the monitors and the chatter in the hallway.

"Why did you keep your relationship a secret from me? If you both respected me as much as you claimed, I never would have found out like that," he said firmly.

He was right, and whatever excuses I've been using, none of them mattered anymore. All I could do was express my regret and apologize.

My heart raced, but I forced myself to sit. "At first, neither of us were sure about our feelings. We didn't say anything because we were trying to figure out what to do. The more time we spent together, the clearer it became that we had real feelings for each other. We wanted to make sure that our relationship was solid before we said anything."

"So, are you planning on staying together?"

"I'd like to build a life with him, and I know it's asking a lot, but I would like to have you in that life too."

I moved the tray closer to his bed when he reached for the water. He brought the straw up to his mouth to take a sip. He set it down and rubbed at his clean-shaven face. "Then who am I to judge and tell you who you're allowed to be with?"

My pulse thundered in my ears. "Uncle Beau, what are you saying?"

I was so confused and an emotional mess. I wanted to make sure I understood him correctly.

He chuckled. "Never in all the years I've known the

boy have I seen him look at anyone the way he looks at you. It would take some serious balls to jeopardize his entire sports career if he weren't completely in love with you. I'm not happy that the two of you kept this from me. I was blindsided and not proud of how I threw my weight around. But now that I've had time to process it, I let my own anger cloud my judgment. I said some things I regret. I was quick to judge and quick to dismiss your feelings," he confessed. "I've always respected Rhett as a player, and I might not agree with everything he does, but I can see how much he means to you."

I blinked. I couldn't believe what I was hearing. "Uncle Beau, are you giving me your blessing?"

He nodded his head, a small smile on his lips. "It's not up to me to decide who is good enough for you. That's for you to decide."

His words settled in my chest and filled me with relief. "That means the world to me. Thank you."

"And I want to be perfectly clear on this," his expression turned serious, "I consider him a step up from the hockey puck you were dating."

I laughed. "I'm really sorry about the scandal. We didn't mean for any of this to come out that way. As much as I want to blame Levi, I take full responsibility."

"Why don't you meet with the media team and draft up a press release? Tell the story from your heart. I can see how genuine your feelings are. No one will question if the marriage is real or not." His eyes softened. "I feel, as your godfather, I need to warn you. There will be challenges. You are married to someone in the public eye, so it won't be easy."

I wiped my eyes. "There is only one problem. I asked Rhett for some space, and he didn't take the news very well. I'm not sure where we stand."

"Oh, sweetheart," he said, covering his hand in mine. "Let me make this right."

My throat felt tight. "It's not your mistake to fix. I did this. He tried to fight for me, for us, and now I have to do the same for him. I need to show him that I choose us, and I will be there for him no matter what." Tears welled up in my eyes and my heart was beating fast. This next part was going to be hard, but there wasn't a doubt in my mind that this was the right decision. "I just want you to know that I appreciate the opportunity you've given me, but I need to resign. It's not fair that I get to keep my job when he doesn't. This isn't a punishment. I need you to know that. I'm not doing this to get back at you. Regardless of what happens, I will always be your niece. But I need to see if there is a future between us and if there is, then I will go where he goes."

I planned on telling him once he was fully recovered, but once he started initiating this conversation, the words just started spilling out of my mouth.

He sighed, his gaze dropping to the floor before meeting mine again. "I'd be willing to change my mind about the trade, but unfortunately, I know he is already in talks with a few teams. I don't know what the status is."

My jaw went slack. "You would consider keeping him?"

He nodded his head. "He is an asset to the team and a damn good player. I can't afford to lose him. I'll see if there is anything I can do once I get in touch with a few people."

Relief flooded through me. I had to blink a few times to make sure I wasn't imagining this. It was almost too good to be true. "Thank you, but please take care of your health first, okay? You heard what the doctor said."

He rolled his eyes. "I would be making a couple of

phone calls, not running in a marathon. I think I can handle it."

I adjusted the blanket again, covering his legs. "Just promise me you will put your health first."

"I promise, as long as you do the same. I can see the exhaustion in your eyes, and I've noticed you haven't been eating."

"It's been a rough few days, but I promise to do better."

"Good." He turned his head to the side and closed his eyes. "Now, if you'll excuse me, I'm going to take a nap. These drugs that they're pumping into me are making me tired. Why don't you go and regroup? Come up with a plan on how you're going to get your guy back."

I walked over to the window and adjusted the blinds to help him sleep. "Nice try, but you're not getting rid of me that easily. I can do that from here. Go ahead and take your nap; I'll be here when you get up."

He settled into his pillow. "Whatever."

Once he drifted off to sleep, I pulled out my phone and started formulating a plan. Somehow, someway, I would make this right.

CHAPTER 28

RHETT

I climbed out of the car and walked up the familiar driveway.

Cruze stood at the door, her face breaking into a warm smile. "Hello, my boy." She threw her arms around me and kissed my cheek. "Where is that beautiful lady of yours?"

I gave her a sad smile. "Afraid it's just me tonight."

Her lips turned down. "It's cold out. Let's get you inside and warm you up."

Once I reached the foyer, I kicked my shoes off and hung my jacket on the hook.

"Your parents are in the sitting room. Can I get you anything?"

I shook my head. "No, thank you. I'm good."

I followed Cruze into the formal living room, where my dad was sitting in his favorite chair, engrossed in paperwork. He looked up as soon as I entered the room.

"Thanks for coming, son," he said, adjusting his reading glasses to the bridge of his nose. "Have a seat."

My mother pushed the book aside while she was

reading and stood to greet me. "Are you alone? I thought you might bring Natalie."

"Just me. What did you want to talk to me about?"

"I think you know," my dad said, getting straight to the point. "You've been getting quite a bit of… shall I say, less than flattering media coverage lately."

"Bad press is better than no press, right?"

He took off his glasses and glared at me while holding them under his chin. "There has been an intense interest in your personal life. People are calling into question your character and have expressed disappointment in your decision-making. The press is having a field day with this story. We need to take control of the narrative."

What else was new? I'd been a disappointment my entire life.

"Control the narrative for who? You or me?"

He stared me down. "Rhett, talk to me. What's going on?"

I sighed heavily, running a hand through my hair. "I'm getting traded."

"You're getting traded because you married Natalie?" my mother asked, stepping back in shock.

I didn't answer. I just shook my head.

"Can he do that?" She started pacing the room, and I could see her putting on her lawyer cap, mentally searching for a legal way around this.

"It's his team. He can do whatever he wants."

He made that perfectly clear.

"Where will you go?" My dad folded his hands in his lap.

I leaned my hip against the sofa and crossed my arms. "New York has expressed an interest."

"What about Natalie?" She walked toward me.

I closed my eyes, trying not to think about that part.

I've been so consumed with figuring out my next steps that I haven't had much time to focus on my feelings. Which was good because every time my mind would start to drift to her, my heart would only hurt more.

My mind kept going back to our last conversation. Even though I understood why she was so scared, it didn't lessen the pain. It was one thing to understand why she did it. It was another to accept it.

I ran a hand down my face. "Natalie and I are over or on a break. I don't even know at this point. She asked me for space but didn't say for how long, so I don't know where we stand right now."

They both shared a look, and the room went silent for a minute.

"You don't know if you're together or not?" my mom finally asked.

"It's complicated." I looked down at the floor. "I pretty much got pissed off and told her I wasn't going to stick around and wait for her to decide if she wanted to be with me or not."

That was the part that pissed me off because we didn't need to take a damn break. She promised me no matter what, and instead of sticking by my side and supporting me, she ran at the first sign of conflict. What did that say about her? About us?

"Is there anything I can do to help?" My dad leaned forward in his chair. His willingness to help shocked me. I figured they would have been thrilled.

I looked up in surprise. "With Natalie?"

Dad nodded and gave me a small smile. "Sure, or with your contract situation. Whatever you need."

I blinked at them. "I assumed you guys would be happy. You never approved of me playing football. This is one step closer to getting me behind that desk you have waiting for me. If I can't find a team, then I'll be unemployed."

That was a stretch because there were already teams that had expressed an interest. Unfortunately, most of those teams were terrible and in places where I had no desire to live. Leaving Atlanta and the team I loved, fucking sucked.

My dad laughed. "Rhett, I never believed for one second that you would ever consider coming to work for me. I used that threat because it was the only one that seemed to scare you. You're a grown man now. I couldn't control you as a kid. You think I'd be any better at it now that you're an adult?"

I looked at the framed photos lining the wall. Snapshots of Ford and my dad on the campaign trail, pictures of Reagan when she graduated law school. Then there was me, in my football uniform, with sweaty hair and a goofy smile. No matter how many MVPs or championship games I won, I always felt like I was coming up short in their eyes.

"Control? No, but there was never any doubt that if I did dress up in a suit and tie, that would have made you happy. I've always been a disappointment to this family. I didn't go to your alma mater like Ford. I didn't graduate at the top of my class like Reagan. I played a sport instead of going away to law school like everyone else in my family."

Ever since I was a young boy, picking Pop Warner over political science, I felt the weight of their disappointment. The life choices I made were never going to live up to their expectations. They have never come out and said they were disappointed, but I felt it in every sigh, hard glance, and shake of a head.

My dad's jaw ticked. "You have never been a disappointment to me. Your mother and I have worried about you ever since the day you put on your first pair of shoulder pads. Football is a dangerous sport." He rubbed his temples. "You could get seriously injured; that's always been our biggest worry. We have never been ashamed of you or your career. While it may be different from what we had originally hoped for you, we can still appreciate the dedication and commitment it takes to play the game at your level. We have been amazed by all you have accomplished."

I studied my father as if seeing him in a new light. I always assumed he just disapproved of the path I'd chosen, that they were both displeased that I chased a dream instead of following a safe and more predictable career.

"Rhett, we love you unconditionally." My mom sniffed. "We don't care what you do for a living as long as you're happy. That's all your father and I want for you."

It dawned on me that this was the first serious conversation with my parents in a long time, maybe ever. I felt that knot in my chest loosen.

My dad cleared his throat, and as I stared into his eyes, nothing but love was reflected back at me. "Maybe we haven't said it enough, but we've always been proud of you, Rhett. I know we haven't always been easy on you, but that's because you were more challenging than Ford and Reagan, so we had to treat you differently. There hasn't been a second in your life where we haven't believed in you. You always found a way to be successful. It was always your way, but you always made things happen."

I glanced down at my hands, feeling ashamed for assuming the worst all these years. "Thank you, both. You have no idea what those words mean to me."

My mom reached out and took my hand. "Sometimes, things happen for a reason. I know you wanted your marriage to Natalie to work. I'm sorry things didn't go as planned. Maybe some space will be good. It will give you both time to figure things out."

"You'll get through this, son." Dad's voice was filled with emotion. "You are strong and capable, and you have friends and family that love you. No matter what, we are here for you. We'll support you in any way we can. That's what families do."

"Are you seriously considering New York?" My mom didn't seem thrilled with that idea. I wasn't either, but they had a strong offensive line with a great quarterback. I think I would do well there.

I hung my head, feeling a sense of defeat wash over me. "My agent is already in talks with the team, but nothing is set in stone yet."

"That's so far away." She wiped at the tears in her eyes.

"It would only be during the season, and it's a short, direct flight," I said, trying to reassure her. I didn't know who I was trying to convince more, me or them.

"What about Natalie?" my mom asked. "I don't know her very well, but you seemed so happy together."

Sadness swelled in my chest. "I don't know, Mom. She's worried about her uncle and his health. She thinks she's doing me a favor. She won't listen to reason."

"Oh, my sweet boy." My mom patted my leg. "Sometimes, you have to let things fall apart in order for them to fall back together. Give her a little bit of space. Maybe she'll come around."

I rubbed at the cramp in the back of my neck. "I hope you're right, because, Mom," I looked her in the eye, "even if things don't work out with Natalie, I'm not marrying Claire. Ever."

She ducked her head in embarrassment. "Got it."

———

"How are you holding up, buddy?" JP squeezed my shoulder, and Mav patted my back as they sat down.

"Fucking fantastic."

They both leaned forward and rested their elbows on their knees. "Tell us what you're thinking?" Mav asked.

I cleared my throat. "I got an offer from New York."

JP handed me a beer. "That's great."

I swallowed, staring at my hands. "Doesn't feel great. I don't want to go to New York. I hate the city and the cold. Not to mention, the subway stations always smell like shit."

"Are those the only reasons?" Mav asked, narrowing his eyes.

I stared down at my blue Nike sneakers. "No."

"I didn't think so." JP rubbed his knee. "Maybe there is a way you can reason with Beau."

I looked between my friends. "You both know that will never happen. He hates me, and I don't think I would be able to handle seeing Natalie every day knowing we couldn't be together."

JP shifted forward. "So, you're just going to give up?"

They acted like I had a choice.

"I'm not giving up on anything. I already lost her," I reminded them, in case they forgot the part where she left me.

JP was quiet for a moment. "Then maybe moving to New York will be the fresh start that you need."

I glanced out the window at the city of Atlanta. Something in my chest tightened. Starting over with a new team was scary enough; living in a new city without my friends around was worse. But I'd still get to play ball, and maybe being away from her would make it hurt a little less.

"That's why I'm considering the offer." I took a sip of my beer and set it down.

Mav sat up. "Have you ever thought about going to her before making any final decisions?"

I scoffed. "After the way she left it. No."

He shook his head. "She was upset and reacting with emotion. Trust me, nothing is worse than when a woman feels backed into a corner." Mav's face scrunched up like he was reliving a memory. "I've learned that a little bit of time and space can make a huge difference."

I turned to him. "Why does everyone think space is a good thing? I don't understand it."

These two acted like they were enjoying this.

JP tapped my head. "Sometimes, people need time to sort through their own stuff. It doesn't mean she doesn't love you."

"I sure as hell don't need space," I snapped. "Why can't she believe in us like I do?"

Mav put his hand on my shoulder. "This isn't about you. It's about her. She's dealing with a lot. You both are. Maybe she didn't communicate it clearly enough, but it sounds like she is trying to be smart about this. You have to respect her feelings. It might be the best thing for both of you in the long run."

"I'm not smart enough for this conversation." I picked up my beer. "Are you guys on my side or not?"

They both laughed.

"You don't have a lot of experience with relationships, so let me dumb this down for you," Mav said. "Women don't know what they want. They think they do, but at the end of the day, they just want someone to love them and to put them first. But if you push her when she asks for space, you could end up driving her away. Just be patient. Sometimes, you have to let go for a while."

I swear to God, the man got off on fucking with me. "I'm going to ask you one more time. No more cryptic sentences and long-winded answers. Do I stay and fight or let her go?"

"If you let her go, there is no going back," JP said. "Just because you sign a new contract doesn't mean you have to lose the girl. You can still keep your place here. Plenty of players live and play in two different cities. Where you play doesn't make being with her impossible."

I had no idea if they were right or wrong. All I knew was that I wanted to be with her more than anything. Maybe if I gave her the space she asked for, she would realize she didn't want to be without me.

Leaving my team was going to suck, but let's be real for a second. Football wasn't forever. I only had a few years left if I was lucky. Then what? Maybe get a job in broadcasting? That didn't sound appealing, but it was better than going to work for my father.

And after being with Natalie, I knew I could never marry a woman I didn't love. So, where did that leave me?

My phone buzzed on the table. I picked it up, and my eyes widened. "It's her."

They leaned forward, but I snatched up my phone and read the message out loud before they could grab it.

> **Natalie**
> I'm just checking in to see if you're okay.
> Beau and I talked, and I feel like we are in a
> good place. His recovery is going well, but
> I'm worried about you. I want to see you
> and talk to you. You probably hate me, but I
> hope you will give me a chance to say what
> I need to say. Regardless of what happens, I
> will always love you. Let me know when
> you're ready.

"Holy fuck!" My heart was pounding so fast. I looked at my friends, who were both grinning at each other.

"That sounds positive." JP's eyes lifted to mine.

"Are you going to text her back?" Mav asked.

I pursed my lips. "I think I will take your advice and give her some space to come to her senses."

Mav's head jerked back. "You're kidding, right? I gave you that advice when I thought you needed to win her back. That text is a game changer."

"It sure is, and now we are playing by a different set of rules," I said, staring down at her message and reading it again.

"What the fuck is wrong with you? You better have the team doctor check your head for brain damage. You're seriously going to string her along after that?" JP pointed to my phone.

"She hurt me. She needs to understand that I'm not going to just roll over whenever she feels like stomping on my heart. I might be a little sensitive, but if the situation was reversed, I'm pretty sure her girls wouldn't be telling her to just give in."

They looked at me like I'd lost all my marbles.

"Okay, let's circle back a bit." JP ran a hand through his hair. "Relationships are about compromise. She made a mistake, and it sounds like she's owning up to it. The mature thing to do would be to text her back and hear her out."

"I will." I sat back and crossed my arms. "When I'm ready."

JP shook his head. "It's your funeral."

Mav pinched the bridge of his nose. "Don't say we didn't warn you."

I didn't want to just give in. How could I possibly trust that she wouldn't do this again? Things happened, and while this wasn't all her fault, I didn't want to make it so easy for her.

I never once doubted if she was the one. That's what made it so hard to accept. I thought we were on the same page. But when I needed her the most, she left me. My friends were right; I had zero relationship experience, and the only reason I was acting this way was because she hurt me.

I wasn't doing this to punish her. I was giving her time to ensure this was what she wanted. As much as it killed me not to text her back, I needed to get my emotions in check. If I did get her back, I wasn't going to lose her again.

CHAPTER 29

RHETT

I was digging a hole to plant a new shrub in the front yard of the Born to Love residence when my phone rang with an alert. I pulled it out of my pocket, and my throat closed when I looked at the headline.

NFL WIFE SETS THE RECORD STRAIGHT. IMPLICATES NHL STAR LEVI JAMES IN ABUSING PRESCRIPTION DRUGS.

My name is Natalie Daniels, I am married to NFL player Rhett Daniels. I am writing to address a recent story about my personal life. It has come to my attention that there are false reports suggesting that I was still involved with Mr. James when I married Rhett. I want to emphasize that this story is entirely untrue and has resulted in significant distress. Levi James and I had ended our relationship last January due to his infidelity. It's unfortunate that my reputation and my husbands have been questioned based on statements from a man seeking revenge.

The accusation that my husband attacked Mr. James is also completely false and misleading. Levi is spreading these rumors to try to cover up the fact that he's been using an illegal substance for the past two years. I have submitted documents supporting these claims to the NHL Players Association. They have launched a thorough investigation.

My husband is a well-respected figure known for his integrity and contributions to the community, so it was important for me to tell the truth. I want to personally apologize to his fans and the entire Atlanta Arrows organization for the confusion that this has caused.

My jaw went slack. I couldn't believe she did this. I was reading the rest of the article when my phone dinged with another alert.

A smile broke out across my face as I looked at the picture. Natalie posted a photo of us on Instagram and tagged me. It was a picture of us lying in bed. We were watching a movie, and a bowl of popcorn was between us. The caption read, "My favorite place in the world is next to you, even when you're not paying attention to me."

If that wasn't a declaration, I don't know what was. She was making us official. No more hiding. And in true Natalie fashion, she didn't stop there. She's been sending me small gifts all week. The best one so far, was an autographed pair of Air Jordans, not just any pair, but a limited edition from 1985. The kind that came with a certificate of authenticity. They were exclusive and hard to find. I had no idea how she pulled it off, but I couldn't stop grinning just thinking about how much thought she put into these little surprises.

The skin on the back of my neck prickled with awareness. I turned, already knowing it was her.

She stood just a few feet away in a cute yellow dress, her long blond hair cascading down her shoulders, and a pair of sunglasses sitting on top of her pretty head.

My heart pounded so loudly she could probably hear it.

I held my phone up and pointed to the screen. "You really threw your ex under the bus. You realize he's going to be in big trouble, right?"

Natalie's smile was wobbly as she stepped forward with her hands behind her back. "He put your career and your reputation in jeopardy. That's not okay. I didn't fabricate anything. I just told the truth."

"You didn't need to do that. I was planning on handling it all on my own."

"Oh, yeah?" She smiled. "What did you have in store for him?"

I took the rag from my back pocket and wiped my hands off. "Do you really want to talk about him right now?"

She shook her head. "No, I came here to talk about us."

It had been two weeks since she left me. Two weeks of gifts and food orders from my favorite restaurants. Two weeks of voicemails and emails saying she was going to win me back. I could make it easier on her and tell her she had already won, but where was the fun in that?

"Have you been enjoying all the gifts I've been sending?" she asked, folding her hands in front of her.

I took a small step forward. There was too much space between us. "So, you're the one who bought me a pair of limited edition Jordans."

She pursed her lips. "Who else do you think would send them?"

I shrugged. "I was just checking to see if it was you or one of my many mistresses."

She took a step closer, and you could feel the air thicken between us. "I'm so sorry, Rhett. I freaked out. I didn't know what to do. I was worried about you, about Beau, about everything, and I handled it all wrong. I know you said you were done, and I don't blame you if you are. I'm here to ask for your forgiveness and see if there is a way to change your mind."

"Change my mind about what?" I asked, moving closer to her.

"About us. I made a huge mistake."

Yeah, she did, and I've spent the last two weeks going through the motions. I've been so torn up that I didn't know what to do with myself. While what she did was shitty, I didn't want to keep punishing her for it either.

"Mistakes are a part of life. Trust me, I've been making them since the day I was born," I said, deciding to go easy on her.

She swallowed. "I hated that you were kicked off the team and forced to start a new life in a new city because of me."

"The only kind of life I want is the one where you are in it."

I also wanted to pull her into me, drag her home, and make up for lost time.

"I want nothing more than a life with you too. I regret leaving that day. I should have stayed. I should have talked to you about my concerns and given us a chance to work through them instead of asking for space."

"Do you think it would have changed anything?"

I held my breath, hoping to God, she would give me the right answer. I've been miserable and angry, but I've always been honest with her and never gave up faith.

She nodded. "Yes, because I could have saved us both a lot of misery. It was unfair, and it wasn't right." She pressed a hand to my chest and looked up at me like she expected me to move away. "I've missed you. I've missed having your arms around me. I miss laughing with you and waking up next to you. And most of all, I miss knowing that you're mine. Do you think you could find it in your heart to forgive me and give us another chance?"

"Are you sure that's what you want?" I placed my hands around her waist.

She smiled at me. "I'm so sure that I got you this." She reached into her pocket and placed a beaded bracelet in my hands. I looked down and realized it was just like the one my niece made me, except this one spelled out a different message. My heart pounded in my chest as I read the words. "Will You Be My Husband?"

I looked up to see tears streaming down her face. "Are you proposing to me?"

Her hands were now shaking as she wrapped them around mine. "I figured I would give it a try this time and see if we could give ourselves a better ending."

"Natalie, I appreciate all this. I really do."

She pressed a finger to my lips. "I messed up."

"You did."

"I hate what I did to us. I hate that I doubted us. I won't do that again. I won't hurt you. I promise to only love you from here on out."

"What about Beau?" I asked.

I didn't want to spoil the mood, but I had to know. I needed to hear the words. I didn't want to question her decision. I needed to know that she chose me because that's where her heart led her, not because he gave her permission or thought it was okay to love me.

She touched my cheek and smiled up at me. "Beau convinced me that I could fix this. He might have given me his permission, but I didn't need it. I was always going to choose us."

Unbeknownst to Natalie, Beau had called me and

asked me to meet with him a week ago. He filled me in on their conversation and apologized for overreacting. He also called my agent and told him not to allow me to sign with another team. He even offered me a bonus to stay. I told him I would consider it. I was waiting on Natalie. I wanted to see how this was all going to play out. If she was done with me, there was no way I could stay. I wouldn't be able to handle seeing her and not being able to be with her.

My contract with New York was in an unsigned envelope right next to the annulment papers I received from my lawyer yesterday. I was giving her until the end of the week to make a decision.

"What do you want, Natalie?" Never in my life do I ever remember fearing an answer to a question like this.

"Everything. I want everything with you."

It was taking everything in me to stand still and not tackle the woman. I didn't want to keep doing this dance with her. I didn't want to keep playing these stupid games where I made her prove to me over and over again that she wanted a future with me.

I closed my eyes and rested my forehead against hers. "Thank fucking God, because I want you too."

Her hands gripped my shirt and held on for dear life. "I've never loved anyone like you before, Rhett."

I pulled her close. "That's funny because I've never loved anyone *but* you."

She moved her hands up to my face. "What about your trade? Where will you go? I need to know where to start looking for a new job."

I smiled. "How do you feel about Atlanta?"

Her eyes widened with so much hope. "Does that mean you're staying?"

I shrugged. "I mean, New York is still an option if you would prefer to live there."

"No. I hate the cold."

I pulled away just enough to see her face. "I want a divorce."

Her eyebrows pulled together. "What did you just say?"

"I don't want you to stay married to me because of some stupid arrangement. I want a second chance."

She smiled, but her stare was unwavering. "You realize you stole my thunder, right? I proposed first."

I winked and dropped to my knees. "When I asked you the first time, it was out of need. Now, it's because I want you by my side. You are my entire world; there is no one else for me."

"There is no one else for me either," she said, quietly stroking her finger down the side of my face.

I squeezed her hand and paused for a minute to pull myself together. "I need you, Natalie, because without you, nothing makes sense. I used to be afraid of commitment. The idea of marriage used to send me into a panic. But I realize now that's because I didn't have any idea what love felt like until I met you. Since the night we met, not once was I scared. Never hesitated or doubted if you were the right person for me. In fact, the only time I was truly scared was when you left me. I can't ever lose you again."

"You won't." She ran her fingers through my hair.

"I love you, Natalie. I know I'm not perfect. I'm going to screw up from time to time, but I promise to spend the rest of my life trying to make you happy. Will you be my forever? Marry me for real this time?"

Her small hand trembled. "On one condition."

I raised a brow. "Name it."

"I want a house with a yard and a pool."

That was fine by me. More space to get creative when I was in the mood.

"Done."

"I'd also like kids someday."

I didn't even blink. "I'll give you as many as you want."

"I'm sorry," she said in disbelief. "Did you just agree to kids?"

She obviously was expecting some pushback. "Sure, I think we should start trying right away. I'm not getting any younger."

She tilted her head to the side. "Did you just agree to have a family with me just so you could get laid?"

I laughed. "I'm saying yes because I love you. Now, are you going to say yes to my proposal or keep handing out ultimatums?"

She moved her hands to my face, the smile on hers never fading. "Yes, I will marry you. I will say yes a thousand times if that's what it takes to prove to you that I'm going to stand by your side forever."

She got down on her knees, threw her arms around me, and sealed it with a kiss. My world never felt right until she came along. The night I met her, everything started to make sense. Now, I don't just live for football and nights of fun. I live for her smile, her laugh, and how her eyes light up when I walk into a room.

I live for her.

EPILOGUE

NATALIE

EIGHTEEN MONTHS LATER

THE ENERGY IN THE STADIUM WAS OFF THE CHARTS AS I scanned the crowd in a sea of blue and orange colors. I was in one of the luxury suites, surrounded by friends and family, while my husband played his heart out on the field. I adjusted myself to get a better view, where one of our players was sprinting forward and dodging tackles. The crowd roared, and the official blew the whistle, signaling a first down for the Arrows.

I took a sip of my water when I felt the baby kick again. "Take it easy there, little one." I rubbed my pregnant belly, feeling ready to pop at any second.

The offensive line huddled in a circle while our quarterback, Brent Wilson, barked out plays and signals. The team lined up, and I noticed Rhett crouched forward, ready to take off. The ball snapped, and Rhett ran, leaping across the line of scrimmage, veering around the defensive players, looking for an open spot. I could hear everyone screaming his name as he ran a perfect route, earning another first down. Completing two quick first-down conversions was a good sign that the Arrows scoring drive was underway.

I was trying to focus on the field when I felt a sharp pain. I looked around the suite. My hand instinctively went to my stomach.

"Natalie, are you okay?" Rylee asked with concern, filling her expression.

"I think it's starting," I whispered, trying not to panic.

Her eyes widened. "Stay calm. I'll be right back." She jumped over JP, who was stuffing his face with nachos, and ran over to where Dr. Sterling was sitting, just a few seats down.

Rhett made sure my doctor had season tickets so she would be here just in case. My due date was a week away, but according to my last exam, they thought there was a good chance I'd go early.

I tried my best to stay calm, but the contractions were becoming too intense.

Dr. Sterling sprang into action and rushed over. "Natalie, how far apart are your contractions?" she asked, looking at her watch.

"I don't know, but they feel pretty close." I winced when another one hit.

Her hands went to my stomach, and I looked around the suite. "They are two minutes apart."

"Is that good or bad?" I asked, squeezing the armrest for dear life.

"We need to get you to a safe place where you can deliver."

"What?" I shouted, noticing the rest of our friend group was surrounding me. "Why can't I go to the hospital?"

JP's hands went to my shoulders while Maverick ran over to get my uncle Beau.

"This baby isn't waiting. We need to prepare now." She helped me from the chair while JP guided us out of the room. Maverick opened the door while Uncle Beau talked with one of the security guards. I waddled my way to the elevators, trying to focus on my breathing and not the fact that I was about to deliver my baby in a freaking football stadium. I guess there was a first time for everything.

I could hear the cheers and boos as we made our way to the medical room. It wasn't the ideal place to deliver a newborn, but at least it had a bed and medical supplies.

Kinley and Rylee helped me lie down while Dr. Sterling pulled her equipment out of her bag. She was calm and focused while I was freaking out.

Uncle Beau came up to my side. "Stadium security is notifying Rhett."

Another sharp pain shot through me. "Please tell them to hurry."

"Just focus on the baby," he tried to assure me. "He'll be here in just a few minutes."

Those minutes felt like hours while Kinley and Rylee each held one of my hands. I tried to smile through the pain, but every time a contraction would hit, I would cry out for Rhett.

"Try to get comfortable," Kinley said and placed a cool cloth along my forehead.

Comfortable? Was she insane? It felt like I was being ripped apart.

The guys stood off to the side, looking petrified, when the door suddenly burst open. There was my husband, still in his uniform, his helmet under his arm and his eyes wide with worry.

Relief washed over me at the sight of him.

"I'm here, baby." He rushed to my side as Kinley and Rylee stepped back, allowing him to take over. His presence was a balm to my frayed nerves.

"Rhett," I panted, "the baby is coming."

"I know." He squeezed my hand. "And I'll be right here with you."

Dr. Sterling asked everyone else to leave the room and started giving me instructions on breathing and pushing.

"Okay, Natalie." Her voice was calm as she held my legs open. "It's time to start pushing."

My eyes flew to my husband. "Rhett, I'm scared. What if something goes wrong?"

He brushed my sweat-soaked hair from my forehead. "Everything is going to be fine."

With each push, the pain got worse. Rhett's voice and Dr. Sterling's calm instructions seemed to fade into the background as my screams grew louder.

"One more, Natalie. You're almost there." Dr. Sterling's voice was firm as she kept giving me words of encouragement.

Gathering as much strength as possible, I took a deep breath and gave it one final push. A second later, the room was filled with the most beautiful sound in the world.

"It's a boy!" Dr. Sterling announced, holding up our son. Tears streamed down my face when she covered him in a towel and placed him on my chest.

He squirmed at first, but then his cries softened as he nestled against me. I was so exhausted I could barely speak, but I could stare at the small miracle in my arms forever.

"He's so tiny." Rhett's voice was thick with emotion as he kissed his forehead.

"He's perfect, isn't he?" I looked down at our son, feeling my heart fill with so much love. He was perfect, with a dusting of dark hair and big, curious eyes that squinted against the bright lights.

"Welcome to the world, little man," Rhett whispered, taking his tiny hand. "We've been waiting for you."

Dr. Sterling quietly cleaned up, giving us a moment to ourselves. The room seemed to fade away, leaving the three of us alone. I traced our baby's features, soaking in every detail.

"We're finally a family now," I said, passing our son off to his dad.

I saw the first tear fall when I placed him in Rhett's arms. His hands trembled as he cradled our little bundle with so much care that it melted my heart. I never loved him more than I did at that moment.

Our baby's cries softened, and Rhett gently rocked him.

The door opened slightly, and a few of Rhett's teammates and coaches peeked their heads in. "We won and wanted to come meet our newest fan."

Rhett laughed and hoisted the baby up in the air. "Thanks, guys. I feel like I gained more than just a win today though."

When they closed the door, I sat up and adjusted the blanket over my son. "I'm sorry you had to miss the end of the game."

Rhett touched my face. "This was way more important."

The door opened again as Uncle Beau and our friends came back into the room.

"He's beautiful." Uncle Beau came to my side, his smile was filled with pride. "And look at that, he's got more hair than me."

"Are you guys going to finally tell us the name?" Maverick asked.

Rhett insisted on keeping it a secret until the baby was born. He looked at me for permission, and I nodded.

"Meet our son, Landan." He held him up proudly so everyone could see.

Landan was a combination of Landers and Atlanta. Two things we both loved.

Uncle Beau's eyes filled with tears as he stared back at me. Everyone made their way around my makeshift hospital bed. Our son might have been born in one of the most unexpected places, but I'm so glad our big, crazy family got to be a part of it.

As I looked at my husband, I knew wherever life took us, we would be okay.

———

Dear Reader,

I hope you enjoyed Fumbled Arrangement. I wanted to give you a glimpse into Rhett and Natalie's future, so I wrote a super fun bonus scene. All you have to do is click on the link below and scan the QR code with your phone, sign up for my newsletter, and you'll get an email giving you access.

Sign-up HERE
Already Subscribed? CLICK HERE

Or Scan:

LET'S CONNECT

Are you on Facebook? If you said yes, then I highly recommend joining my reader group. We play games, talk about books and life in general. It's a great place for me to get to know my readers on a more personal level. You can join here:

https://geni.us/izHU

Want to stay up to date on my new releases, sales and comings and goings? You can find all my social media links on my website here:

https://geni.us/sjonesauthor

―――

THANK YOU

Thank you so much for reading. I know you have many other books to choose from, I am so grateful you took the time to read mine. If you enjoyed it and if you get a chance, I'd be so grateful if you could leave a review.

I can't wait to share more stories with you.

Love,

Sandy
Xoxo

ALSO BY S. JONES

Fumbled Love (Maverick & Kinley)

Fumbled Beginning (JP & Rylee)

THE HARD SERIES

Hard to Love (Chase & Emily)

Hard to Stay (Brad & Lexi)

Hard to Leave (Jack & Chloe)

THE PROTECTIVE SERIES

Whatever It Takes (Quinn & Charlotte)

Whatever You Need (Marco &Amelia)

Whatever You Want (Logan & Ava)

ABOUT THE AUTHOR

S. Jones is a contemporary romance author from Upstate New York. She has a strong passion for writing and reading stories that will rip your heart out before it's put back together again.

If she's not buried in her writing cave, she's usually reading or planning out her next vacation.

She loves to travel to different places and spends all her free with her husband, and two college age children.

When the weather permits, you can find her outside walking her golden retriever, or enjoying a nice cocktail by the pool. She loves cooking and entertaining for her family and friends.

When she's not holding a glass of wine in one hand and her kindle in the other, she loves to hear from her readers at:

authorsjoneswrites@gmail.com